Living in Glass Houses

Living in Glass Houses

Zoe McKnight

Cover design by Steve Comando

For Mom and Dad

Acknowledgments

Many thanks to everyone who's ever read any article, blog, or short story I've ever written and given me the confidence to pursue this venture. Thank you to all of my writing buddies, especially to those who've taught me how to be a better writer.

To all of my friends and family. Deepest gratitude to Alicia Jerriho, Kenyon Kee and Tamarah Reel for lending me their ears, thinking out loud with me, for being my sounding board, reading draft after draft and most importantly for encouraging me to do what I love.

And finally to Justin for supporting my dream to write this book and always being in my corner.

1

Jonathan

They pulled onto her parents' block to find their circular driveway lined bumper to bumper with late-model cars. Jonathan was pleased to see this—the more people in attendance meant the less focus on him. The backyard was sprinkled with guests, most with drinks already in hand. Music hummed in the background, loud enough to add ambiance yet low enough so as not to interfere with conversation. Roslyn regarded every little detail. He parked his pick-up behind a black S-class; its gleaming trunk provided a chastising reflection of Jonathan's dirty hood.

"Do you think it's too tight?" Lauryn tugged on her A-line skirt before carefully adjusting the blouse she'd changed into and out of twice before they'd left her house.

"Nope, you look fine," Jonathan said.

"You didn't even look."

"I was there when you put it on, wasn't I? You look good. Stop fussing, it's just a barbecue." Why she insisted on wearing a dress and heels just to traipse around grass was beyond him.

She reached for his hand as they entered the curving flagstone pathway leading to the backyard. Clusters of people mingled around linen-draped high-top tables. What had come to be known as the traditional barbecue scent—a strange mixture of burgers, charcoal, and citronella—was replaced with the aroma of steak, seafood, and lamb. At the far end of the yard were three banquet tables adorned with ivory and black linens. Behind them stood several servers, all dressed in black so they could easily be distinguished from the guests, most of whom donned crisp whites, creams, yellows, and pinks. Jonathan's dark blue jeans and navy blue polo shirt stood out— like the smell of lamb at a backyard barbecue. Lauryn looked to Jonathan, her eyes sending a clear, *I told you so* message. He shrugged, grabbed a shrimp kebob from the tray of a passing server, and slurped a pineapple from the tip of the stick as he thought, *What man wears white pants to a barbecue? Hell, what man wears white pants?*

"Ah, my first-born finally decided to grace us with her presence." Roslyn appeared behind them, her four-inch heels placing her statuesque frame eye to eye with Jonathan. She kissed Lauryn on the cheek and squeezed Jonathan's free hand. "Now, what took you both so long?"

Lauryn stood a tad taller and squeezed her stomach a bit tighter. "Church ended a little late today. Then there was traffic on the LIE."

"Traffic? Eastbound at this hour? Anywho, how was the service? Did you send Father James our best? I just couldn't tear myself away this morning. The landscaper was late, then the caterer brought the wrong silverware. It was a mess. But I'm glad you could go in our stead. Well, *my* stead. Your father rarely attends anymore."

"Well, you know dad can't sit still but for so long."

"Don't I know." Roslyn rolled her eyes, then set them on Jonathan. "It's been a long time. When was the last time we saw you?" She wagged a chastising finger at him. "You never come around anymore."

This, all of this, was the reason he rarely came around—stuffy, pretentious people all crammed into one space discussing boring right-wing crap. He'd tried to fit in for Lauryn's sake, tried to be a good sport and rub elbows with her parents' friends, but no sooner than he'd reveal that he wasn't a member of a fraternity, that he'd gone to a community college, and was now a basketball coach, they'd lose interest and conveniently be drawn away to another conversation. Some would feign interest by asking condescending questions, like Roslyn's accountant who was so bold as to ask Jonathan what college basketball coaches grossed these days. That was the last time Roslyn had seen him.

"Just been busy with work is all." He shifted on his feet as he looked past her, hoping another server would make it his way.

She appraised him, her eyes briefly resting on the tattoo peeking from beneath his sleeve. "The season's only a few months, though, isn't it?"

Lauryn wrapped her arm around Jonathan's waist and leaned against him, grateful she'd insisted he shaved that morning. Although he preferred a more rugged look, she thought he looked especially handsome with a sharply lined mustache and goatee. She reminded her mother that he taught fitness classes at the college when he wasn't coaching—a fact Roslyn acknowledged with a haughty nod.

To Jonathan's delight, a waiter carrying a silver tray came their way. He scooped up another shrimp kebob and Lauryn reached for a chicken slider. Before it could reach her lips, Roslyn frowned.

"Sweetie, maybe you shouldn't. It looks like you're putting on a pinch of weight." Roslyn leaned in and whispered in her ear. "Remember what I told you. When in doubt—Spanx." Her attention was drawn away. "What is that girl doing? I told her not to bring out the fruit salad until six. Oh my, I'll be right back." She strode away.

Lauryn turned to Jonathan. "I told you it was too tight." She squeezed her cheeks in an effort to create slack in her skirt.

"You're fine. Stop it."

Her self-appraisal ended when two of her childhood friends swooped in and regaled them of tales of a recent vacation or a good sale on some boots or maybe it was about a pair of boots they'd bought on vacation. Who knew? Jonathan was no more interested in their conversation than he was in being there. Lauryn was swept away and in due time he was left posted up against the bar, grateful she wasn't glued to his hip for once. Multiple cocktails eased his discomfort and he even managed to find common ground with the bartender, who was probably the only person there impressed with the fact that Jonathan coached a NCAA Division III team. They talked sports until the sun set and the backyard became illuminated with rattan globe string lights and lanterns.

Just as he was mulling over a reasonable excuse to leave, Roslyn approached him with Lauryn in tow. "I have someone I want you both to meet." Her eyes sparkled with excitement. She waved to a short, white-haired man standing a few feet away. He was surrounded by a flock of women who appeared to be hanging on his every word. "Dr. Leed! Come."

What now? Here goes Roslyn again, posturing by introducing him to her well-appointed, professional friends. Either her way of reminding Lauryn she could do better or of telling him he wasn't good enough. Or both. To his face she campaigned for their marriage, but who knew what she said to her daughter behind closed doors.

Dr. Leed excused himself from his fan club and made his way to the hostess. "Ah Roslyn, my dear, I so enjoy your functions. I always meet the most interesting people."

Roslyn linked her arm through his. "Doctor, this is my daughter Lauryn, the one I was telling you about."

Lauryn and Jonathan exchanged curious glances as they took turns shaking Dr. Leed's hand.

"Ah yes," Dr. Leed said as he reached inside his jacket. "We should definitely set up a consultation." He retrieved a business card and handed it to Lauryn. "But I can answer any questions you both might have. It's actually quite simple of a procedure."

"Procedure?" Lauryn asked.

"Oocyte cryopreservation. Egg freezing." The proud smile on Dr. Leed's face receded. "I thought you and your fiancé were looking into it."

Lauryn turned to Roslyn. "Mom?"

"What?" Roslyn said. "I looked into it for you, sweetie. For the *both* of you. Dr. Leed is one of the best fertility specialists in the state of New York. He can help you. This way you'll have them available whenever you both are ready."

"Mom!"

"Now, why are you turning all red? I'm just trying to help."

Jonathan snatched the card from Lauryn's hand and ripped it in two. "This is some bullshit. We don't need a damn fertility specialist."

Dr. Leed looked to Roslyn, his face was awash with confusion. "Um, excuse us for a moment, doctor." She plastered a smile to her face, then ushered him away before turning back to them. "How dare you embarrass me like that in front of one of my guests? What's wrong with you?"

"We need to talk—inside." Lauryn led the way back to the kitchen. Inside, some of the waitstaff stood around, leaning against the counter and laughing amongst themselves. As soon as they saw Roslyn, they quieted, stood erect and scrambled to grab utensils or anything that resembled work.

Roslyn shot them daggers. "How long have these trays been sitting here?" She stabbed a crab cake with a plastic toothpick and examined it closely. "Just as I thought—it's cold. They should have been out there a long time ago."

They mumbled apologies as they grabbed trays and darted towards the sliding doors.

She turned to Jonathan and Lauryn. "Now, what's the problem with you two?"

"Why the hell are you recruiting fertility doctors? Did anybody ask you to do that?" Jonathan felt ambushed. If Lauryn's face wasn't beet red, as it often turned when she was upset, he might have believed she was in on the whole thing.

Roslyn, however, never became frazzled. "In case you forgot, Lauryn here is thirty-seven-years old. A woman her age has an eighteen percent chance of conception. Eighteen! And it drops to ten after she turns forty. You guys are running against the clock. Why not take advantage of all of the technology—"

"Because this is none of your business! We're not married and we're not even *thinking* about having kids. You have a lot of nerve—"

"*Married.* Hmph." Roslyn grabbed a hand towel and wiped up a ring of water, which to an indiscriminating eye would have been completely camouflaged amongst the fluid swirl of the silver granite countertop. "That's a whole other story. Don't even get me started on that."

A server stepped back inside the kitchen, carrying an empty tray. She took one step toward the refrigerator before Roslyn barked. "Outside! Don't you see we're having a private conversation?" She turned back to them. "Listen, drag your feet if you want to, but what you're not going to do is deny me of grandchildren simply because *you* like to take your sweet time." She took Lauryn's hands in hers. "Now listen to me for a

6

change and go see Dr. Leed. I'll call him tomorrow to see if I can smooth this over. I'll just tell him that—that Jonathan had too much to drink. Yes, that's it, too much to drink."

"You don't get it, do you?" Jonathan said. "We're not going to see any doctor and you need to stay out of our business."

Roslyn glared at him before turning to her daughter. "Are you just going to stand there and let your boyfriend talk to me like this? God knows I raised you better than that. First your brother, now you. You'll both be the death of me, I swear." She raised an exaggerated palm to her forehead. "I'll never make it to sixty, dealing with you two."

"Mom, you were out of line." Lauryn's eyes darted all about the room, everywhere except up towards her mother's. "I told you, it will happen in due time. I don't need this pressure from you. It's bad enough—"

"What? What? Say it. It's bad enough that your best friend is having a baby? Or that your little cousin, Sheila is pregnant with her second? Look around you, girl, everyone is having children. That's what you're supposed to do—get married and have children! Your sister would die for the opportunity and here you are letting it slip through your fingers because of him."

Jonathan slammed his glass down on the counter. "I'm out of here, I don't need this shit. Let's go."

Lauryn grabbed his hand and followed him out of the kitchen.

"You remember, Miss thing," Roslyn called, "you only have one mother!"

They rode home in silence. He'd been a fool to believe he would make it through the day unscathed. Marriage simply wasn't on Jonathan's radar. It was touted by most people as the beginning of a new life, but to him it signified the end. The end to individual thoughts, priorities, and space. Right now he still had choices. If he felt like being alone or blowing his bonus on a set of Titleist golf clubs or even flirting with the cashier at CVS, he could and without any guilt. Marriage changed everything. And marriage to Lauryn? That would be a task.

But he did understand her plight. She was five years his senior and the only one in her circle not yet married or at least engaged. She'd been a bridesmaid in at least three weddings last year and was a godmother four times over. The ticking of her biological clock kept her up some nights and the pressure from her mother didn't help. Her younger brother, Brandon, was gay and had made it clear there would be no children in his future. Her younger sister had struggled with sickle cell anemia most of her life and as fate would have it she married a man with the sickle cell trait. So to avoid the risk of passing the disease onto a child, they made a painful decision not to have children. Their names were now on the bottom of an extremely long adoption waiting list. Therefore, the pressure for grandchildren rested on Lauryn's shoulders and she passed it onto Jonathan's.

As if she were reading his thoughts, she blurted it out. "Do you ever plan on asking me to marry you?"

There it was. Or rather there Roslyn was. He'd driven a good ten miles away, yet her presence still lingered. Her words danced around in her daughter's head, bringing Lauryn's insecurities to the surface.

"C'mon, don't start that again."

"I want to know. We've been together a long time now. Don't you want a future with me?" This was a question she'd rehearsed in the mirror several times before. His eyes remained straight ahead, glued on the road although they'd been brought to all but a stop by traffic.

"Of course I want you in my future, but that doesn't mean we have to get married right away."

"I don't mean right away. It doesn't have to be today Jonathan, I just want to know that we're on the same page. I want to marry you, I have no doubts in my mind about that."

"And I want to be with you, I have no doubts in my mind about that either."

"So, then what are we waiting for?" A year ago his answer would have sufficed, but she needed more. She couldn't go back to her friends and tell them he'd only said he wanted to be with her.

He shrugged. "I don't know . . . "

His gesture incensed her. A shrug meant indifference. A shrug was a response one offered when asked what they wanted to eat for dinner or what movie they wanted to see. It wasn't an answer the man of one's dreams gives when asked about marriage. She needed and deserved more. "You don't know?" Her eyes grew wide.

"I don't know, Lauryn. I just don't know and don't start getting all upset, either. Just relax."

"Relax?" Relax was a distant cousin to a shrug. "How can you tell me to relax when we're talking about my future? Our future! How long am I supposed to sit tight while you decide what you want to do, Jonathan? It's time we take this to the next level, I'm tired of waiting. What's the damn hold up?"

"You're getting worked up over nothing—"

"And you're not taking this serious enough. Tell me what the problem is, we can fix it. You need to tell me something or—"

He whipped his head towards her. "Or what?"

Lauryn froze. Her internal script came screeching to a halt. She'd been ready to spew the bullet points lined up in her mind, but realized she'd treaded into ultimatum territory— someplace she didn't want to go. A place her friends had casually suggested she visit if all else failed. Although she'd feigned agreement at the time, she knew in her heart she would never have the guts to do it. There was entirely too much on the line and her inner gambler was a coward. Her voice was low and timid. "I just don't understand . . ."

"In due time, Lauryn. You just can't rush things like this. Look at your friends. Yeah, they're all married, but how many of them are happy? Either they're cheating or they think their husband is cheating or they're sleeping in separate bedrooms. What is that? What we have is much more solid. A piece of paper doesn't mean anything." He reached over and squeezed her left hand. "Let's not argue, okay? Or else your mom wins. Let's just go home, get in bed, and forget all about today, okay?"

She stared at his profile and couldn't help but admire the sharp lines of his jaw and the way the corners of his deep-set eyes crinkled when he was frustrated. She decided that arguing about getting married wasn't going to get her to the altar any faster. *In due time.* She had to be patient. He would come around.

2

Blair

She could hear rumblings from the loud bass in his media room. Normally it annoyed her, but tonight offered assurance that her husband would be distracted as she made her exit. She kept one eye fixed on its door as she rummaged through her overnight bag, checking to see if she'd remembered her cell-phone charger. As usual, she hadn't. Her nerves were always in disarray when it came time to pack for her weekend getaways. She sprinted upstairs to their master suite, tugged it from the outlet near the bed, gave the room a quick once over, and rushed back downstairs. When she reached the bottom of the steps he was standing there.

"Leaving already?" He stood at the foot of the stairs in a pair of baggy basketball shorts and a plain white t-shirt. Dangling from between his knuckles were two empty long-necked beer bottles.

"Yeah." Her eyes darted to her unzipped bag, resting on the floor a few feet away from him.

Vaughn stepped towards her and wrapped his large hand around her waist. He pulled her close and attempted to kiss her on the mouth but she turned her head to the side and his lips landed on her cheek. It was the type of kiss he hated. The type he'd been getting a lot of lately. "What's wrong?"

She shifted on her feet. "Nothing, I just want get on the road before it gets late. I'll call you tomorrow, okay?" She rushed to zip the bag shut. Before she could slide the strap over her shoulder, he told her he had it and lifted it by its handles before walking her to the garage.

A moment later she was seated in her car, eager to release her foot from the brake and head to the highway. But Vaughn delayed her. He was leaning through her window, his forearms resting on the jamb as he engaged her in idle chatter. "So what are you guys getting into this weekend?"

She told him she was going wine tasting with her sister. Wait, had she used that excuse already? Were there even vineyards in Pennsylvania? Didn't matter, he'd soon forget what she said anyhow. It must have sounded plausible because he told her to have a good time and sent her sister his best. Only after the garage door had closed behind her and she inhaled the nighttime air, did she finally exhale.

When she reached the first red traffic light, she removed her wedding band and tucked it in a tiny velvet pouch. Soon red oak trees and suburban silence became replaced with traffic lights and activity. She rubbed her bare finger and gnawed her bottom lip as she pulled onto the highway. No matter how many times she'd taken this same road, heading towards the same destination, guilt had a way of creeping into her backseat and hovering, pressing heavy against her conscience. She tried her best to muzzle it, for Vaughn didn't deserve her guilt. No, she was not going to feel bad. So what that he'd called her at lunch time, *just to hear her voice*, and had surprised her last week with front-row tickets to Madame Butterfly. He probably didn't even pay for them. Just made a call as he always did, cashing in on his celebrity. An opera and a phone call did not a good marriage make. It was a good performance, though, and arranging for her to meet the cast had been an unexpected bonus. Guess it didn't really matter how he secured the tickets. He'd listened, for once. Even sat through the three-hour performance with her, the first time in a long time they'd done anything together. It reminded her of how things used to be way back when, when they were inseparable, before his true colors were revealed.

Seemed so long ago, their years together at Syracuse University. It was only at the insistence of two of her college roommates during sophomore year that they even met. Blair had entered the dormitory lounge she shared with four other girls and found two of her suite mates, Lisa and Renee, blasting their mixed CDs above the roar of the blowdryer and television. It had been Blair's plan to hole herself up in her room and spend some much-needed quality time with her accounting textbook. Much to her chagrin, she was still unacquainted with the difference between debits and credits; anything less than a B would have dropped her GPA below a 2.5 (an already low set bar for her business management major) and she'd lose one of her grants. When she tried to explain this to her suite mates, they didn't want to hear it and gave her twenty minutes to change her clothes, add some curl to her flat bob, and be ready to go with them to the homecoming game.

It didn't take much convincing, for she promised herself she'd dedicate her entire weekend to studying for the dreaded midterm. A practice which had gotten her into GPA trouble in the first place. It turned out there was an agenda above and beyond cheering for the Syracuse University football squad. Renee, her newest suite mate who'd just transferred from some

SUNY school Blair couldn't recall the name of, had her crosshairs set on the team's star wide receiver. He was in her psychology class and had invited her to the game earlier that week. Blair was later to learn that his invitation was in fact a casual, 'you should check out the game' as opposed to 'I'll have tickets waiting for you at the gate' like Renee had told them.

The excitement of the game, the crowd hysterics and the sea of orange fanfare trumped Blair's date with income statements and balance sheets. That night, at Renee's insistence, they went to an after party off campus. It was there where Blair's friendship with Renee ended and her relationship with Vaughn began.

Renee had spent the entire night trying to draw Vaughn's attention by batting her eyelashes, suggestively stroking his forearm, and offering him sips of her cocktails. Blair and Lisa figured they'd be walking back to their dorm alone that night and were ready to do just that until Blair and Vaughn found themselves standing across from each other on a ridiculously long bathroom line. When his turn came before hers, he offered her his spot, much to the displeasure of the tipsy undergrads lined up behind him. She accepted, truly seeing him for the first time that night and quickly understanding Renee's infatuation with a man who hadn't said but a few words to her. He had a perfect blend of pretty boy features and rugged good looks. She shook the thought from her head as she washed her hands, ready to go find Lisa and head back to their room. But when she stepped back into the hall, he was still there, leaning against the wall waiting.

She smiled. "It's all yours."

He bit his lower lip. "Is it?"

"What?"

"You heard me?" He smiled, his lips curled into a playful sneer.

"You're crazy."

14

"Wait." He stepped in her path and leaned his long arm against the wall, creating an alcove with his body.

"What?" Her neck strained to take him all in, as he was a full foot taller than she. Even so he was close enough that she could smell the sweet, sugary scent of his gum. She took a step back.

"Where are you going? Can I talk to you for a minute?" he asked.

She took deep swallow. She was treading on dangerous ground. Not only because he was the object of Renee's affection, but because she'd heard all the stories, not of him per se, but about men like him. The so called Big Men on Campus. In all of the after-school specials her mom had forced her to watch, this story never ended well. They would take advantage of the meek, quiet plain Jane who wore glasses and clutched her books to her chest with one arm and covered her braces with the other while she giggled. Not that Blair was that girl. After all, she was no straight-A student, had a wide circle of friends, and she was pretty, very pretty in fact, but she was completely inexperienced with men. Yes, she'd had a couple of boyfriends in high school and one special friend during her freshman year, but never had a full-on adult relationship. Vaughn, however, was grown in every sense of the word. Although he was only nineteen, he had a deliberate and mature way about him, which set him apart from his peers. And the look in his eye told her he wasn't interested in coffee in the student union, study dates at Starbucks or afternoon movies. She knew any woman who took him up on his offer would have to be ready and willing to take it all the way, and that was one thing she had yet to do.

"I think Renee is waiting for you," she said in an effort to deflect.

"Who?"

She couldn't help but laugh. Renee had spent the entire night telling them about the chemistry she and Vaughn had, how he'd offered her a ride in his new Mustang, and here it was he didn't even know who she was. "Renee Charles. You were just talking to her. The tall girl with the curly hair."

"Oh her." He dismissed her existence with the wave of a hand. "She's way too thirsty."

Blair felt an urge to defend Renee's character, but he was right. Renee was aggressive. Once she set her sights on a man, job or even a pair of shoes, she wouldn't stop until she had it. "Well, maybe you should go tell her that 'cause she has her eyes set on you."

"And what about you? What do you have your eyes set on?"

"My bed. I'm tired and my feet hurt," she blurted out, instantly regretting her candor.

"I can take care of that."

Her brows raised.

"Not like that," he said. "Get your mind out of the gutter. Come, I'll give you a ride home."

She declined. That ride home was Renee's, even if he couldn't recall her name. He insisted and told her to wait for him there as he went to the bathroom. Instead, she went to find Lisa, who told her she should go with him. She said not to worry about Renee, who they'd both known for only two months, and who also had exchanged phone numbers with at least two guys since Blair had been gone.

"Are you sure? What if she really likes him?"

"She doesn't," Lisa insisted. "He's just a challenge. As soon as she sleeps with him, she'll be on to the next one. Shoot, by the time we get back to the room, she'll hardly remember his name. Trust me. Let him drive you back." Lisa pointed. "There he is. Ooh! And he's looking for you girl." She gave Blair a playful shove. "Go!"

Sure enough, there was Vaughn. He was easy enough to spot at six-feet-four inches tall. He had his jacket in hand and was searching the crowd. That night she rode in the Mustang, which turned out not to be new as Renee had boasted, back to his dorm room where they talked until the sun came up. He made no effort to touch her or even broach suggestive conversation. Rather they talked about their respective childhoods and future plans. She learned he was from a small New Jersey town. He'd accepted the scholarship to Syracuse over those from more respected football programs because it was his father's alma mater. His father was a former NFL player (of marginal recognition) turned successful IT executive who earned a handsome enough living so his wife could stay at home and raise their three boys. All three were exceptionally athletic. Vaughn, however, was the only one they believed had enough talent to take it all the way to the pros. He confessed his fear of disappointing his family by not making it into the league. She'd soon come to learn that, unlike her, he was a straight-A student and that was without the assistance of die-hard Orangemen professors who'd been known to grant unearned A's and B's to student athletes. It was that night she fell in love with him, without so much as a stroke of her arm or a kiss on the lips. From that point on, they were inseparable on campus. By the following semester, she'd given herself to him and he became her world. It wasn't until their senior year when things changed. Rumors swirled, not only about his likelihood of being drafted, but about him and other women. It began with late-night phone calls to his room and clusters of giggling girls who appeared at games and lingered afterwards near the locker room. Soon it escalated to taunting prank calls, racy voicemail messages, panties in his laundry bag, and a case of Chlamydia he couldn't explain how he'd given her. There were dramatic tear-filled break-ups and dorm-room hysterics, which often resulted in a week of her ignoring his calls until she'd eventually succumb to his charm-filled apologies and vehement pledges that it wouldn't happen again. But it always did, not always in the form of pure indiscretion, but in subtle hurtful ways she couldn't even blame him for. It wasn't his fault women fawned all over him. Some of the advances were subtle, like those from the female trainers and managers. Others much more overt, from the groupies who hung around after the games half dressed and eager to please. The times he traveled to away games were the worst and always filled her with angst. But she managed to hang in there under the belief that once they graduated and got off the campus, away from his notoriety, everything would change. So when he was drafted later that year, she didn't share his joy. Her friends and family told her to hold on. *He's just going through a stage, He'll grow out of it, Just be patient*, they all told her. And she did and in doing so reaped the benefits of his success. Money became no object. They lived in a beautiful house, drove luxury cars, and shopped excessively. Vaughn rationalized his adulterous behavior by spoiling her, giving her any and everything she wanted. Everything but a faithful man.

An unexpected pregnancy brought about a temporary change of heart and a fervent guarantee he'd be faithful. When he almost lost Blair in a car accident and then lost their child to a sixth-month miscarriage, he searched his soul and realized he'd been given a second chance and he needed to solidify their union. So a month later he placed a five-carat emerald-cut diamond on her finger. She took the proposal as a sign of renewal, a new life, and a chance to start all over.

Blair saw a new man in Vaughn. He became a doting, attentive husband who made it his business to make her feel secure. After a shoulder injury left him on the bench for half of a season, he decided to retire and launched a career as an ESPN sportscaster. Although he presented it as a sacrifice on his part, claiming he'd be home more often to ease Blair's mind, she knew it wasn't just for her, as Vaughn prided himself on being the best at everything he did. The doctors assured him his shoulder would never heal completely, which meant his game would be forever curtailed. Before he'd become a sub-par player or get traded against his will, he decided seven years had been enough and he'd retire while still on the top. Although his intentions were mostly selfish, Blair was grateful he was home more often and hopeful they could work on starting a family. The prospect made her drunk with happiness. Happy until the day her sister called her at work.

"Blair! Is it true?" Her sister's panicked voice filled the airwaves.

"Norah?" Blair held the phone to her ear with her shoulder as she scrolled through a file cabinet, wishing she'd committed to one form of organization or another. Half of the drawer was alphabetized, the other half was filed by industry. "What are you talking about?"

"What they're saying in the news. Someone just showed me the paper. Did you know about this?"

"Know about what? What happened?" Her annoyance rose. If Norah was calling her to tell her about another celebrity break up as if she knew these people in real life, she was going to hang up.

"God, you don't know, do you?" She could all but see her sister's large eyes wide with terror.

Blair pushed the drawer shut then spun around to face her computer. "You're starting to scare me. What? What are *they* saying?"

"Get a copy of today's Post. It's in there, on the cover," Norah said.

"I don't have the paper." She glimpsed at her watch. "It's already two-thirty. Where am I going to get a paper now? Would you just tell me already? I don't have time for this."

"It's not a game Blair. It's about Vaughn."

Blair's chest began to pound. "Is he okay? What happened?"

"Are you sitting down?"

"Tell me!" In a mere moment, her thoughts went into rapid-fire. She pictured his bloodied body lying at the scene of a five-car pile-up. Then she conjured an image of him clutching his chest before plummeting down a flight of steps. And finally of him pleading for his life as a band of thugs stole his jewelry and took turns pounding on him in the dark corner of a parking garage. The one thing she hadn't imagined was what Norah would tell her next.

"It says that—that he's the father of some girl's baby. Some secretary at ESPN—"

Blair gripped the phone tightly, pressing it so hard against her face, her earring stabbed her cheek. "What? A baby? Is this your idea of a joke?"

Norah took a deep breath. "I wish it were. It's here, in today's paper. I mean, who knows if it's true, but . . . "

Blair Googled Vaughn's name. There—beneath the cerulean blue link which read, *News for Vaughn Hill*—were multiple sites: The Post, Access Hollywood, Celebuzz and E!Online, each with a separate link to the same story. She clicked on the first and there it was, just as her sister had reported, the nineteen words that would send Blair into a tailspin. Her worst fear was realized in black and white for the world to see. *Former NFL Pro Bowler, Vaughn Hill, has been named as the father of a young ESPN secretary's illegitimate child.* She clicked *More* and felt her heart twist with each word as she read vague details about this unnamed woman whom he'd met at the studio, dated for a few months and who now claimed was the father of her twelve-week-old son. There was more, but each word blended into the next, creating a sea of black and white scrawl.

She grabbed her coat and purse and bolted for the door. As she made her way out of the office, there were stares, more of the same stares and whispering she'd noticed, but had disregarded, earlier in the day. Now she knew why. All of her co-workers knew. They were all laughing behind her back, pitying her or maybe even believing she deserved it. She had never truly been accepted at the firm; she was completely under-qualified and had no public relations experience yet carried the title of VP and all without so much as an interview or resume. They all resented her, that she knew, but the envious glances, subtle snubbing, and self-serving artificial friendships had all been worth it, a small price to pay to have something of her own, something else to focus on besides her miserable marriage. Ordinarily she'd have been able to ignore the snickers, but today she was embarrassed and ashamed. It fueled her fury.

A short forty-five minutes later, Blair was pulling into the circular driveway of their twelve-thousand-square-foot home. She stomped into the foyer, flung her coat and tote on an armchair, and kicked off her pumps.

"Vaughn!" she called as she bounded up the stairs, two steps at a time.

He wasn't in their bedroom. Back downstairs she went, first checking the den, then the kitchen and his media room. She found him sitting behind his desk in his office, the phone cradled to his ear. When he saw her, he held up his hand with a raised index finger.

"Nothing yet? . . . come on Stu . . . I know . . . but you need to handle this . . . yeah, I'll be here . . . "

He slammed the phone down. "So, I guess you've heard. Tried calling you, but—"

"But what?" She marched towards his desk. "What the hell is going on, Vaughn?"

"I barely know that woman. Stu is trying to contact her attorney or publicist or whatever the fuck she has and get this cleared up."

"Did you sleep with her?" Her face twisted into an angry scowl.

"Now don't tell me you believe this shit."

"Did you sleep with her?" She repeated with exaggerated emphasis on each word.

"Lower your voice. Rosa's going to hear you." She walked back to the door and slammed it shut. "Answer the question, Vaughn."

"No." He shook his head. "No, I didn't sleep with her, I told you I barely know her."

"That never stopped you before."

He wagged his long finger at her. "You're doing it again. What did Dr. Lane tell you? You have to stop bringing up the past—"

"How the hell do you expect me to forget the past when you keep repeating it?"

"Calm down." He rose out of his seat. "I told you—it's not true."

"It never is, Vaughn."

Unless he'd been caught red-handed, he would never admit it. Hell, he'd barely wanted to confess the times she'd caught him red-handed. A few years back, when Blair found out he'd taken a mistress to Las Vegas, she drove to the airport to confront them. She stood at the gate with her arms folded, impatiently waiting for the large metal doors to open, release the passengers and deliver Vaughn into her wrath. She watched each woman that passed as she held her breath, waiting to see what this one would look like. Then out she sauntered—a meticulously groomed, petite brunette. The type of woman who traveled in high heels, tight clothes, and a full face of makeup. Vaughn followed shortly after, with his monogrammed Louis Vuitton carry-all draped over his shoulder. Blair was incensed when she saw he was carrying the brunette's hot pink Juicy Couture tote in his hand. In her eyes, the bag was nothing more than a tacky adult version of a Hello Kitty book bag. His taste in mistresses was dreadful.

At first, he didn't recognize Blair, who stood to the side wearing a black sweatsuit and oversized dark shades; her hair was slicked back into a long dark ponytail. She shouted his name as he passed her. His immediate expression was a pleasant, *hey, funny running into you here,* but was quickly followed by a flash of horror as he became aware of the circumstances—that he was deplaning with his mistress in front of his wife. He performed the typical I've-been-caught-cheating song and dance. First there was a lot of stuttering and attempts to explain. If she remembered correctly, his lie that day had been that the woman was actually his new personal assistant and they were just returning from a charity game in Nevada. Then came the age-old flipping of the script. He laid into Blair for stalking him and causing a scene and of course, for being insecure. His mistress quickly fled the scene. Shouted accusations and flimsy excuses flew through the terminal. People stopped and stared and eventually airport security forced them to take their matter elsewhere.

Back then it had taken Vaughn a solid forty-eight hours before he admitted he'd been unfaithful. What had she hoped to accomplish in accusing him today when all she had were words on a computer screen and text in a newspaper. Vaughn would go down fighting. Recalling this, Blair shook her head and left the room.

"Get back here!" He went after her. By the time he reached their bedroom suite, she already had a suitcase laid out across the bed. He stood in the doorway and threw his hands up. "Ah, here we go again with this nonsense."

"I'm done. Not dealing with this anymore." She paced back and forth between the walk-in closet and the bed, haphazardly tossing clothes into the suitcase.

"Dealing with what?" He raised his hands in frustration. "Why can't you just believe me?"

"Because, I don't! I don't believe a fucking word that comes out of your mouth. I don't believe you, I don't trust you. Not anymore." She nearly pulled the top drawer of her bureau off its tracks. She snatched a fistful of panties and tossed them in her luggage.

"How are you going to take her word over mine? I'm your husband!"

"Yeah, you're my husband all right, the same husband who's been cheating and lying to me for years." She turned to him, a black sweater with the tags still attached waving in her hand. "When does the shit end Vaughn? When?"

He started emptying the suitcase and returning her clothes to the bureau. "C'mon now, would you just put this stuff away and calm down."

She slapped his hand. "Leave it."

"So just damn everything I said, right? You convict me just like that. I'm just guilty as charged, huh?" He said, his temper was rising.

"With your list of priors? Yeah, you're guilty all right." She disappeared into the closet, angrily raking through the hangers.

"You need to believe me when I tell you—"

"Why should I? Why? What about the times I did, just so you could go out and do it again and again?" She dumped another messy pile of clothes onto the bed. "You say you love me, you make all of these promises, but you're full of shit. You're selfish, Vaughn! It's always about you and what you want."

"Oh really? It's all about *me*? Really, Blair?" He swept his arm through the air. "Look around you. Have you ever had to work a day in your life for any of this. Anything you ever wanted, you got—just like that. Never had to lift a finger, wash a dish, or so much as iron a damn shirt in all the years we've been together." He snatched the shoe from her hand and waved it in her face. "You prance around here in these eight-hundred-dollar sandals and do whatever the hell you want, whenever you want, because of me. Because of everything *I've* given you."

"I have a job—"

He laughed. "Yeah? Can that job cover half of this mortgage? Could that job have paid off your student loans? C'mon, Blair. I asked you for one thing." He stabbed the air with his finger. "To believe me when I tell you I didn't sleep with that woman, and what do you do? You go off the deep end, packing your stuff. I'm tired of the drama. You know you're not going anywhere, so cut the bullshit."

"How do I know you didn't sleep with her? How do I know that? This is different than all the other times, Vaughn. If she's pregnant, do you know what that means for us?" Her voice cracked. Cheating was one thing, but the thought of another woman giving him what she couldn't cut deep.

"She's not pregnant 'cause I did not sleep with her. Why can't you understand that? I told you I was done with all that mess. You're so freakin' hard-headed, don't want to believe anything I tell you."

She squared off with him, arms akimbo, the top of her head barely reaching his shoulders. "So why would she lie? Why would she go this far if it wasn't true or there wasn't any chance it was? Ya know, it's real easy to prove if the child is yours."

He glared down at her. "You expect me to get inside her head? I don't know why women do what they do. Maybe she's looking for a quick pay day, hoping I'll slide her some cash to go away—"

She slapped her hands against her hips in frustration. "But if you never slept with her, why would she think that would work?"

"I don't know, Blair. Why don't you ask her? Since you have all the damn questions. Why don't you find her number, call her and ask her? Hell, it wouldn't be the first time. Look, I have enough on my plate already. Don't have time to be arguing with you."

"You can't just dismiss me like I'm some hired hand. I'm your wife, or did you forget?"

"Then start acting like it and get on my side for once!" He slammed the suitcase shut. "Now put this shit away and pull yourself together."

"You can't talk to me like that." The conviction in her voice waned. "I don't have to put up with this you know."

He started for the door, turned around and said, "Neither do I, and don't *you* ever forget that."

A moment later she heard his car peel off. Blair was left seething. How had she allowed herself to get in this situation? Playing by the rules and doing the right thing counted for nothing. She was trapped. On the outside looking in, she had it all, when in reality all she had was a helpless, miserable existence.

Hours later she sat on the bedroom balcony enveloped by the warm Indian-summer air. A wine glass dangled between her fingers and an empty merlot bottle sat at her feet. She wished she could cry, anything to release the frustration which consumed her, but she had no more tears. The well had run dry.

"Hey, baby." She turned to find Vaughn standing in the doorway. She rolled her eyes and turned back around. He approached her, then swept her jet-black hair to the side, leaned over her shoulder and whispered, "I'm sorry."

She responded with a sip of wine.

"I didn't mean those things I said."

Lies. It wasn't the first time he'd berated her and it wouldn't be the last.

"I was just stressed out about the whole situation, but you'll be happy to know Stu got to the bottom of it and she retracted her story. He says I have a case for slander if I want to pursue it."

"Libel."

"What?"

"You mean libel, not slander."

"Whatever. I have a case if I want to pursue it, but I don't. I'm just glad it's over."

"Me too," she said, her voice void of emotion.

"So, we're good now?" It was more of a statement than a question. "Change your clothes. I'm taking you to dinner. Oh, and I have a little something for you." He pointed to the dresser. On top sat a small black box adorned with a silver bow. He kissed the top of her head. "Go ahead and get ready. We have reservations for eight-thirty. I'm going to hop in the shower."

An hour later they sat across from each other at his favorite Thai restaurant—the one she hated. The distraught, tear-stricken face she'd worn only an hour before was replaced by the attractive, demure one she always presented to the world. MAC had done wonders to conceal the dark circles beneath her almond-shaped eyes. Her long lashes fluttered when she was complimented by the owner, who always made it his business to greet them after they'd been seated. No one was the wiser as the handsome couple sampled grilled chicken satay and exchanged strained banter over the dim candlelight.

"What a beautiful bracelet, Mrs. Hill," the server had gushed. "You're a very lucky woman."

Vaughn beamed. Blair offered her best artificial smile. "That I am."

It was that night Blair promised herself she would never again be made to feel so worthless. The time had come for her to let go of the fantasy and accept her marriage for what it really was—an arrangement, a business deal, a meeting of minds. Their vows clearly meant nothing. She'd finally gotten the message. It was loud. It was clear.

The memory of that day was one she turned to whenever her guilt got the best of her. It silenced her conscience and justified her behavior. Her excitement grew when she glimpsed her favorite sign, *Pennsylvania Welcomes You*. Just a little while longer and she'd be in Philadelphia where Dylan would extinguish the final embers of her guilt.

3

Elle

Luke was called into the office on Saturday morning. He agreed to cover appointments for his partner, who was under the weather, leaving Elle to lounge around his house, waiting for his return. Had she known he would have been gone so long, she would have brought some work with her. Three manuscripts awaited her attention at home. She'd promised herself she would finish reading at least one over the weekend so she wouldn't be forced to stay at the office past eight. But who was she kidding? Leaving early, or even on time for that matter, was never going to happen. Overcome with boredom, she sat at his desktop, surfing the web. For what, she wasn't sure, but her hope was that something, anything in the world-wide-web would pique her interest until he returned. Periodically she checked her Facebook page, only to be greeted by that dismal notification that told her none of her friends were online and available to chat. Even her overseas friends—whom she collected from years of international travel with her diplomat father and globetrotting mother—weren't online. Just as she was about to log off, a tiny red notification popped up in the corner of the screen, indicating that Michelle, her cousin, had tagged her in a picture. A tiny bit of angst filled her as the computer buffered. She never knew with Michelle. It could have been anything—a photo from their vacation in Vegas last year or a picture that had absolutely nothing to do with Elle, but one Michelle just *had* to make sure she saw, or even a naked shot of the two of them as four-year-olds bathing in her aunt's claw-foot tub.

She held her breath and was pleasantly surprised to find it was of Michelle's last birthday. Elle had thrown her a surprise party on a rooftop lounge in the meatpacking district. Ah, that was a good night. Elle, Jonathan, his girlfriend Lauryn, and Blair along with most of Michelle's friends all had an amazing time. She stared at the photo, appraising her image in the way one does when first seeing a picture of herself that she hadn't even know was taken. Funny because she remembered feeling good about her hair before she left the house that night, yet in the picture it was overtaken by frizz—the arch nemesis to curly-haired girls everywhere. Those women in her office with bone-straight hair, whether by nature or by the way of a professional blow out, endlessly complimented her curly locks, telling her how they wished they had her hair. Whereas she envied them, for humid air and unexpected rain only mildly impacted their smooth tresses, but would cause Elle's to swell and she'd go from looking like a corporate professional to a bohemian artist in a matter of minutes. But in defense of her ethnically-ambiguous tendrils, they suited her olive complexion and set her apart from most other women. And when they were behaving, she rather embraced them.

She had to admit that beyond her hair it had been a high moment; as she further examined the picture, she was pleased with the way she looked. Her outfit wasn't just the perfect combination of style (wrap dresses had a way of flattering most women) and color (red, although she rarely wore it, was always an attention grabber), but it paid tribute to her early morning workouts. Seeing pictures like this one every so often encouraged her to stick to her sometimes excruciating five a.m. spin classes.

She concluded that the tagged picture was a thumbs up. The hair was a clear miss, but the ensemble was a win. A fact which ordinarily would have garnered a draw—meaning she wouldn't untag herself, but it definitely would never enter profile picture territory. However, this picture earned an honorable mention because she had looked surprisingly happy on the heels of her heart-wrenching break-up with Marcus. It was possible those good spirits were brought on by the half-empty martini glass in her hand, but it was a far cry from the place she'd been only weeks before.

As she studied the photo, trying to recall the last time she'd worn that dress, she knocked over her glass of water. She began to blot the drenched papers on Luke's desk with paper towels when an ivory business card caught her attention. It was from Van Cleef & Arpels. Below the saleswoman's name it read, *Precious Stones*. She flipped the card over and saw *$25K* scribbled on the back—in Luke's handwriting. Her heart raced. Luke didn't wear jewelry, nor was he one for material things. What could he possibly be looking to purchase for twenty-five thousand dollars from a jewelry store? She studied the card. Her emotions vacillated from pure excitement at the prospect of an engagement ring to downright shame for getting giddy over a simple card. She sat at his desk, resisting the urge to slide open the top drawer and search for more solid evidence. Her fingers cradled the edge of the wood, sliding it open slowly, then pushing it back shut. She did this for more than fifteen minutes, hoping he'd walk in the door it any moment, putting an end to her mental chess game. But he didn't come. So she did the best next thing and called Blair, who promptly told her it couldn't mean anything but an engagement ring and insisted that Elle should be clicking her heels with excitement.

"Have you been drinking? I can't marry him. I haven't even known him a year."

"And?" Blair said.

"Maybe I'm getting beside myself, maybe it's nothing. Maybe he's looking at jewelry for his mom or sisters or somebody," Elle said.

"Or maybe even for you. Or it could be some other type of precious stone. So, back to my original point—you should be happy. And what's it say on the back of the card? Twenty K?"

"Twenty-five." Elle ran her fingers across the embossed logo on the face of card.

"Well, damn. I doubt the man is about to drop twenty-five thousand dollars on his little sister. Besides, didn't you say he was cheap?"

Elle sighed. Blair had an annoying tendency to jump to conclusions. If one said they were hungry, she'd hear them say they were starving. In the same way she'd somehow concluded Luke was cheap because Elle told her he drove a Toyota and lived in a three-bedroom Cape. Although his net worth was considerable, he lived way below his means, simply because he chose to. Another reason she adored him.

"He's not cheap. He just doesn't blow his money."

"Well, I think it means one thing and one thing only. He's about to propose!" she exclaimed.

"Can you just be rational for a minute? We've only known each other for months, Blair. What middle-aged, level-headed man would propose to someone he's only known a few months? It just doesn't make sense."

What Elle wanted to hear was that this middle-aged, level-headed man loved her, although he'd only known her a few months. She needed to hear someone else say it. If the words were cast aloud in a voice other than her own, maybe she could believe it.

"What's so far fetched? Both you and Luke are grown. You both know what you want already. Does it really take another year or two to figure out if you're right for each other?" Blair answered her own question. "No, it doesn't. When I met Dylan, I knew in weeks he was someone I could spend the rest of my life with. In weeks. I didn't need more than that, I just knew. And I'm sure Luke knows. I mean what is there not to love about you? You're beautiful and smart and funny . . . the list goes on. What man wouldn't want to marry you? You have to stop wasting time on what makes sense."

Blair had said exactly what Elle wanted to hear, but still a voice inside told her it wasn't the case.

She went on. "So, if the man went to Van Cleef & Arpels to look for an engagement ring for you after knowing you less than a year—so what? Look how long you knew Marcus and see what happened. Time means little when it comes to affairs of the heart."

Elle knew that she wasn't the only one Blair was trying to convince.

"But what if this is just a rebound thing? What if I'm not over Marcus and Luke is just the transition guy?" Elle asked.

"Do you love him?"

Elle loved everything about him. She smiled every time he entered her thoughts. A grin crawled to her face as she recalled the day she'd first seen him. It was all clear in her mind's eye—the overcast skies on that Saturday morning, the forest-green corduroy jeans she was wearing, even the smell of the examining room, a sterile blend of rubbing alcohol and Pine Sol. She first glimpsed Dr. Luke Cartright when he poked his head in the exam room to say he'd be with them in two minutes. As a favor to Michelle, she'd agreed to take her goddaughter, Simone, to her pediatrician appointment. In the time it took him to place a stethoscope and conduct a routine ear exam, Elle became smitten. Initially for superficial reasons like his deep-set hazel eyes, the distinguished graying of his temples, and his bright slightly imperfect smile. But as she listened to his exchange with Simone and witnessed his effortless brand of humor and wit, she knew she had to learn more. Fortunately, something about her must have intrigued him as well, because he invited her for a cup of coffee.

A week later, over several Chai tea lattes, they spent hours talking. She learned he hailed from Georgia, had attended medical school in Maryland, was the oldest of three children and was very close to his parents. He'd been raised in a small Baptist town just outside of Atlanta. All of his family still lived close to his hometown and were itching for him to move his practice back down south or at the least somewhere within the bible belt. They'd been disappointed when he decided to attend Johns Hopkins University. During his residency he met and married his ex-wife. They had their son, Ryan, soon after and then moved to New York to be closer to her family. Twelve years later, they realized their love for each other had fizzled and made a mutual decision to go their separate ways. She had moved to New Jersey with Ryan, and Luke remained in Long Island. They maintained a healthy relationship despite the divorce.

Luke was handsome by any measure, but he also had a boyish charm to him. He dressed simply, mostly in khakis and polo shirts. He possessed a southern charm which armed his vocabulary with lots of please, thank you and pardon mes.

He treated everyone he encountered with an equal measure of respect; was on a first-name basis with his office cleaning lady, the cashier at Dunkin' Donuts and all of the car-wash attendants. He loved his job, was exceptionally good at it, but seldom, if ever, would he mention his profession to those who didn't know. A trait Elle found refreshing, as she'd spent so many years in corporate America surrounded by men who wore their titles as badges of honor. As if somehow their white collars made them better than everyone who didn't earn their living out of an office. In the wake of Marcus, the consummate corporate professional, she was especially pleased to meet a man not of that world. Something about spending his days surrounded by toddlers, puzzles and lollipops kept Luke grounded and she loved that about him.

Their respective careers kept them busy, but didn't prevent daily phone calls, intimate dinners and long weekends. They soon came to spend most, if not all, of their free time together. She'd given him the abridged version of her relationship with Marcus, he recapped the final days of his marriage and confessed he wanted to remarry one day.

Despite his years living in New York, he remained a bright-eyed optimist and encouraged Elle to take a peek through his rose-colored glasses. He brought out an easy-going, relaxed version of her. Her whole life had been goal driven. No sooner than she'd accomplished one, were her eyes set on the next. For her, idle hands were uncommon, there was always a need to fill them with a new project or a hobby. That's how she believed it should be and in dealing with Marcus, another career-driven type-A personality, her life was always on the go. They'd behaved like human chess pieces, constantly shifting and calculating their next move. With Luke, there was no next move. He took each day as it came. He was serious about his profession, but managed to assuage even the heaviness of conditions like measles and pneumonia with his light-hearted demeanor. He introduced her to activities like white-water rafting, rock climbing, and hang gliding, all things she'd sworn never to attempt. He encouraged her to trade in her pumps for a pair of cross trainers and she embraced it, even agreeing to take a week off from work and accompany him to Cambodia, where he traveled once a year to volunteer medical care to impoverished children—a deed that made the two or three times she'd volunteered at a Thanksgiving soup kitchen seem so small. They had nothing in common, yet completed each other in the strangest of ways. She felt alive when she was around him. Yet, she couldn't help but wonder if it was all too good to be true.

"Well? Do you?" Blair asked.

"I do."

"Well, take advice from a woman who's been to hell and back. Don't let him slip through your fingers. Seriously Elle, stop looking for excuses to not live your life."

"You're right." Elle heard herself say, but wasn't quite sure she was convinced.

4

Jonathan

"All right, guys. Good game! Let's call it quits for tonight. See you all tomorrow." Jonathan ended the evening's practice then grabbed his towel from the bench and headed for his office. As he changed out of his gym clothes, he checked his voicemail.

Jay, what's up. I'm gonna pick up Curt and Pat, we'll be over around nine-thirty. I'll bring the brew. Later.

Perfect ending to a long week. Lauryn was back at her place for the weekend and he had good money on the heavyweight fight tonight.

Hours later, back at his apartment, Jonathan heard a key in his door. From his couch he watched Lauryn come through the front door, balancing two shopping bags in her hands.

"Oh babe, you're home. Thought you had practice." She rested the bags on the kitchen counter. He approached apprehensively. It was Friday, wasn't it? What the hell was she doing there? She greeted him with a quick kiss.

"Ended it early. What's all this?" He peeked inside the Trader Joe's bags.

"Was shopping and figured you could use a few things for your fight party. It's tonight, right?" She pulled out chips, salsa, a bag of grapes, two six-packs of Heineken and a bottle of wine.

"Grapes, babe?" he asked.

"I know you're all about your protein shakes, but you should start eating more fruit. They're sweet. Taste." She dangled a vine of plump, green grapes in his face. "Plus they're a good source of vitamin K."

Vitamin K? Where did she get this shit from? "Nah, no thanks. And what's with this wine? None of the guys drink Moscato, ya know."

She took the bottle from his hands and placed it in the refrigerator. "That's for me, silly. You know I don't drink those . . . what do you call them? Greenies?"

"For you?"

"Yeah. What time is everyone coming? I want to change out of these clothes first."

"Around nine." He watched her kick off her patent leather pumps and remove her gray pinstriped blazer. "*You* want to watch the fight?"

"Of course. You always say you wished I liked sports. Well tonight you can teach me all about boxing. The rules and stuff." She popped the cap off one of the beer bottles, wrapped it in a napkin and handed it to him. "Now, who's fighting again?"

"Um babe, it's just really going to be the guys tonight. Nobody's bringing their girlfriends. It's just the fellas. You wouldn't really have a good time . . . "

"I always have a good time with you. Who's coming? Chuck and the rest of them? I like them. It'll be fun." Her cell phone rang. "Just a sec baby, I have to take this."

As Jonathan listened to her handle a minor work crisis, he struggled with how to tell her she couldn't stay. This was his time. He'd been looking forward to the fight all week. It was his time to kick back and relax with his friends. She'd been at his house the past seven days straight. When he was at work, she texted him pretty much all day and made a habit of calling during both her lunch hour and commute home. The walls were starting to close in on him. Tonight was his to do with it what he wanted.

"Lauryn," he said after she ended her call. "I don't think it's a good idea if you stay tonight. It's going to be loud and we'll be drinking and acting up. You don't want to be around that."

She turned on the faucet, retrieved the plastic yellow gloves she kept under the sink, and began to wash the dishes in his sink. "It's no different than going to a football or basketball game. I can handle it. You think too much, Jon." She playfully flicked him with some soapy water.

He leaned against the refrigerator and mulled over his choice of words. "No, Lauryn, it's not the same. This is just the fellas tonight. Like when you and Cory have your girls' night, the wine and chick-flick thing you do. Boxing, especially a main event, is like a man's chick flick. No girl's allowed."

She turned off the water and stared at him. "So you want me to leave? Is that what you're saying?"

He stammered. "Not exactly, I mean . . . not leave, like get out . . . just more like, the guys might be put off if—"

"So, you want me to leave. Just say it, Jonathan. If you want me to go, I will."

"Just for tonight, babe. You understand what I'm saying, right?"

She gaped at him, then pulled off the gloves and gently draped them over the edge of the sink. "Okay. I'll go . . . I'm sorry, I didn't think I was going to be in the way, but I . . . I understand." Her voice cracked. "I made some wings and those mini-egg rolls you like. They're in the bottom of the bag. Just make sure you heat them up in the oven, because if you put them in the microwave, they'll . . . they'll get . . . they'll get soggy."

Damn. As much as he'd tiptoed, he managed to crack yet another eggshell. "Baby, don't cry now. I wasn't trying to hurt your feelings, I just—"

"No, it's okay." Her voice was now muffled as she cried into his shoulder. "You just want to be with your friends. I shouldn't have assumed that meant me too."

"Lauryn, stop crying." He dabbed at her tears with a paper towel. "I was being an ass. Of course you can stay. You stay, okay? I didn't mean what I said."

"You're just saying that." Mascara streaked down her left cheek.

"No, I want you to stay, seriously." He kissed her forehead, then her lips. "You go wash your face. I'll put the rest of this stuff away and make sure I put the egg rolls in the oven . . . not the microwave."

No sooner than the bathroom door closed behind her, he slammed a silent fist down on the counter. Again. Those damn tears were always his downfall. He berated himself for not standing his ground. For falling for the same crap yet again. Watching a woman cry was something he just couldn't get used to. It tugged on his heart strings in such a way. What was he going to tell his friends? Most of them liked her because she cooked and appeared easy-going. Some even admitted their envy because their wives and girlfriends weren't so accommodating, but they only saw the shiny, polished edition of Lauryn, not the clingy, insecure version who invited herself to his fight party. Soon they would.

Two hours later, Jonathan and five of his friends were sprawled out in his living room with their eyes glued to the TV screen. Lauryn flitted back and forth to the kitchen, strategically slipping coasters under beer bottles and wiping away water rings from the coffee table. Chuck, his closest friend, shot Jonathan a glance every time Lauryn asked another question and threw his hands up when she asked when was half time. When a buxom blonde in boy shorts and a halter top circled the ring holding a sign above her head, Pat couldn't help himself. "Man, if I got a piece of that right there, I'd wear her ass out!"

Both Jonathan and Chuck shot him a reprimanding glance.

"What?" Pat said before Chuck elbowed him and nodded towards Lauryn.

"Oh. My bad, I forgot she was here."

"*Wear her out?* Pat, don't you have a girlfriend?" Lauryn asked.

"Uh yeah, but I was just sayin' . . . like if I was single, I might wanna . . . like get with her or something," Pat stammered.

"With *her?* She has her chest all out. I mean, why do they even need a half-naked woman in the ring announcing the rounds anyway? You'd think they'd have it up on a screen somewhere. It's kinda primitive, actually. I wonder if her parents know she's running around half dressed—"

"Lauryn." Jonathan's tone was firm. He got up, stepped behind the couch and stood beside her. His face said it all.

"What?" Her expression was innocent. "I'm just saying."

He whispered in her ear. "Nobody wants to hear about that. They just wanna watch the fight, okay?"

"Now I can't speak? Everyone else gets to comment, but I've got to keep my mouth shut?"

"How much have you had?" he said, pointing to the half-empty wine glass in her hand.

"What? You think I'm drunk now? Because I have an opinion, I have to be drunk?"

He reached over to take it from her hand when she flicked her wrist back, splashing what was left of it on Pat's head.

"Hey!" Pat jumped up. "What the hell?"

Lauryn brought her fingers to her mouth. "Oh my God, I got Moscato all over you. I'm so sorry, let me get a towel." She ran off to the kitchen.

While Pat dried himself off, Jonathan grabbed Lauryn by her forearm. "Lemme talk to you." He led her into the bedroom by her elbow and shut the door. "What the hell are you doing?"

"What? I spilled a little wine is all. It'll dry. Besides it's a white, it won't stain."

"It's not just the wine. It's the coasters and the commentary and all the freakin' questions. What are you tryna do?"

"I was *trying* to spend some time with you. I didn't realize I was annoying you. I guess I should have just left earlier, when you—"

"Oh!" They heard an eruption from the living room.

Jonathan sped back out to find all of his friends on their feet hollering with excitement. "What? What happened?"

"KO!" Chuck regaled. "Hooked off the jab, took him straight down. You missed it, man."

They recapped the knockout and HBO replayed it from a thousand different angles, but to Jonathan it all tasted like leftovers. Soon after, his friends departed one by one while Lauryn sulked in the bedroom.

"Well, let me get out of here," Chuck said.

"You don't have to leave. We still have a six-pack in the fridge, or we can even run down to Lucy's and get a drink there—"

Chuck waved his hand. "Nah man, your old lady has you under wraps tonight. Another time. Oh, the next fight is gonna be at my house and no chicks allowed."

Jonathan closed the door behind him and thought, *she got me again.*

5

Blair

Sunday came way too fast. She and Dylan had planned to see the new Matt Damon movie, to have dinner at an Indian restaurant he'd heard rave reviews about, and she'd promised to help him find a gift for his mother's birthday. None of which happened. Rather, they spent the entire weekend holed up in his house eating Chinese take-out and watching movies they'd already seen a hundred times. Was moments like this when she wished she was a good cook, well even a decent cook, so they wouldn't have to leave the house for even the twenty minutes it took to pick up the food. In between sex, watching movies, eating, and having sex during movies, he would try to sneak out his favorite board game, which she had to be coaxed into playing, for Dylan always beat her at Scrabble. She would complain it wasn't fair, her versus him, the college professor with an inflated vocabulary. But even with all of his Ph.D. pursuing intelligence, he never made her feel stupid for not knowing the definition of mercurial or how to spell curmudgeon. At a certain point she would insist he spend some time on his dissertation. She'd pretend to sleep while she watched him at his desk, chewing on the cap of his pen, feverishly flipping through the pages of a book, and highlighting sentences in between his keystrokes. Always true to his word, he'd lay down his pen in precisely three hours and join Blair back in bed. At his house she didn't mind sacrificing her French manicure by washing dishes and cleaning up. Once she even offered to help him with his laundry, although it soon became evident that she wasn't well acquainted with Maytag appliances. Although he'd told her on more than one occasion that she completed him, she never quite felt like she was enough; besides good sex and conversation, she wasn't sure what else she brought to the table. Pretty women were a dime a dozen and he could have anyone he wanted. Handsome, single, intelligent men were commodities in Philadelphia. Especially ones with olive-green eyes and wavy, chestnut-brown hair, coifed just enough not to raise eyebrows from his boss, but just messy enough to make him relatable to his male students and desirable to his female students. Why did he want her? Her, with a wedding band tucked away in a velvet pouch at the bottom of her overnight bag. And they really had nothing in common. He was an intellectual with advanced degrees, who sat on a Sunday-morning panel discussing global economics and was a mere thesis away from having *Doctor* appended to his name. Meanwhile she'd graduated with marginal grades and couldn't even name the U.S. Secretary of State if her life depended on it. While they'd both been raised in lower-income homes, he'd pulled himself up by his boot straps and put himself through college and grad school. She'd met a man who paid for her education and provided well enough that there was no need for her to ever go back to school. He taught business courses at Drexel University and was slowly but surely working

45

his way up the ranks, predicted to soon be one of their youngest department chairs. Although he now had means to be proud of, a far stretch from his humble beginnings in the slums of Philadelphia, he was frugal and lived simply, as was evidenced by his eight-year-old car and basic cable package. Perhaps it was his stark contrast to Vaughn's privileged upbringing and ostentatious life style which drew her to him. He was simple yet perfect.

She was having the Sunday afternoon blues as she repacked her bag. It never ceased to amaze her how she spent five days anticipating two days, and spent one of those two dreading the next. She tried to shake the thought of the Jersey bound turnpike, the winding road which led up to her home and the garage she'd pull into, right in between Vaughn's truck and sports car. If he was home he'd be in his media room watching football coming out only to eat and grab some beer. Or maybe he'd be out and about, perhaps at one of his 'meetings' with some tall, thin simpleton who hung on his every word then ran to the bathroom to brag to her friends that she was about to have sex with the infamous Vaughn Hill.

It was time to go. The sun was setting and she needed to get back on the road. As was their pattern they grew quiet preparing for the inevitable. In his doorway they stood with her bag at their feet, their hands clasped, and her face buried in his chest. They stood, inhaling each other, quietly acknowledging it would be a long time before they would share another such weekend. They'd stolen time for dinners, movies, and day excursions, but entire weekends were rare. It was hard for Blair to take overnight trips and her lies were beginning to run on repeat. It was nerve racking. Each time her cell phone would ring or a text message would appear on the screen, her gut would wrench. Was today the day? Would she be found out? When she learned it was nothing, she'd exhale a sigh of relief and make a feeble commitment to stop. But like a teenager who lies to her mother or shoplifts from a department store and gets away with it, she couldn't bring herself to quit. The rewards were too high. Sporadic yes, but oh so satisfying. How could she give this up? How could she give *him* up? Especially now. It was all she had, the only thing which mattered, the only thing that made her feel alive.

In spite of the circumstances, she felt lucky because what she and Dylan had was rare. It was the stuff love letters were made of. He hated that she was married, had implored her to leave Vaughn and start a life with him, but accepted her resistance and offered her time to figure it all out. That only made her love him more. If only she'd met *him* in college, her life would be completely different. Less lavish yes, but different.

She'd promised herself the last time that she wouldn't ruin their final moments together with thoughts of Vaughn, so she shook them away and squeezed Dylan around the waist a bit tighter. She told him she loved him and he told her he missed her, although she hadn't left yet. Their lips met one final time before he watched her walk to her car and blow him a kiss before driving away.

She'd have to remember to stop and grab a couple of bottles of wine on her way home.

6

Elle

Elle sat on the edge of her bed, sorting through her mail. She and Michelle had both just spent the last hour burning calories in a kickboxing class and Michelle was packing them back on as she chewed on the tip of a floppy Twizzler. Elle checked her voicemail to learn she had no messages, but two missed calls. One of which was from a number she knew very well, but hadn't dialed in ages.

Michelle plopped down on the ivory, tufted bench at the foot of Elle's bed. The pile of laundry, which had just been meticulously folded, toppled to the floor. "Really Michelle?"

Michelle shrugged as if to say *whatever* before picking up the clothes, stopping at pair of light blue medical scrubs. She waved them about. "Lookie here. Dr. Sexy's pants. I swear you always get the good ones."

"Good ones?"

"Yeah. First the investment banker, now a pediatrician. I need to drink what you're drinking."

"Oh please," Elle said as her thoughts trailed back to that missed call. What was he calling to say? How come he hadn't left a message?

"It's true, and to think I've been taking Simone to Dr. Cartright, I mean Luke, for years. Who would have ever thought you two would end up together. The truth be told, I always—" She stopped short.

"What?"

"Nothing."

"What, Michelle? *Truth be told* what?"

She shrugged. "Nothing, I just always thought that you and Marcus would end up together. You two just seemed so . . . so right for each other. I don't know . . . "

Elle loved her cousin, but she wasn't exactly a good source of relationship advice. She'd spent most of her twenties and thirties strung out on one pretty boy after another, so hers was the last person's opinion that should matter. But her admission laid heavily on Elle's heart because she had always believed the same thing.

"You know what?" Michelle gnawed off half of the remaining Twizzler in her hand. "I really admire the way you can just move on. I can't do that. I mean it's obvious, isn't it? I'm still putting up with Jason's selfish ass. Wish I had your strength."

Elle wanted to laugh because if her cousin only knew the half. If she knew that as soon as she left, Elle would lie in bed for the next few hours staring at the ceiling, fighting the urge to return Marcus' call while reminiscing on all the good times they had shared, then she wouldn't admire her. The phone call had come at an especially delicate time because she was still in a state of flux over that card on Luke's desk. She'd watched him closely in the weeks following. Every time he suggested they go out to dinner, her radar went off, wondering was it going to be the night he popped the question. What should she say? How would she handle it? She'd made a mental list of the logical reasons she should say no and even the few illogical reasons she should say yes. Her conversation with Blair replayed over and over in her head. Did it really matter she hadn't known him a long time? She did love him. He had everything she wanted in a man. Was she in fact, as Blair put it, 'getting in her own way'? It ultimately didn't matter because a proposal never came and she felt a fool for ever believing it would.

Elle shrugged. "Those gray suede pumps you wanted to borrow—they're at the top of my closet." Switching the discussion to clothes was sure to make Michelle drop the topic.

It did. "Where?" Michelle asked.

"The top shelf. The orange Charles David box. And make sure that's all you take. I'm watching you."

Michelle grabbed the box and tucked it under her arm before planting a kiss on Elle's cheek. "Thanks, cuz. Who needs the mall, when I've got your closet?"

No sooner than Elle heard the front door close behind her cousin did her phone ring.

She was greeted by a familiar voice. A deep, inviting one which still riveted her even after all of this time.

"Hey, lady."

Damn, she thought, why was it that the mere thought of an estranged someone could conjure him up, whether on a random street corner or in an out-of-the-blue email or even on the phone on a lonely Saturday night when her new boyfriend was out of town.

"Hey," she said.

"How are you?" His voice brimmed with familiarity as if they'd spoken only days ago.

"Good. Everything's good."

"Did I catch you at a bad time?" Every time he called was a bad time. An awkward time in which she was forced to scramble for the right response. One which indicated indifference, yet maturity. He clearly didn't respect her requests for him not to call anymore. A fact which both annoyed and pleased her at the same time.

"Just getting some work done." She instantly regretted her reply, fearing it somehow implied her life had been relegated to staying home on Saturday nights with her nose in a book. So she quickly added. "Until Blair gets here. We're going out."

"Anything good?"

"Good?"

"The manuscript you're reading. Anything good? Worth publishing?"

"Eh."

"So," he said, "you and Blair have big plans tonight?"

"Going to a lounge downtown."

"Which one?"

"Café Seven," she lied. The tail end of a 7/11 commercial served as the inspiration of her fib.

"Oh, is that new? Never heard of it."

"I think so."

"Where is it? Maybe I can meet you guys there." The ease of his words and delivery of his suggestions disturbed her. It was the same trait that had first attracted her to him, but now made her skin crawl. He was so damn self-assured. Did he really expect them to clink wine glasses over conversation and pretend as if she still didn't hate him?

"I don't think so."

"What's the name again? I'll look it up." She heard him clicking keys in the background. He could search Yelp as much as he liked. Good luck finding the lounge and even better luck getting her to meet him.

"Marcus, don't."

"Don't what?" His tone was light and inquisitive as if he was clueless, a term which could never be used to describe Marcus Stone.

"Do this."

"C'mon, don't be like that. What's the harm in two old friends having a drink together? That's all, I don't want anything more."

Friends? Oh now they were just old friends? This was his way—to offend her, to get her riled up so she'd lose sight of the big picture and get all emotional. But before her logical self could come up with an aloof, mature response, she blurted out, "We can't just pretend as if nothing's happened. You already know that."

"Just a drink Elle, that's all I'm asking for."

There was silence.

"Two friends can't have a drink now? You're making this harder than it needs to be. C'mon, Café Seven you said? I can meet you there around eleven-thirty, twelve. How's that sound?"

"You're not listening—I'm not meeting you."

He sighed. "I don't know why you have to make everything so difficult."

"*Me?* I'm making it difficult?"

"Yes, you."

This was the point where most women would gush about the new love in their life, enthusiastically rubbing it in their ex's face, but that would only accomplish two things. For one, it would incite a proverbial duel between Marcus and Luke. Men, like children forced to share their toys, had a way of gaining renewed interest in a woman once it was known that other men had interest in the same woman. And two, it would have Marcus believe that if it weren't for Luke, she'd give him another chance. Besides, the less he knew about her personal life the better.

"I have to go," she said.

"I really wish you'd reconsider, but I'll leave it alone. You know where to find me if you change your mind." There was no defeat in his voice. She even detected a hint of arrogance. The kind which believed she'd be calling him as soon as her pride wore thin. Whatever it was she thought she'd heard affirmed her resolve.

"Good night, Marcus."

7

Blair

Blair sat in her doctor's office, mindlessly twisting her wedding band around her finger. Dr. Oh had gone to retrieve the results of her blood test. What was taking him so damn long? She gripped her kneecap to stop her leg from shaking. The doorknob turned slowly.

She heard her gynecologist just outside the door ". . . yes, give her ten milligrams and have her come back in two weeks."

Would he come on already? she thought. This was her time. To hell with all of his other patients. By the time he closed the door behind him, beads of sweat streamed down the sides of her torso.

She perched at the end of her seat. "Well?"

He read from a manila folder. "Okay, it appears the bleeding was nothing serious." She felt a *however* coming on. "Nonetheless, your cervix is weak. Like we discussed the last time, your probability of miscarrying is higher than average. You have to take it easy, Blair. If you want to carry this baby to term, you're going to have to follow my instructions." He gave her a list of do's and don'ts before advising her to avoid stress, for it was just as bad as the wrong physical activity.

Blair sat in the parking lot watching her doctor's patients come and go. Most were women accompanied by their husbands or boyfriends. Men who'd probably sit in the waiting room holding their hands as they waited to enter the examination room and exclaim over ultrasound pictures of tiny heads and feet. No such man sat with Blair as she clenched her insides, willing her womb not to bleed so as to preserve the life growing within her. She called Elle and recounted her doctor's visit.

"Well, thank God it was nothing serious," Elle told her. "But he's right, stress is a killer."

"My middle name is stress. How the hell am I supposed to avoid it? Now, with everything that's going on. "

"Something has to give, Blair."

"You're right. It's gotta stop." Blair flipped down her sun visor and studied her reflection in the mirror. The circles beneath her eyes were growing darker. She'd have to remember to get some lighter concealer.

"It does, but are you ready to tell Vaughn you want out?"

She flipped the visor shut and slumped back in her seat. "I want to, I really do. Just don't know how. He's going to make it so hard. But you're right, this can't go on anymore. Dylan is patient, but for how long? What happens when he gets to the point where he's had enough?"

"Has he said anything?" Elle asked.

"No, it seems the more I'm with him, the better it gets and the more guilty I feel. I know I shouldn't. I really don't owe Vaughn shit, but with this whole baby thing, it's just a mess."

"And you didn't tell Dylan yet?"

"Of course not!" Was Elle crazy? "Not until I figure out what I'm going to do."

"Well honey, I know that you know this, but you have to say something to somebody soon . . . or you have to make a decision."

Blair sat up straight in her seat. "I'm not having an abortion, Elle. That's totally out of the question. You remember what the doctor said. After that last miscarriage, this could be my last chance."

"But you're running out of time."

"I know, but . . . "

"But nothing. If . . . well, *when* Vaughn finds out you're pregnant and it's not his, there are no words to describe what's going to happen. A messy divorce will be the least of your problems. You need to start working on your exit strategy now, because it's only going get worse."

"I don't care anymore. I'm not scared of him." She could all but see Elle's raised eyebrows.

"So then tell him."

"Are you crazy?"

"Well Blair, if you're not having an abortion, then he's going to find out eventually. What are you going do? Wait until you're waddling around the house and say 'Oh, by the way, this isn't gas in here, it's a baby. Oh, and did I mention it's not yours?'"

"This is funny to you?" Blair asked.

"It's not! I'm just trying to lay it out for you. You either get rid of it and no one is the wiser or you keep it and tell them both. If it were me, I'd pack all of my stuff and file my papers before the end of the first trimester. At least then you're out of harm's way. Who knows what he'll do to you."

"He's not violent."

"Oh no?"

"He only pushed me that once, but that was after I threw a candle at him. It doesn't count." Blair had pushed that memory out of her mind. For some reason it still bothered her to hear people speak ill of Vaughn, even if they spoke the truth.

"Whatever," Elle said. "Point is, you don't want him *pushing* you when you're eight-months-pregnant. Your doctor just told you to avoid stress. Umm . . . crazy husband plus illegitimate baby makes for stress in my book."

"Damn, Elle, you make everything so black and white. It's not that simple. I'm not like you, I can't just flip a switch and move on."

"I'm not expecting you to be like me, but I'm scared for you. I think you're taking this way too lightly. You're underestimating Vaughn. We don't know what he's capable of."

"I hear you."

"Do you?"

"Yeah, I do. Listen, I have to go. This *conversation* is stressing me. Doctor's order," Blair quipped.

"Okay, be a smart ass. I'll talk to you later."

What Blair didn't tell Elle was what she actually feared the most—walking away empty-handed. An illegitimate baby would destroy all hopes of a fair settlement and she refused to leave with nothing. Oh, it sounded horrible, she knew it, but when she was alone with her thoughts, she could admit that it was the money that gave her pause. Blair could see herself sitting in court, with a big round belly, pleading with the judge for sympathy, imploring him to award her half. Picture that. If they even made it that far. As soon as Vaughn found out, there was no question in her mind he'd toss her right out with little more than the clothes on her back. And where would she go? Back to her mother's house? The same house Vaughn had all but paid for. Or maybe to her sister's house where she could share a bedroom with her niece, who'd have to drop out of the ivy-league university Vaughn was paying for. And of course there was Dylan. She loved him and knew he loved her, for he'd told her many times, but was it enough to support both her and a baby? Was it even possible on a professor's salary? A salary already compromised by alimony payments to his ex-wife. Oh no. Dylan didn't have the resources. It was easy for Elle to tell her to file papers and leave, for Elle had skills, an MBA and a career. What did Blair have but a useless BS in business and an unmerited PR job which paid a mere ninety thousand dollars a year. A job she'd be a fool to believe she could keep after Vaughn's publicist's husband—her boss—got wind of what happened. After all of the years of bullshit she'd endured, she deserved her fair share. Without it, everything would have been in vain—the last ten years, arguably her best years, all down the drain because of a technicality. No. The type of asshole Vaughn had become he would only feel remorse by writing a check each month.

8

Jonathan

Lauryn couldn't help but be irritated by the sight of her best friend, Cory, prancing around with that eight-month-pregnant bulge. She was fighting a losing battle to be happy for her, struggling even to be mature. They were at buybuy Baby picking out last-minute registry items for Cory's baby shower which, unbeknownst to her, was only a week away.

"What do you think of this?" Cory held up a yellow and purple butterfly crib mobile. "Cute, isn't it?"

Lauryn nodded. Did she have to get confirmation from her on every damn thing she picked up? It's a baby store; everything is cute.

"Are you okay?" Cory asked.

"Mmm-hmm."

"You think I should wear my kelly-green dress? You know,

the one with the empire waist. Or the white pantsuit?"

Cory hovered the scan gun over a box of Evenflo baby bottles.

"What?"

"To my shower. Now, I don't want to know when or where, but I need to be prepared. Since you know all the details, tell me which is better." She waved the scanner back and forth. "Damn, this thing doesn't work."

Lauryn took it from her hands and lined up the red laser with the bar code. It beeped. "Whichever, Cory, you look nice in both."

"I know that, but which is better? I mean if it's outside, I'll want to wear the dress. If not, then the pants. Or maybe I should just go buy something new." She grabbed a package of silicone nipples and handed it to Lauryn. "Here, you scan it. Doesn't work when I do it."

Lauryn no longer cared if it was a surprise or not. "Wear the pants."

"So, you guys rented a hall? It's the Oyster Club isn't it? I love that place! They have the best mimosas, not that I can have any, but you can drink a couple for me, friend."

"Right."

Cory brought her hands together for a series of tiny claps. "Ooh, I'm so excited, I can't wait. Just don't tell me when, I want to be surprised."

Lauryn offered a weak smile. Most days she was able to handle Cory's need to be in the spotlight, but today she couldn't wait to get away from her. When her cell phone rang, she welcomed the distraction.

"Hey baby, what are ya doin?" Lauryn's spirits rose instantly at the sound of Jonathan's voice.

"Hey you. I'm at the mall with Cory. What's up?"

"I hate to do this, but I can't make it tonight," he said.

She'd had a feeling she would be receiving this call, but couldn't hide the disappointment in her voice. "Why not?"

"One of the guys on my team, his car broke down on the turnpike and I have to go help him out."

"Well, what time do you think you'll be done? We can push the reservations back." She was lying. Cory would have a hissy fit if she dared suggest it.

"Well, it's already seven and I haven't even gotten on the road yet. We'll go to dinner next weekend. Tell them I'm sorry," he said.

She fought the urge to protest. Nagging and complaining would be boat-rocking, and it would only delay her proposal. "Okay, I'll tell them. I love you."

"What happened?" Cory asked.

"Nothing." Lauryn quickly shoved her cell phone back into her purse.

"Who was that? Who just gave you that long face?" Cory asked in the same manner she would when they were kids, when she would jump into attack mode, ready to pummel anyone who'd hurt her best friend's feelings. Any transgression against Lauryn—as mild as a push on the playground or as mean spirited as high school gossip—could warrant Cory's wrath.

"It's nothing. Jon can't make it tonight, is all. One of his players had car failure."

"And what does that have to do with you?"

"He has to go and help them," Lauryn told her.

Cory planted her hands on her hips. "On a Saturday night? That's bullshit. He's a coach, not a mechanic."

"He has a very close relationship with a lot of his players. They see him as more than a coach. He's like their big brother."

"Oh, whatever. How long does it take to change a damn tire? He can still make it to dinner. Didn't you tell him it's the grand opening? Those reservations were damn near impossible to get. Doesn't he know that?"

"I didn't tell him. It's really not that big a deal. You guys go ahead without us." Lauryn reached for a floral baby bag. "Now this is really cute. Add this to the registry."

Cory grabbed it from Lauryn's hand and placed it back on the shelf. "Doesn't go with my color scheme. And yes, it is a big deal. Look at your face. You've been looking forward to it all week. Isn't that why you're all gussied up today with those spiral curls?"

"Drop it. It's okay, I'm fine."

Cory seethed. "You let him get away with murder. When are you going to finally put your foot down? If Dean ever cancelled on me for some eighteen-year-old, I'd rip him a new one and he knows it, which is why he's always where he's supposed to be. You need to take a page out of my book and stop being such a freaking martyr, Lauryn. Look where it's gotten you? Waiting years for a ring from a damn basketball coach." She pulled a tube of gloss from her handbag and applied it to her lips. As if on cue, the sparkle from her princess-cut engagement ring danced mockingly before Lauryn's eyes. "I keep telling you that you can do so much better, but you don't want to listen—"

"Just drop it, okay?"

Cory shook her head, her expression a mixture of pity and disappointment.

Her relationship with Jonathan had always been a sore point between them. Cory's life perfectly mirrored the blueprint which their mothers—who'd been both best friends and rivals since high school—drafted for them at birth. Lauryn's life was impressive by many standards, yet it paled in comparison to her best friend's. Things which Lauryn struggled for, came easy for Cory. While Cory made the tennis team on her first try out, Lauryn had to spend her entire summer practicing just to make junior varsity. When Lauryn finally was promoted to senior buyer after two years and six interviews, it was a bittersweet congratulations she gave her friend whose promotion came in a mere six months. Relationships were no different—Cory's twelve-month engagement record was one Lauryn would never catch up with. She'd sucked up a lot through the years, equating most of her ill fate to poor luck, which is why she dealt with Cory's insensitivity, reasoning that she couldn't be mad at her friend simply for living the life she wished she had.

———

Jonathan felt a pang of guilt as soon as he hung up the phone. He wasn't in the habit of lying, but Lauryn wouldn't have understood if he'd told her the truth—that he couldn't stand to spend another evening with her highfalutin friends. It was a set-up, another method of double-teaming him to get him to propose. He knew the drill. Lauryn would sit silently, while Cory would casually enlighten them as to the joys of married life. Her husband, Dean, an alpha male everywhere except at home with his wife, would pretend to discuss sports, home repair and other masculine topics with Jonathan, but his agenda was transparent too. His job was to convince Jonathan that a man was incomplete without a wife and a family. Besides the fact that the women in their lives were best buds, they had absolutely nothing in common. Dean was a white-collared, ivy-leagued, trust-fund baby; fortunately so, otherwise his receding hairline, freckled cheeks and pudgy midsection would never have garnered a second glance from Cory. Before she, rather she and her mother, decided it was time to settle down, all Cory had dated were tall, hard-bodied, thick-haired, athletic types. The kind whose good looks and meticulous grooming were in stark contrast to their basement apartments, flimsy resumes, and low credit scores. So Dean it was and with him came a massive historical Colonial in Chappaqua (a fact Cory often embellished by claiming they lived across the street from Hillary Clinton) and a powerful surname she tossed around as it fancied her. Most recently to secure a four top at an exclusive new, celebrity-owned restaurant. Jonathan had half-heartedly agreed to the double date and although he dreaded it, had every intention of going. Up until that morning when—as if the weather seconded his motion to stay home—torrential rains poured down. There was a sharp chill in the air. The last thing he wanted to do was spend his Saturday night battling traffic and hunting for parking in midtown Manhattan, only to break bread with two people who didn't like him. He clicked the remote. *Ah, the game is on.*

9

Elle

On a lazy Sunday morning, Elle and Luke were eating breakfast together on his deck. The pre-noon sun shone down on them as Elle thumbed through a newspaper and Luke read the latest John Grisham novel.

"Want some more juice?" Luke asked as he dog-eared his page and got up. Engrossed in an article about a small earthquake in South America, she mumbled a distracted 'No, thank you'. Just as she was reading about the subpar relief efforts, she looked up to find Luke kneeling before her, his expression full of cautious anticipation.

"Elle." He took her left hand in his. "I know it hasn't been long, but . . . but you're the first thing I think about when I wake up and the last thing I think of before I go to bed. I can't . . . rather, I don't want to picture a life without you in it. So, what do you say? Will you marry me?"

He slid a platinum solitaire on her finger; it was exquisite. As much as she had anticipated the moment, she felt awed at the reality of it. She looked down at the ring, then at him and then back at the ring. Her words were caught in her throat. Was this really happening? At eleven in the morning on a Sunday, while they both were still in their pajamas with the television humming in the background. It was so unexpected, but so much like Luke. Cool and easy and natural.

"Well? You're scaring me here." His long eyelashes fluttered with anticipation. "Interested in becoming Mrs. Luke Cartright?"

Against her will, an image of Marcus flashed through her mind. In a rapid stream of memories, she recalled everything from the moment they'd met up until the day, three and a half years later, when the walls all came crashing down around her. She remembered the pain, the tears, and the self pity she'd wallowed in for months on end. Then she looked down at Luke's face. His warm sensitive eyes and expectant expression stared back at her. She concluded he would never hurt her the way Marcus had. Although common sense might dictate otherwise, she decided to take a leap of faith and for once make a decision with her heart rather than her head.

"Yes!" she exclaimed, surprised by her own enthusiasm. "Yes, I'd be honored to be Mrs. Luke Cartright." He wrapped his arms around her and she knew she'd made the right decision. To hell with Marcus. She was right where she belonged.

10

Blair

Vaughn's meeting ended early, allowing him to beat the rush hour traffic and make it home earlier than usual. As he made his way up the stairs, he heard what sounded like heaving. He found Blair in their bathroom on her knees, embracing the toilet seat.

"Babe, are you all right?"

She whipped her head around, then quickly wiped her mouth and stood. "What are you doing home so early?" she asked as she flushed away the evidence of what had become her any-time-of-the-day sickness.

He told her his meeting ended early and pressed his hand against her brow. "You're burning up."

"I'm fine. Must have had something that didn't agree with me. You know how sensitive my stomach is."

"What did you eat?" He followed her into the bedroom.

She told him she had a chicken salad for lunch, and it was probably bad. When he suggested they go to the doctor, she insisted she was fine, that she just needed some fresh air and planned to go lie by the pool. He watched her descend the staircase. Once she was out of sight, he went straight to the top drawer of her bureau.

11

Jonathan

Tim, the athletic director, made the formal introduction in the doorway of Jonathan's office. "Bree, this is Jonathan Moore. He coaches men's basketball."

Jonathan muttered a distracted greeting, barely raising his head, as he shuffled through the paperwork on his desk.

"Oh, no, don't get up," Bree said.

He looked up, seeing her for the first time. She was tall. At least five-foot-eight. Even through her loose t-shirt and shorts he could see that she was exceptionally fit, but not in that taut, boy-like way female athletes often were, with broad shoulders, narrow hips and tiny breasts. Her arms and legs had just enough hint of muscle tone to reveal a commitment to the gym, yet she was endowed with perfectly appointed curves above and below her narrow waist. She was the perfect blend of woman and athlete. Her shoulder-length hair was drawn back into a loose ponytail, a soft row of bangs grazed her eyebrows.

He could tell she wore no make up. Her high cheekbones had their own natural shade of blush.

"I'm sorry. Just wrapped up in some paperwork here. It's nice to meet you," he said before locking his gaze with Tim's. If he looked at Bree any longer, it would border on gawking.

"No problem." Her raspy voice drew his eyes back to her.

He was suddenly grateful he'd just gotten a hair cut the day before. "Welcome aboard. I'm sure I'll see you around campus."

She paused in the doorway and shot him a furtive glance. "I sure hope so."

A full two weeks passed before he saw her again. One evening after practice, he bumped into her on line in the cafeteria.

"Hey, Coach Jonathan." She nudged him with her elbow as she balanced a beige plastic tray in her hands.

He smiled broadly before catching himself and tempering his reaction. "*Coach Jonathan?* Real cute. Does that mean I have to call you Coach Bree?"

"Only if you plan on joining my team. Holding cross country try-outs next week. Should I plan on seeing you?" she asked.

"I'm more of a sprinter, actually."

"So you like to move fast?"

He grabbed a banana from the counter, more out of nerves than a sudden need for potassium. They reached the cashier and she pulled out her wallet. His pleasure in not seeing a ring on her left hand brought another goofy smile to his face. "I got this," he said, handing the cashier his campus ID card.

"No, I can't let you pay."

He instinctively placed his hand over hers. A sudden surge of something he couldn't describe ran through him. "No, I got it. Consider it an apology for being rude when we met."

She smiled. "Okay, but only if you sit and eat this apology dinner with me. Unless you have someplace to be."

He did, but for some reason, eating a chicken wrap on a plastic tray with her seemed more appealing. They sat tucked away in the corner, a good distance from the student center dinnertime clamor. Idle chatter developed into two hours of getting to know each other, drawn to an end only when the cleaning crew interrupted to tell them the cafeteria was closing.

12

Blair

It was late on a Friday afternoon. Blair had left work early to get a head start on her extended weekend plans with Dylan. She had yet to concoct a story for Vaughn, but figured it would be a seamless get-away because he'd mentioned something about going to the casinos with his brothers. As she crossed the street at the corner of 28th Street and Park Avenue South, she noticed a black town car traveling slowly besides her. It made a quick right turn in front of her and came to a sudden halt. The rear window rolled down and six pink balloons cascaded out. Ah, Dylan really outdid himself this time. He remembered how that was her all-time favorite scene from Sex and the City. It was a brazen move, there out in the heart of the city during rush hour, but how could she not be tickled? She was so in love with this man. She approached the car giddy with expectation. But then the door opened and her stomach sank. There she stood, face to face with her husband.

"What . . . what are you doing here?" she asked, imagining that even the tiny bit of color in her fair complexion must have drained away.

"Surprising my beautiful wife," Vaughn said, then flashed a charming smile, the same one which had won her heart over years ago. Now it only irritated her.

"Surprising me? What for?"

"C'mon, get inside." He held the door open.

She looked about helplessly, wishing some random stranger would scoop her up and shuttle her away, but there was no superhero to save the day, so she accepted her fate and climbed into the back seat. "What are you up to, Vaughn? What's this all about?"

He gave the driver a cryptic directive and turned to her. "You've seemed really stressed lately, so I wanted to surprise you."

"By giving me a ride home?"

"Not exactly." He pulled a navy blue silk cloth from his pocket.

She inched back. "What's that for?"

"What's wrong with you? You don't trust me?"

She gave him a look as if to say, *are you kidding me?*

"C'mon, just relax and close your eyes." She reluctantly complied and he tied the scarf over her eyes.

For the next forty-five minutes she inquired about his intentions and he refused her any hints. When they eventually arrived at their mystery destination, she heard the driver get out and open the trunk. He then opened the door for Vaughn, who only untied Blair's scarf after he'd helped her out of the car. She opened her eyes. They were at the American Airlines terminal at John F. Kennedy Airport.

"Vaughn, what the hell?"

"We're going on vaca, baby. A few hours from now we'll be lying on the beach in the Caribbean." His expression was proud, like that of a little boy presenting his mother with a report card full of A's.

All about them, people hustled. Her head was spinning. An hour ago she'd been in the city, relaxed and at peace, ready to steal away time with Dylan. Now she stood on an airport curb, about to leave the country—with him.

She gasped. "The Caribbean? I have to work next week and I told my mom I was coming over this weekend."

Vaughn, never one to take no for an answer, marginalized her concerns. "You always used to say you wanted to go to Turks & Caicos. It's the only island down there we haven't been to. So I called your job and told them you're taking some time off. You'll see your mom when we get back, I had Rosa pack your bags."

Sure enough, there was her expensive luggage being hauled away by two skycaps.

"Vaughn, honey." She stroked his arm and made her best effort to mask her disappointment. "This was a wonderful idea, it really was, but it's all so last minute. Can't we just hold off until next month?"

"Why wait until next month, when we're right here and it's all planned out? C'mon, you'll feel better once you get on the plane and have a drink." He clasped her hand and led her through the automatic doors. "We're running late, we're going to have to hustle to make our flight."

Before she knew it they were rushing through check-in, the security gates and waiting to board. Her mind was fixated on Dylan and how to find the opportunity to speak with him before they left. She needed to speak with him. There was no way she could tell him this news over text. He needed to hear her voice as much she needed to hear his.

Once they reached the gate she told Vaughn she needed to run to the bathroom.

"Go on the plane. They're about to start boarding first class."

"I hate those tiny bathrooms, they make me claustrophobic. I'll just be a second." Before he could protest, she bolted to the nearest restroom, which was directly across from the gate.

As soon as she was inside, she rummaged through her purse for her cell phone, keeping one eye on the door. She couldn't scroll through her contacts fast enough. She tapped send. Nothing. When she tapped it again the screen blinked. All of the bars on her phone flatlined. She paced back and forth in the little space, glaring at the screen, willing it to work. A flight attendant, noticing her frustration, told her she'd have to go back out into the corridor to get a signal.

Just perfect. Absolutely perfect. How was she going to reach him? She could not get on that plane and leave the country without speaking to him. She could not! Oh, how she hated Vaughn. He always managed to make things hard for her and to get his way, even when he didn't realize he was doing it. This rage of hers was commonplace. Every so often she'd get to thinking about him and the way he always managed to win and it would infuriate her. What happened to karma and reaping what you sow? Did these concepts not apply when it came to Vaughn? Was there some patron saint or Greek god looking down and protecting him? Why did he deserve special treatment and she did not. Oh, how she hated him. She glimpsed her reflection and was saddened by what she saw; what had once been a beautiful face was now riddled with furrowed brows, crimson cheeks and frown lines she couldn't get rid of no matter how much Restylane she used. He'd brought out the worst in her; that innocent, vibrant, glass-is-half-full girl was gone and in her place stood a jaded, bitter woman who felt way older than her thirty-two years.

She splashed water on her face and brushed back stray wisps of her dark hair. She willed herself to calm down and retreat from that ugly place. This was typically when she'd keep Vaughn at bay and find a way to put distance between them until she'd calmed. But today that wasn't an option. She'd have to face him and hate him beneath the surface as she sat beside him on the plane. All while the man she loved was at home confirming reservations for a dinner that wouldn't be eaten, and printing out tickets to a show that wouldn't be seen.

As soon as she stepped out of the restroom, her gaze met Vaughn's. He nodded towards the gate. "They're boarding first class, let's go."

Once they were settled in their seats, she did exactly what she'd hoped she wouldn't have to. She sent Dylan a quick, frantic text while Vaughn played with his iPad.

Baby, i'm so sorry 2 have 2 do this like this but i had no choice. vaughn picked me up from work, n took me straight 2 the airport 4 some vacation. i didn't wanna go but i had no choice. not sure when i'll be home but i'll try n call u as soon as i can get away. i'm so sorry n please believe me when i tell u i didn't know anything about this, I LOVE U. She clicked send and felt a tiny bit of relief. She then sent Elle a similar hasty text.

Moments later a flight attendant came by to take their drink orders. Blair ordered a glass of orange juice.

"Jack and ginger for me," Vaughn said, "and add some Ketel One to her juice."

Upon recognizing him, the attendant's voice rose two octaves. The giggling and excessive smiling commenced, but Blair was too distracted to be annoyed. "No, I'm fine, just the juice please."

He kneaded the back of her neck. "You're all tense. You need something stronger than OJ." He flashed a grin at the attendant. "Bring her the screwdriver."

Smitten with Vaughn, the attendant giggled and returned with a glass of orange juice, which had clearly been diluted with vodka.

Blair pushed the glass to the edge of her tray. "I don't need a drink, I'm fine."

"Yes, you do." He popped in his ear piece and hit play, his was of concluding the discussion.

Hours later they landed at Providenciales Airport in Turks & Caicos. Ironically she sought the comfort of the same hotel she'd scorned only hours prior. The traveling, worrying about Dylan, trying to appease Vaughn, and the queasiness building in her stomach were all bearing down on her. She was in need of a good night's sleep. Her only hope was that Vaughn was equally tired and wouldn't try to have sex with her. He fell asleep as soon as they reached their room. For that she was grateful.

13

Elle

Her jaw dropped as she read the frantic text from her friend. Elle immediately called Blair back and was sent straight to voicemail. What could all of this mean? Vaughn was not a man known for romantic gestures and especially not as of late; the distance between them was growing day by day. Oh, this was not good. Was her friend in danger? Had Vaughn found out she was pregnant?

She called Jonathan. "What do you think? What could he have up his sleeve?"

"Up his sleeve? What do you mean?"

"I'm serious. A husband and wife who barely speak don't just up and go on vacation one day. Maybe he found out about Dylan. Maybe there is no trip to the Caribbean."

"What? So, what do you think is going down?" Jonathan said. She was about to reprimand him for chewing in her ear, but decided against it.

"Maybe he knows."

"And he knows and he's going to do what? Wait, is this like one of those movies where the rich man takes his cheating wife somewhere to kill her and get rid of the remains so he doesn't have to pay alimony?"

"Everything's a joke with you, right?"

"Nah, I'm just saying, things like that don't happen in real life. You're watching way too much Lifetime," he said. "Hey, shouldn't you be out shopping for a wedding gown or something?"

"Yeah, and maybe I should take Lauryn with me, so she can look for hers."

"Ah, good one. Point taken. No more wedding talk."

"But seriously, about Blair. I'm scared for her."

He took her off of speaker phone. "Okay, okay. I see where you're coming from, but let's think logically. If he really knew, he would have confronted her already. You gotta remember, men aren't strategic like you women. If we know some shit, it's coming out. Only a woman would have the patience to hold it in, set up some make-believe trip and then do God knows what." She could hear his blender whirling in the background. Jonathan's inability to sit still wore on her nerves. "Maybe he's really trying to make up for being such a bastard all these years. It happens, you know."

"Vaughn's not your typical man. He's manipulative," she said. "Who knows what he's really capable of?"

"Elle, at the end of the day, she's a grown woman who can handle herself. Don't get worked up so soon. Did you call her back?"

"Yeah, over and over. I keep getting the voicemail."

"So we wait and see what happens. She'll call or text you soon enough. She's probably lying on a beach somewhere loving life, forgetting all about Dylan and enjoying all the good stuff Vaughn's money can buy."

"What's that supposed to mean?"

"Nothing."

"It means something. What are you saying?"

Jonathan sighed. "Nothing, I just think that cheating sucks, but it's a lot easier to deal with when the cheater is a millionaire. That's all I'm saying."

"So it's okay, it's okay for him to be unfaithful as long as he has money? You don't really believe that, do you?" she asked.

"No, I'm saying that men . . . well, people cheat every day. There are women out there dealing with husbands who cheat on them left and right, husbands who make fifty-thousand dollars a year and rely on them to split the rent. I'm just saying, if it's gonna happen anyway, at the very least she has a nice set-up to go home to."

"Wow! I don't even know what to say."

"Take it in the spirit I say it. Not passing judgment, just stating the facts and I'd bet money that's exactly the way Vaughn sees it. Hell, it's probably the way she sees it, which is why she stays. It's all relative, Elle."

Maybe if Jonathan knew the whole story, that Blair was pregnant with another man's child, he would have been more concerned, but she could never tell him. She already told him too much. Blair would kill her if she knew Elle had told him about the affair at all. What if Vaughn knew and this was all some type of set-up? He definitely could. For all his faults, he was a smart man and he'd know what signs to look for since he'd practically made a career out of infidelity. Elle couldn't think straight.

"My battery is about to die." She told him. "I'll call you later."

14

Blair

Blair reread a Mademoiselle article at least three times before she even had a sense of what it was about. Her eyes glazed over the page; her ability to concentrate was fleeting. She looked up, squinting despite the coverage of their oversized aqua-blue umbrella, and saw her husband approaching with two drinks in hand. She couldn't help but still admire his good looks. He maintained the physique of a man ten years his junior. His skin glistened under the sun, his muscular thighs and chest provided the perfect frame for his taut abs. His arms were perfect, shoulders were broad, even his calves begged noticing. His gait oozed confidence, he knew what a sight he was to behold. His rugged good looks and infectious smile were just icing on the cake. Blair was no slouch; she was attractive by any measure, plus she was one of those fortunate women who managed to maintain a flat stomach, cellulite-free thighs and a perky bum without stepping foot into the state-of-the-art gym Vaughn had built into their basement. But she didn't have Vaughn's charisma or his personality. Being the center of attention made her uncomfortable, whereas Vaughn thrived on it. He was always on, always ready to entertain idle conversation and bask in attention.

"Here, baby," he said, handing her a frothy white drink in a plastic cup. The stem of plump red cherry dangled over the edge.

"Is it virgin?"

"Nah."

"It's too early for liquor." She handed it back to him. "You drink it."

"We're on vacation. It's never too early."

"I'll pass. And I think I've had enough sun, I'm going back to the room." She started packing up her beach bag.

"I'll come with you."

Damn. She could not get away from him for even a minute. He hadn't let her out of his sight since they'd arrived. She needed to call Dylan. He still hadn't replied to her text message.

"No, you stay, I know how you like to lie out. I'm just going to take a shower and get ready for dinner. You know how long it takes me." She leaned over and kissed his forehead for good measure.

"Nah, I'm done too. Let's go."

As soon as they got up to their room, she rushed to shower and dress. By the time she was done, Vaughn had drifted off on the couch. This was her chance to get away. She called Vaughn's name in a loud whisper. When he didn't stir, she grabbed her clutch and scurried down to the lobby. Her cell-phone battery had died and Vaughn had conveniently forgotten to pack her charger. At the first pay phone she saw, she dialed Dylan's number. *Please pick up. Please.* Her heartbeat quickened as she anticipated the sound of his voice. She was greeted by his voicemail, which was to both her dismay and relief, for the coward in her really didn't want to hear his voice. No matter how much she apologized, it wouldn't take the sting out of what had happened. The thought of Dylan on a romantic vacation with his ex-wife, or any woman, made her ill, and he had to feel the same way. Would this be the straw that broke the camel's back? Had he had enough of the sneaking around and lying? Did he still think she was worth it? The beep interrupted her thoughts. She breathed into the phone. *It's me. I don't know if you got my text. If you didn't, I need to explain . . .* She went on to explain all that had happened, feeling a mix of relief and anxiety.

When she turned the knob to their suite, Vaughn was standing at the door with his arms folded. "Where did you go?"

"Down to the lobby," she said, "to make reservations for dinner."

His stare was full of suspicion. "Why didn't you just call from here?"

"I thought maybe they had some menus down there I could look at." She flopped down on the couch and casually flipped through a magazine. "Are you going to get ready or what?"

He shot her a pensive look before proceeding to the bathroom. As soon as she heard the sound of the shower, she exhaled. Although lying to Vaughn had become commonplace, it was still difficult. Especially when he gave her that look, the one which pierced through her, as if he were reading her thoughts. Her concerns shifted to back Dylan. Would he believe she was still sleeping with Vaughn? Up until now he'd believed her when she told him she was not and it was the truth, for the most part. She hadn't been sleeping with Vaughn, at least not voluntarily. There had been a few isolated incidents when she couldn't avert his advances, nights he either came home tipsy or was feeling especially amorous. On those occasions she just laid there and waited for it be over. Vaughn either didn't notice or didn't care. But she could never admit this to Dylan. He wouldn't understand. The fact of the matter was, Vaughn was still her husband and with that came certain responsibilities that Dylan should expect, not like, but expect.

"Blair, it's time to get up." Vaughn tugged at the sheets. "C'mon, get up or we're going to miss the boat."

Blair rubbed her eyes. Vaughn stood over her, already dressed in a pair of baggy swim trunks and a white tank top.

She sat up, stretched her arms over her head and yawned. "What boat? It's not even seven o'clock. What are you talking about?"

"I booked us a trip on one of those day cruises. It goes to a small private island. We'll have lunch, go snorkeling and stuff . . . "

Her daily bout with nausea had already set in. "Ah babe, I don't know if I'm up for all of that."

He sat on the edge of the bed. "C'mon, just get dressed. You can take a nap when we get there."

She shook her head. "Vaughn, I don't know. I'm really tired. Is there a later boat?"

"I don't know. Don't think so. It doesn't matter, we're booked for eight. Just get up, would you?" There was a knock on the door. "I ordered us some breakfast."

One look at the scrambled eggs and she wanted to vomit, but somehow she managed to pick at the toast and drink enough juice to appease him. As he scarfed down his food, she mustered the energy to get showered and dressed. Maybe some fresh air would do her good.

To her surprise, she made it across the water without feeling ill. Vaughn was right—the island was breathtaking. How she would have loved to have been there with Dylan. It was fringed with pure white sparkling sand and spattered with tall, bowed palm trees. Curtained yellow-and-white striped cabanas were sprinkled across the shore. A row of men and women wearing peacock blue short-sleeved button-down shirts and crisp white pants stood waiting, holding trays of colorful, tropical drinks. Blair was troubled to realize there was no ramp and they had to jump right into the ocean to disembark the catamaran. She shot Vaughn an uneasy look before several of their boisterous cruise-mates leapt right into the warm, blue water and she learned it was only three feet deep.

They ambled towards the shore feeling the warm, soft sand beneath their toes. Once there, a tall bronzed server offered Blair a hurricane glass filled with an electric-blue drink replete with slices of orange, pineapple and strawberry tucked into the rim. In response to the apprehensive look on her face, he silently assured her it contained no alcohol.

She and Philip, as she would later learn was his name, came to a subtle understanding that all he was to bring her for the rest of the day were virgin drinks of the like. Vaughn, thankfully, didn't notice and was pleased to believe that she finally agreed to consume alcohol. For some reason he always took issue with people who refused to drink with him, as if his sipping on Scotch as they sipped on ginger ale was tantamount to him being a drunk. The day went without incident until he tried to convince Blair to go scuba diving.

"What's wrong with you?" he asked as he massaged sunblock into his calves. They were lying in their cabana a few yards from the idyllic crystal blue water. The waves crashed against the shore, each time drawing away more of the warm white sand. They were two of the twenty people who were fortunate enough to have the beach all to themselves.

"I just don't feel like it."

"But look how nice this water is. We're on vacation, for God's sake."

"So you go," she said.

"It's no fun by myself."

She pointed towards a lively group of sunbathers a few yards away. "Go with them."

"I don't want to go with them, I want to go with you," he whined.

"But I don't want to, I'm not feeling well"

He studied her. "What's wrong with you?"

"Feeling a little seasick."

"Seasick?" He threw up his hands. "We've been on land for hours already."

"Sometimes it takes a while to shake it, I just need to rest for a little bit. But I don't want to ruin your time, so you go ahead without me." She put on her sunglasses and reclined back on the plush, white beach chair.

He surveyed her again, then shrugged. "Suit yourself." He started off towards the group which couldn't contain their excitement over the prospect of diving with Vaughn. She watched him sign a few autographs and pose for pictures. Good, he's in his element. He'd be distracted long enough for her to get some rest and figure out how she was going to work things out with Dylan once she returned home.

She woke up, what turned out to be hours later, to find Vaughn back by her side, sitting at the edge of his beach chair.

"You really should have come, babe. It was amazing. You would've loved it." He brushed sand from his shoulders, which, along with the rest of him, was already two shades darker. She looked down at her pale thighs, thinking she could really use some sun herself.

"Glad you enjoyed yourself." She sat up. "Get any good pictures?"

He dangled the colorful rubber camera around his wrist. "Sure did. Really missed you, though. It's been a long time since we've done anything fun together."

She nodded before pulling a magazine from her beach bag.

A wistful expression cast across his face. "What do you think happened to us?"

She gave him a wry look. "You know what happened to us."

"I know, I know, I haven't always been the best husband. But that's in the past."

"Is it really?" She flipped through the pages, searching for an article she hadn't already read.

"Don't give me that look. Yeah, it's in the past."

"Look, let's not get into it. It's too beautiful out here to be arguing over nonsense. Let's just agree to disagree, okay?" She landed on an article titled, *Rekindling the spice in your marriage.* Hmph. She turned the page.

"We're not arguing." He took a deep breath. "I've been doing a lot of thinking lately, about you and me . . . and us."

"Yeah?" She flipped another page.

"Do you mind?" He took the magazine from her hand and placed it beside him. "Yeah, and I've realized some of the reasons why I did what I did."

She liked the way he used the word 'did', as if his transgressions were limited to one singular occurrence. Part of her wanted to know what it was that he had realized, but at the same time, she didn't want to revisit the past. There was nothing he could say which would matter at this point. The damage was done.

He went on. "I know what you're thinking—you've heard this song and dance already, right?"

She folded her arms. "Yup."

He looked away then raked his long fingers through the sand near his feet. "I had a long talk with my mom not too long ago." He dug out jagged pieces of seashell. "Know what she told me?"

Blair shrugged.

"Told me my father had an affair once." He tossed the shells back out towards the ocean. "It lasted a couple of years, actually. Some woman he'd met at work. My mom found out and he denied it, of course, but she'd hired a private investigator and had all the proof she needed, so she gave him an ultimatum and he ended it."

Blair whipped off her sunglasses. "What! Your dad? I never would have thought he . . . he doesn't seem like the type. They seem so happy."

"They are—now. But things were rough for a few years. Really rough. Remember when I told you how my mom used to go back and forth to Arizona when I was a kid, to take care of my grandmother?"

"I remember."

"Well, turns out she wasn't in Arizona. She was away upstate at a facility."

"A facility? For what?"

"After she found out about the affair, my father told her he was in love with the woman and wasn't sure if he wanted to stay married. She was devastated and . . . "

His voice cracked, " . . . and she tried . . . she tried to kill herself."

"Oh Vaughn, oh my God." She reached for his hand. "That's horrible."

She instantly thought of Elaine, a kind-hearted woman, who'd had always treated her as if she was her own daughter. *Tried to kill herself?* A wave of sadness washed over her.

"So all the time I thought she was away with my grandmother, she was actually in a clinic trying to get over what my father had done. You know they've been together since they were fourteen, he's all she ever knew. The thought of him leaving her was too much to handle. She had a nervous breakdown."

Blair instinctively squeezed his hand and stroked his arm. He felt both oddly foreign and familiar at the same time. She hadn't touched him affectionately in over a year. As her fingers ran over the contour of his shoulder, her flesh tingled and she felt a curious surge through her core.

"I didn't know then, of course, because I was just a kid, but now that I look back, I can see the difference in her from before she went away and after. She's seemed so much more fragile and weak and of course that explains the pills she started taking for her nerves." He made air quotes with his fingers.

"What made her tell you all of this?"

"I don't know, we were having dinner the other night and she started asking questions about you and me and when we were going to try and have another baby. I told her things weren't going so well, how you seemed really distant and how it was probably my fault because of everything I've done. She thought it was something I should know, but made me promise not to tell my dad she told me. She doesn't want me to look at him any differently."

"Do you?"

"Yes and no. I'll admit I was pissed at first. To know he put my mom through all of that, to think she could have died, because of something he did. It tears me up, I mean, where would I be without my mom?"

"But you're not mad at him anymore?"

His eyes were downcast. "I don't know. Some days I am, others I know I have no right to be."

"Because?" She knew the answer, but wanted to hear him say it.

"Because, I'm no better. I could have driven you to the same thing if you were a weaker woman. I see that now. When I did what I did, I was only thinking of myself, I figured what you didn't know wouldn't hurt you." He turned and looked at her for the first time. "And if you did find out, I thought I could make up for it with stuff, material things. There's no getting around it, I was a hundred percent wrong. You didn't deserve that."

Her mouth opened, but nothing came out.

"You don't have to say anything. Just to think I could have hurt you the way my dad did my mom, it really breaks me up. I don't ever want our children to look at me the way I looked at him, to be disappointed in me."

He turned his body to face her and reached for both of her hands. "Blair, look at me. Believe me when I tell you I'm so sorry for everything I ever put you through, going way back to Syracuse. I love you and want this marriage to work. I need you to give me another chance."

She stared back at him and thought, *is this just another apology?* One brought on by grief over his mother and the romance of the setting? She'd seen more apologies than she cared to remember, but something about this one was different. It seemed genuine; his expression was contrite. She was looking at the face of the same nineteen-year-old she'd fallen in love with many moons ago.

She took a deep breath. "Vaughn, I love you, you know that, but we've been through so much—"

Her heart was thawing, she had to regain her resolve, so she avoided his gaze and looked away. "I'm afraid to get back in a comfort zone just for it to happen all over again."

He gently touched her chin then guided her face back towards his. "I know you're scared, baby. You have every right to be, but I'm not asking you to give *me* another chance, give *us* another chance. Don't you think we're worth it?"

He'd pled for forgiveness in the past, promised to do right by her and had not. Was she falling for the same trap? She searched his eyes. They were wide and woeful. His smile was silly and fragile, an expression she hadn't seen since clear back to the day he'd first invited her on a date, when he was fearful she might say no. She even saw traces of his mother's face. He adored her and through her, finally saw how painful and damaging infidelity could be. For once he could understand how his cheating demoralized Blair, how it crushed her self esteem and ruined their marriage. Finally he recognized it. It was a shame his revelation only came after learning his mother's story—but he now knew all the same.

"That's part of the reason I planned this trip for us. I wanted us to get away and be alone, get to know each other again. We're drifting apart and I can't let it happen, I can't lose you anymore than I already have. We've gotta fix this, you're the only thing that matters. Believe me when I tell you that."

That face. That handsome, endearing face, the one she had once loved so much. Memories of the day they met, the first time they made love, the night he first told her he loved her, their wedding day—all of it came barreling back in a flash. He had been her first love, the father of the children she'd lost, her rock, her support. If only he hadn't done those things they would have been perfect together. How could she forget it all and move on?

"We're worth it, I know we are," he said. "That's why I want us to start over fresh by renewing our vows."

"Our vows?"

"Yeah, what do you say, baby? We can do it tomorrow. I'll make all of the arrangements."

She couldn't find her voice. He placed his palm over her stomach. "We can even try and have another baby, start our family."

Tears streamed down her cheeks. She still loved him. Why had he waited so long? If only he'd said these things to her before she'd met Dylan, before she fell in love with him and before she became pregnant with his child.

"Excuse me, Mr. and Mrs. Hill." They looked up to see the cruise coordinator. "Sorry to interrupt, but we'll be boarding soon to go back to the mainland. May we get any of your bags for you?"

Back in their suite, she allowed her emotions to lead the way. For the first time in over a year, she didn't flinch when he touched her. His kisses felt good, natural, real. There was no protesting when he undressed her, laid her on the bed and entered her.

She cried that night, not out of frustration, or anger or sadness, but out of calm. It just felt so right. This was where she was supposed to be. Who would have thought she needed to travel over a thousand miles in order find home?

15

Jonathan

He was exhausted, but doing his best to keep up with her. How she managed to maintain both perfect form and steady conversation was beyond him. After the ninth consecutive lap, Jonathan broke into a trot.

"Let's cool down," he said.

"Run out of steam?" Bree teased as she began jogging backwards.

"Listen, Flo Jo, not all of us spend our days and nights running around the track."

She slowed to join him. "Okay, I'll take it easy on you."

He caught his breath. "You're killing me, lady. When I agreed to join you for a little air after work, this is not what I had in mind."

"Well, you were all suited up. Figured a fellow athlete like you would like this."

She arched her back and clasped her hands behind her head. "Doesn't this nighttime air feel good in your lungs? This is my favorite time of day. After everyone has left and the students are back in their dorms. So nice and quiet."

The sun was setting and the sky was streaked with bands of orange and red, a sight one knows he must appreciate quickly before it's soon replaced with a blanket of darkness.

"Ya know, there's another way you can get that calm and quiet you seem to like so much. It's called going home."

She smirked. "You're just a regular old court jester, huh?"

"I try." Something about Bree brought out the silliness in him. Maybe because she was lighthearted and easy to talk to; she was someone he could be himself with.

Their conversation was more of the same they'd had in the cafeteria. She explained that she'd moved to New York after her job was eliminated due to budget cuts at her college in north Florida. She told him she knew absolutely no one in New York and admitted she hadn't even stepped foot in Manhattan since she arrived. To which he replied by rattling off the names of landmarks she should visit. It was then when the conversation took its first turn. "So you're going to just give me some directions and send me on my way? All by my lonesome?" she said.

He knew it was the point where he should change course and discuss work or what's good in the movies or even the weather, anything to avert the direction it was heading. But he couldn't or rather he didn't want to.

"You're right. I guess I can't do that, can I?"

"No pressure, of course." She pulled the band from her hair and shook her head from side to side. Her dark-brown locks tumbled down onto her shoulders. His words were caught in his throat. God, she was beautiful. Out there in the dark, wearing a dull gray sweatshirt, with her skin beaded with sweat —she was beautiful.

"It's no pressure at all. Might be cool to give a tour to a New York City virgin," he said.

"Virgin? Ha, haven't been one of those in years."

Another turn.

"I'm gonna leave that one alone. How about this weekend we go check out some sights? The Empire State Building, Times Square, Central Park, you name it. How does that sound?" He felt a pang of guilt with each word. He thought of Lauryn for the first time that evening. What the hell was he doing?

"Sounds like a date," she said. "I can't wait."

Why did she have to use that word? All of their flirtatious banter had lingered in a gray area, one he could easily push out of his mind later. The word *date* framed it, brought it to the forefront of his mind and face to face with his reality.

"Something wrong?"

He smiled. "Nah, not at all. It's getting late, though, I should be getting on my way home. You should too."

She told him she wanted to run a few more laps and was already looking forward to the weekend. Then she trotted off. He watched her as she ran, his feet temporarily frozen on the turf. Why was he so intrigued by her? He wanted to know more, more about her past, more about who she was, why she was single and most importantly what she thought about him. As he walked back to the locker room, he found himself smiling, eager for Saturday to arrive so he could spend a whole day with her and learn the answers to all of his questions.

Saturday came. Jonathan was mildly chagrined that he'd taken so much care with his appearance; he was wearing a new button-down shirt, his favorite jeans and a healthy dose of cologne. It was not a big deal, he told himself. He was just being hospitable to a new colleague, yet another example of his being a good person. He repeated this mantra to the reflection in his rearview mirror. It was innocent and it definitely was *not* a date. He looked up and watched her emerge from her building and approach his truck, which coincidentally had just received its first waxing of the season. Should he get out and open the door? Or was that corny? No, but it would be 'date-like' behavior. But if he didn't, what would she think? She didn't strike him as a disciple of Emily Post's rules of etiquette, but still. Sometimes all it took was one misstep for a woman to write a man off. Before he could resolve his cognitive debate, she opened the door and was easing into his passenger's seat. Without warning he was enveloped by her fragrance. She leaned over and kissed his cheek. The hairs on the back of his neck stood. How was he going to get through a whole day with this woman?

"Thanks for picking me up," she said. "I would've been totally lost on the subway."

"I couldn't let that happen." He said in an exaggerated southern twang. "Who would explain to your ma and pa how you disappeared in the big city?"

She waved a tiny fist at him. "You're going to stop making fun of my people if you know what's good for you."

In the hours which followed, they ascended the Empire State Building, Bree was awed by the bustle of Times Square, they window-shopped in Soho, then lunched at a sidewalk cafe in the village. By the time it grew dark, they were strolling along the outskirts of Central Park, discussing everything under the sun from politics and sports to their favorite characters on the ThunderCats. He'd heard people describe moments when they wished time could stand still and had believed those statements were reserved for teenage girls and hopeless romantics, but now he knew exactly what they meant and it both scared and thrilled him. Was Bree feeling the same thing?

Only when a passerby asked him for the time did he even glance at his watch. It was a quarter past eleven. It had been nearly seven hours since he'd picked her up.

"Look at that. I made it almost eight hours in Manhattan without getting mugged," she joked.

"You know why, right? 'Cause you're accompanied by a big strong man. If you were alone, you'd be in an alley somewhere begging for your life."

"Big strong man?" She looked from side to side. "Where? I haven't seen one."

For the first time that day, he touched her. It was only a playful shove, but that's when he knew just why he'd refrained from doing so. Like that moment in the cafeteria when he'd placed his hand over hers, it had been brief and innocent, yet titillating. He had to get out of the situation, it was feeling way too good. There was still time to pull out. He hadn't crossed any lines yet, he could still drive her home, drop her off and then go see Lauryn. He'd climb into her bed and she'd remind him of all the reasons he loved and wanted to be with her. Yes, that's what he should do. Go home. Now, before it was too late.

They hailed a cab and rode back downtown in silence. Silence was his friend. His thoughts needed to remain clear and focused on what he had at home. Lauryn loved him, she respected him and was good to him and would never do anything to hurt him. Her life revolved around him. She needed him. He could not disappoint her. He *would not* disappoint her.

Bree interrupted his thoughts. "Why are all of those people lined up outside of a church at this hour?"

He explained it was a former church turned nightclub.

"That's eerie. Kind of sacrilegious, don't you think? I tell you, you northerners are something else."

He pointed a playful finger at her. "Now you're going to stop talking about *my* people or else."

"Or else what?" She inched closer to him.

He got another whiff of her scent. Damn. He searched for the verbal equivalent of a cold shower. "So, what did you think? Tell me your take on the Big Apple?"

"I liked it, but I really enjoyed the company more than anything."

Another inch closer.

"Yeah?"

"Yeah." Her voice was void of all humor.

"That's what's up. Maybe next time we can go to the Met or the Museum of Natural History. You'd like those."

No sooner than the words left his mouth, he knew he'd screwed up.

She shifted in her seat, crossed her legs and turned towards him. "I would love that."

It was almost midnight by the time they reached his car. Lauryn would be texting or calling soon to say good night. That was sure to sober him. But as they drove back up towards Westchester, he couldn't help but wonder what was going through Bree's mind. She liked him, that much he knew, but was she aware of Lauryn? He'd never told her directly that he was in a relationship, but she had been within earshot while he'd spoken about Lauryn at work and she must have noticed the framed picture of them on his desk. He'd never said anything because it simply never came up in conversation. While he hadn't been trying to conceal it, he knew making it known would have jeopardized the sexual tension between them and that he didn't want to do.

Finally her building loomed in the distance. A minor sense of relief washed over him as he pulled up in front of it. He'd made it through the entire day and all had remained above board. No inappropriate comments or behavior. See, he was capable of just being Bree's friend. Maybe they could even go out together again.

"Well, m'lady, back home safe and sound, just like I promised." He refused to put the car in park. A foot on the brake implied it was just a drop off, there'd be no long drawn-out conversations while his engine idled.

She told him she had wonderful time, then leaned in towards him. He held his breath as her face neared his. He was both relieved and disappointed when she only planted a soft peck on his cheek. As she fumbled through her purse for her keys, he admired her profile from his peripheral view. She smiled, then dangled them in front of him. "Here they are."

She bid him a good night and was gone. He sighed a heavy sigh of relief, proud of himself for doing the right thing. As confirmation of his wise decision, he sent Lauryn a text message telling her he loved her and to have a good night. Before he reached the highway his phone vibrated.

You know you didn't have to leave, read the text.

He quickly wrote back. *Oh really?*

Yes, really.

Didn't wanna keep you up. He typed.

And what if I wanted you to keep me up?

A chill surged down his spine. *Did you?*

You can always come back.

He made a U-turn at the next corner.

16

Elle

It was 3:34 a.m. Elle was jolted awake by the sound of heavy thumping on her front door. She rubbed her eyes until the blurry red figures on the alarm clock formed decipherable digits. As soon as she realized the noise was coming from her front door, her annoyance became fear. She immediately sprung out of bed and retrieved the .22 from the safe in her closet before tiptoeing downstairs. It wasn't loaded, yet it made her feel empowered enough to bark through the front door.

"Who is it?"

There was no response.

She squinted through the peephole, saw a man's shoulder and jumped back.

"Who's there?" she repeated, her thumb hovering over the nine key of her cordless phone.

"Elle, open the door." She instantly recognized the drunken, slurred voice. "Baby, open the door, I need to talk to you."

Her mind raced.

"Baby, just let me in." His knuckles rapped lightly on the door.

Against her better judgment and mostly out of curiosity, she unlocked the door. She'd never seen a drunk Marcus before.

The cold night air slapped her in the face. "What are you doing here?"

He stumbled past her and collapsed onto her couch. She quickly regretted her decision. "What's your problem? You're pissy drunk."

He steadied his bobbling head and sat up. "Not drunk. Yeah, I had some drinks, but I'm not drunk. I don't get drunk."

"Well, there's a first time for everything," she said, suddenly feeling exposed standing there braless, wearing only a thin t-shirt and leggings as she stood only feet away from her ex-boyfriend, who even in his inebriated state, looked yummy. So she reached into the hallway closet, grabbed a sweatshirt and put it on.

"You have something you wanna tell me?" he asked.

"What?"

"I said, do you have something you want to tell me?" He repeated with an exaggerated emphasis on each word.

"What are you talking about?"

He tugged at the red paisley tie which hung askew around his neck. He was still dressed in one of his power suits. Beneath the navy blue jacket, hung the rumpled tails of a white oxford shirt.

"You know what I'm talking about," he slurred.

"What the hell do you want?"

He pointed a wobbly index finger at her. "You."

God, please don't let him throw up on her new couch. "You need to drink some water or something. Maybe some coffee."

"*Coffee*? I'm here tryna have a heart-to-heart with you and you're talking 'bout some damn coffee?"

The cold air, which had trailed him inside, lingered about her living room. She gripped the panels of her sweatshirt and drew them tightly across her chest.

"What do you want?"

He anchored his elbow on the arm of the couch and rested his chin in his open palm. "So, you gonna answer me?"

"Marcus, just get up and go home." She grabbed him by both of his wrists and tried to yank him up off of the couch, but none of his two hundred and five pounds would budge.

"No!" He pulled back. "Not until you answer me. Is it true?"

"Is *what* true?"

He attempted to stand, but stumbled back into his seat. What to do with him? It would only be a matter of time before he'd pass out on her couch and she'd have to deal with an awkward exchange in the morning. At the same time she couldn't just kick him out and let him drive home drunk. A cab. That was it. She would let him ramble on then call him a cab and haul him out of there.

She went to the kitchen and returned with a bottle of water. "Here, drink this."

He reached for it, then knocked it from her hand. "I don't need any damn water."

"What the hell is wrong with you? I'm trying to be nice and you're being an ass."

"So, you gonna tell me or not?"

"Tell you what Marcus? I don't have time for this. I have to work in the morning. Hell, so do you."

"About you and that guy. The doctor. Is it true?"

How did he know anything about that? Who had told him? They didn't share any mutual friends. Plus, everything had happened so fast. How could he have known and how much did he know? "What are you talking about?"

"Heard you're seeing some doctor. Heard he gave you a ring. Is it true?"

He sat erect and eyed her left hand as if she would be wearing an engagement ring at four in the morning. His face took on a serious, determined expression.

"Huh? Is it?" he persisted.

She studied his face. A small part of her wanted to tell him everything, to rub it in his face so he could really see how much he'd messed up, but it was clear he already knew. Hence, his night at the bar. Marcus drank socially but never, ever got drunk. If he was brought to this point, then hurt and sadness must be the culprit.

"Yeah, it is," she admitted and although it was a moment she'd played out in her imagination many times following their break up, rubbing her happiness in his face fell short of its perceived flavor.

His eyes became glassy, then darted frantically from side to side. What the hell? Was he about to cry? He quickly recovered and took a deep swallow.

"So, you're going to marry him?" he asked in a voice she didn't recognize.

"Yes," she whispered.

He leaned back on the couch, massaged his temples and exhaled.

"When?"

"Don't have a date yet." It was a statement she'd been repeating a lot lately. While most newly engaged women sought to set a date immediately, she'd been dragging her feet, but wasn't wholly sure why. For some reason, telling Marcus she didn't have one made her feel slightly relieved.

He must have felt the same way because his eyes registered a subtle gleam of hope. "No?"

She shook her head.

He sat up and rested his elbows on his knees. "And you're sure this is what you want to do?"

She nodded.

Marcus's hopeful expression withered and a dark shadow crossed his face. She could tell it was equal parts of regret (for having let another man get so close to her), anger (for just learning the truth of it all), and embarrassment (for believing there was no moving on after him).

"Ellie, please think about this some more." He looked up at her. His eyes, which always had a way of appearing slightly remote and detached, suddenly grew warm and sympathetic.

He stood, making a considerable effort not to sway, smoothed out his shirt, and stepped towards her. "Ellie, baby." He cupped her face in his hands, his nose just inches from hers. "I am not drunk and what I'm telling you is the truth."

She wanted to remove herself from his grip and step away, to put space between them, to even kick him out of her home and tell him never to contact her again, but she couldn't. A small part of her wanted to hear what he had to say.

"I know everything I'm saying is old news by now, but what you don't seem to be getting is that despite what I did, I still love you. You're the best thing that ever happened to me, Elle, seriously." The faint smell of Johnnie Walker lingered on his breath. "Always thought any woman who had me would be the lucky one, but Elle . . . I was the lucky one. I'm never going to meet somebody like you again, I know that now."

She made a pitiful attempt to pull away.

"Ellie, please . . . "

By now she was supposed to be over Marcus. Time had passed and much had happened since they'd broken up, yet she still longed to pick up the phone and hear his voice. Thoughts of him always found their way to her mind, despite her hate for him, despite the wonderful man she now shared her life with, despite even that flawless ring which rested in a black velvet box one story above them.

Marcus's eyes bore into hers, instantly drawing her back to the day she'd first laid eyes on him more than four years ago.

She'd been settled in her standard business-class window seat en route to San Francisco for her monthly division meeting. That particular morning she was seated next to a mature woman who, by the time they took off, was already chatting away about her grandchildren. Elle nodded politely as she prayed the old lady would just fall asleep. On her way to the bathroom, she caught the eye of an attractive, well-dressed man seated a few rows behind her. Their eyes met briefly before he turned his attention back to his newspaper. Moments later, when she returned to her seat, Mrs. Annoying was gone and Mr. New York Times was seated in her place. She checked the seat number, confirmed she was in the correct row, and smirked at her new seat mate.

"I believe you have the wrong seat."

He looked up at her. "No, ma'am, I believe I have the *perfect* seat."

Albeit flattering, she found his repartee corny. "What happened to the old lady?"

"Oh her? I just explained to her that my fiancée and I were so disappointed we weren't able to get seats together, so she graciously agreed to switch with me." His expression bordered on smug. "Are you disappointed?"

"Suit yourself." She gestured for him to make room for her to pass.

He stood up to let her sit. His cologne, a spicy blend of sandalwood and lavender, wafted pass her. "Since we'll be sitting together for the next four hours, I think it's only appropriate I introduce myself. I'm Marcus. And you are?" He extended his hand.

She extended hers, grateful she'd squeezed in a lunchtime manicure only the day before. "Elle."

"So Elle." He adjusted the crease in slacks and crossed his legs. "Where are you heading to?"

"San Fran."

"I know that much, but are you going home? On vacation? Lady, don't make me pull teeth now." He smiled. His teeth were all but perfect except for a slight gap in the middle, which she found oddly sexy.

"I'm going to San Francisco for business, I live in New York."

"Looks like we have something in common then. I live in Manhattan. I'm actually going to a job interview."

"That'll be a long commute."

"Cute. No, the company is based out of California, but the position would be in New York. I wouldn't leave the city for anything."

She steadied the grip on her cup of coffee as the plane trembled with turbulence. "I hear you. There's nothing like it."

Their conversation was halted by a flight attendant's voice over the PA system advising all passengers to take their seats until the fasten seatbelt sign was turned off. A message which clearly didn't apply to the heavy-set businessman still rummaging through his overhead bin.

"So, Elle, I guess the next appropriate question would be, what do you do? But to be honest I'm more interested in who you are than how you earn your living. Are you married?"

She was taken aback by his forwardness and a bit ashamed to admit to herself that she liked it. "No."

"Are you seeing someone, a man or a woman?"

"No and no."

"Can I see you?"

"I don't know, can you?" It was a small pet peeve of hers, one of the quirks of being an editor, when people used the word can in place of the word may, because the former referred to ability whereas the latter referenced permission.

He wagged his finger. "Ah, touché. *May* I see you?"

"See me how?"

"See you. Call you at home, not on your cell phone. Come by and pick you up one evening. Take you to dinner or lunch, or a play, hell, even just go for a long walk."

She was intrigued. She hadn't asked him what he did for a living, but could guess it had something to do with sales or perhaps he was a trial attorney, for he had the gift of gab and she could tell he was rarely told no. "That's a possibility, but answer me this . . . "

He shifted in his seat and rested his clasped hands on his lap. "Yes?"

"Are *you* married, gay, involved, have a baby's mother? Any of the above?"

The sexy gap resurfaced. "No, hell no, no and no."

"A handsome man like you? I'm surprised."

"Don't be. I'm very selective." He removed his rimless eyeglasses and placed them inside a black leather case. "There's really not much out there."

"Who are you telling?"

"Well, then we have something else in common."

They talked until the 747 landed in California. Much to her surprise, she'd been disappointed to hear the pilot announce their arrival at SFO. Phone numbers were exchanged, marking the beginning of a three-and-a-half-year relationship.

As with most relationships, things were ideal the first few years. They appeared perfect for one another, as was evidenced by all they shared in common: flourishing careers at Fortune 100 companies, advanced degrees, significant incomes and no children which they were obligated to spend it on. All agreed they made a handsome couple and it seemed it was just a matter of time before their wedding would be announced in the New York Times Sunday edition.

They weren't immune to disagreements or arguments, but nothing was ever serious enough to warrant a break up. It wasn't until the beginning of their third year together when she first sensed something was awry; something about Marcus's behavior made her suspicious. Things like his increased client lunches and dinners, the new lock on his cell phone and earlier-than-usual good-nights calls. Each of which were singularly insignificant, yet telling as a whole. She fought the urge to search through his belongings and hunt for clues of his indiscretion. For in doing so, what a hypocrite she would have been. She disapproved of snooping and always viewed it as the behavior of an insecure woman. Her entire adult life she stood on a soap box and doled out advice based on her belief in quotes like Luke chapter twelve, verse three: *Therefore whatever you have said in the dark shall be heard in the light, and what you have whispered in private rooms shall be proclaimed on the housetops.* Months later, that light eventually flickered and her suspicions came to fruition.

" . . . you can't marry him." Marcus's voice snapped her back into the present. "You hardly know that guy."

Hardly knew him? That was the best he could do? What the hell did he know about her and Luke? So what they'd only been together months. That had nothing to do with anything. Like Blair had said, time matters little when it comes to affairs of the heart.

She pulled away. "It's too late. Marcus. You've got to go."

"Why is it too late?"

"Because it is."

"That's not an answer."

"It's my answer."

"Always have to be such a smart ass?"

"Insulting me is definitely not going to get you what you want."

"Not insulting you. Asking you a question."

As much as she didn't want to be drawn into a heated discussion, she couldn't help but ask. "If you cared so much, then why did you do me like that?"

He grew quiet then said, "Honestly?"

She rolled her eyes. "No, not honestly, lie to me."

He shrugged. "I guess I just wanted to see if the grass was greener. I'm man enough to admit that now. It was wrong and I should've known better. I know that now and all I can say is, I'm sorry. I want to work this out. I want you. Please, just let me try, I promise it'll be different. You have my word."

She didn't know what to make of his apology. It sounded heartfelt and it was the most he'd said to her in person since their break-up, but the cynical part of her couldn't help but wonder if this was just the byproduct of her recent engagement and a long night at the bar.

"Say that you forgive me." He stared at her, his lips curled into a pitiful frown.

"Even if I did, what does that really change? What's done is done."

"It doesn't have to be."

"Look, you have to go." She grabbed the phone and began to dial. "I'm calling you a cab. You can come get your car tomorrow."

He snatched the phone from her hand. "Not ready to go yet. We have to talk about this—"

"There's nothing to talk about. Why can't you get that? Enough already. Now give me back the phone." She grabbed for it, but he held it from her reach.

"Ellie?" he pleaded.

"Don't call me that."

He tried to hug her, then kiss her lips, but she pulled back and pushed him away. "What are you, crazy?"

"I want you to feel how much I miss you, how much I mean what I'm saying—"

"Okay Marcus, you want an answer? Is that what you need to hear before you agree to take your ass home? Well, then here it is. You want the truth? I think you're full of shit. You're a smart man—you've made a career out of valuing assets and calculating risks, yet I'm supposed to believe it somehow slipped by you that I was a good thing? I don't want to hear that. What you are is a self-absorbed ass who's used to getting his way, used to women dealing with your nonsense, but I'm not that woman."

"C'mon now . . . " He peered at her, then stared at the phone as if he didn't know how it ended up in his hand. "Why are you being so damn mean? You must not be over it 'cause if you were, you wouldn't still be so angry. That just shows me that you still care. C'mon, Elle . . . "

Still so arrogant. Still couldn't swallow rejection. No one had ever told him no in all his thirty-five years. "You just don't get it, do you? I'm—getting—married. End of story."

He sat at the edge of the couch and sighed.

"What? So, you're frustrated now? You're mad because this isn't going as planned? Did you really think you could show up here, throw some I miss yous my way and I'd just call off my wedding? Get over yourself. Just go, Marcus. I'm calling you a cab and when it gets here, you're getting in it, end of discussion."

After he'd finally agreed to leave, she retrieved a pack of cigarettes from her nightstand drawer; it was her secret stash. Not that she had to hide it from anyone, for she lived alone, but she refused to leave them out in plain sight for two reasons. First, it reminded her of the addiction, which had taken her eight years to kick, and second, because she smoked only when she was sad. It was the only way she knew how to cope with an emotion she associated with weak people. The kind of people who threw themselves pity parties and deemed themselves victims. Those kind of people had no place in her life, but today she couldn't help but admit she was one of them, so she lit up.

She sat on her deck blowing rings of smoke out into the early morning air. In her heart she knew she'd done the right thing, but was still plagued with doubts. Saying she was done had always been the easy part, but staying true to her word was the challenge. Not a day went by she didn't think about him. She wanted to believe everything he'd said. But why did those words come only after a night at the bar? He'd sounded sincere, her gut told her to believe him. But no, she refused to play the fool twice. She recalled the night she'd driven five hours in a hailstorm, racing away from Maryland after having learned the past three and a half years of her life had been a lie.

Everything had come to light one November when she'd accepted an invitation to spend an extended weekend with some colleagues at her boss' vacation home in Telluride. The trip, however, was postponed at the last minute when a blizzard struck the northwest, shutting down all air traffic in Colorado. She hadn't told Marcus of her change of plans, deciding rather to surprise him, since he'd asked her to go to Maryland with him the same weekend for his cousin James' birthday party. She'd solidified the details with his cousin's girlfriend, Stacy, over the phone. Stacy loved the idea and suggested they didn't tell James, since he couldn't keep a secret.

A few hours later, Elle was on the phone with Marcus.

"I'm jealous," he said. "Telluride in the fall is beautiful. You're going to have a great time, although I still wish you could come with me. Won't be the same without you."

"I know. Me too," she said as she unpacked her ski clothes and replaced them with causal weekend house-party attire. "But I couldn't pass up on a free trip like this. Besides, it's a bad look to tell the boss no."

"Definitely. Whatever it takes to move up the ladder. Are you sure you don't need a ride to the airport? We can drop you off before we hit the road."

"Nah, I've already scheduled a car service. Plus, the airport is out of your way."

"Nothing is out of the way for you, luv. And you know my brother is just itching to take his new Chrysler out on the road."

She declined again. They said their good-byes and a day later, Elle embarked on the five-hour drive to Prince George County. As soon as she turned onto James' street, she spotted a brand new 300M with New York plates in the driveway of a small brick Tudor, confirming she'd found the right house. She exchanged introductions at the front door with Ana, a friend of the family whom she'd never met, before briefly explaining her plan to surprise Marcus. As she rested her bags down, she could hear laughter coming from the next room. Ana told her she hadn't actually seen Marcus arrive, but believed he had. Before she could show Elle to the living room, she was summoned by the cries of her newborn upstairs.

"Was that the bell?" A willowy, dark-haired woman came hustling down the hallway. "Elle? Is that you?"

"Stacy?" Elle recognized the voice from the phone.

There was a look of panic on Stacy's face. "I wanted to call you, but I must have deleted your number."

"Why? What happened?" Elle's eyes grew wide. "Is Marcus okay?"

"I don't know how to say this," Stacy spoke in a hush, "but he didn't come here alone."

Elle's heart pounded. "What do you mean?"

"He's here. With another woman. They just got here, I wanted to give you a heads up, but . . . I didn't say anything to him, though. I'm not in the practice of covering up for a man up to no good, family or not. I just didn't want you to walk into something without warning."

Another woman? Elle was speechless.

Stacy went on. "Now I don't know how you want to handle this, but they're in there." She pointed towards the den.

Elle racked her brain. How was she to handle it? She quickly weighed her options. The first dictated she turn about face and tell Stacy to let Marcus know she'd come and gone—no confrontation at all. The passive-aggressive technique would probably result in a string of desperate phone calls, perhaps even a hasty pursuit on the Beltway. He would jump in the 300M and try to catch up with her as she sped back to New York with her eyes blurred and swollen from crying. He would hope he could convince her to pull over at a rest stop so he could explain himself and plead with her to forgive him. What would become of the girl back at James' house? Maybe she'd scurry off to the nearest Amtrak station, cursing Marcus the whole way for being sloppy or for having lied to her, too.

Ah, there were so many variables. Did the other woman know about her? If she did, did she even care? Or, the worst scenario of all, what if *she* was his longtime love and Elle was the other woman. Could that be?

Option B would require Stacy to call Marcus into the hallway so as to avoid a loud, garish altercation in front of the other guests. Marcus would enter the hall, see Elle, and his face would drop in complete and utter shock. He'd probably shoot Stacy a dirty look for not having warned him, then he would tell Elle whatever he thought she needed to hear in order to smooth things over. He might even suggest they take a ride and talk so as to not disrupt the festivities inside. In the meantime, James or whoever would drop the other woman off at the Greyhound station so no evidence, other than Stacy's mention of her, would exist by the time Marcus and Elle returned. Or maybe the other woman was a co-conspirator who would willingly abscond for Marcus's benefit.

The final option called for her to be true to her feelings and confront Marcus in front of all of his friends and family, letting the chips fall where they may. This possibly involved collateral damage, but why should she care? She was the victim.

What would Blair do? How would Michelle handle it? It didn't matter. Their decisions could not be hers. Blair was married to a womanizing bastard and Michelle bobbed back and forth in a dysfunctional relationship. She could not and would not mirror their behavior because she wanted different results. She had to be true to herself and her feelings and whomever got struck by the resulting shrapnel was not her concern.

"Down here, you say?" Elle started down the hall and stopped when she heard Marcus's voice. She took a deep breath then stepped into the doorway. All eyes shot in her direction. All conversation ceased. Everyone stared as if they'd seen a ghost. Everyone, that is, except Marcus's companion. Her confusion was apparent as she reached for his arm and mouthed, 'Who's that?' He didn't answer. Rather, he darted to the doorway.

"I . . . I thought you were in Colorado?" His smile was tight; a stilted dry laugh escaped his mouth. "What . . . what are you doing here?"

"I came to see you, sweetheart." She brushed his cheek with the back of her hand. "But you don't look happy to see me."

He lowered her hand to her side then shot a fearful glance back to his companion, who sat at the edge of the couch, her face awash with confusion.

The room cleared out quickly; one-by-one, everyone excused themselves, only to crouch outside the doorway with their ears glued to the wall. Only the three of them remained.

"Elle, I . . . I really don't even know what to say. God, this is . . . this is so awkward."

"*Awkward?* Is that what you want to call this? Try fucked up because that's what this is."

"Can we . . . ah shit, . . . I can explain . . . " His eyes shot back and forth between the two women as he searched for the right words.

Elle turned to her. "Who are you?" As much as she tried not to, she couldn't help but acknowledge their striking differences. The woman's head was a mop of unruly golden curls. She had a faint sprinkle of freckles on her round cheeks. She wore a floral print dress over brown opaque stockings and motorcycle boots. A billowy turquoise scarf was wrapped around her neck. She was cute; Elle couldn't deny that, but she was a disheveled mess. The kind of woman she'd likely pass in Washington Square Park sitting Indian style on a bench. The type who didn't bother ironing, rather threw on whatever was clean as she raced out of her studio apartment en route to a pottery class. This was what Marcus liked? Marcus, whose closet could rival a Marine cadet's? Marcus who organized his refrigerator once a week and color coded his sock drawer? He was cheating on Elle with *her*? The woman with the chipped nail polish, scuffed boots and wild hair?

"Nicole," she said. Then she turned to Marcus and asked, "What's going on here?"

Before he could speak, Elle told her that she and Marcus had been in a relationship for the past three-and-a-half years and how it was her plan to surprise him, only she was the one who was surprised.

"Elle, can we speak in private please?" he asked.

"No, we don't need privacy, we're all here now. I think it's the perfect time to get it all out in the open." She turned back to Nicole. "How do you know each other?"

Nicole remained seated, a throw pillow clutched in her hands. She glanced from Marcus to Elle and back to Marcus. His eyes silently pleaded with her to keep quiet. To his disappointment, she told Elle they met at the gym, had been seeing each other for about six months, and a few days prior he'd asked her to go to Maryland with him—and that he'd never told her he had a girlfriend.

Elle grabbed the closest thing to her and hurled it. "You son of a bitch!"

The glass coaster struck his shoulder with a thud. Nicole screamed.

"Calm down!" His hands flew up. "This sounds worse than it is."

Elle charged towards him and swung, her fist connecting with his jaw. Her knuckles stung, but she continued to swing until his brother came out of nowhere, grabbed her from behind, and pulled her back. In an instant the room was full. All she heard were random voices telling her to calm down and relax. Nicole bolted out of the room as Marcus stood in the middle of the den, rubbing his jaw and pleading with Elle to hear him out.

"What, Marcus? What can you possibly say? What?"

"I'm sorry." He rested an open palm against his chest. "I fucked up. I know it, I'm sorry."

Her eyes burned as she fought to keep the tears from escaping. "You're sorry? That's all you have to say? You're sorry? You made a fool out of me. I feel so stupid! Thought what we had was real—"

"It was . . . it is . . . just hear me out for a minute—"

"No!" She tugged at the bottom of her blazer and smoothed down the front of her button-down shirt. "There's nothing to say. I've heard all I need to hear." She shook her head, her anger thawing into disappointment then pooling into hurt. "Are you proud of yourself? Are you? You couldn't just be man enough to tell me the truth? No, you let me drive all the way out to Maryland in the fuckin' rain just to realize what you are. Thank you. Thank you for wasting the last three years of my life."

"Ellie please . . . let me . . . "

Those were the last words she'd heard him say.

Elle looked down to realize she'd smoked the cigarette down to the butt. No, there was no turning back. She and Marcus were done. Even if there was no Luke, she wasn't that woman, the one who took back the cheating man, the one who let a man, or anyone for that matter, get over on her. That's not who she was. Her mind begged her to put it to rest, so she headed to her bedroom to salvage an hour of sleep.

17

Blair

Blair took a deep breath as she unpacked her bags. For the fifth time in a row, her cell phone rang. She silenced the ringer and let it go to voicemail. She wasn't ready to speak to him. Of her seventeen missed calls, three were from Elle, one from her sister and the other thirteen from Dylan. Guilt lay heavily on her heart. How could she face him? What could she possibly say? Just at the moment, Vaughn approached her from behind, wrapped his arms around her waist and kissed her neck.

"So glad we had that getaway. It was just what we needed to get us back on track." He traced the length of her arm with his finger, then held out her left hand. "It looks good on you."

They both marveled at the new diamond-encrusted platinum band on her finger which commemorated, not only their vow renewal, but a renaissance of their devotion to each another. "Are you happy, baby? You've been real quiet since we came home."

She turned and rested her forehead against his chest so he wouldn't see the tears welling up in her eyes. "I am happy, but I'm scared."

He wrapped her in his arms. "Don't be, I won't do anything to hurt you again, I promise."

As they embraced, her cell phone vibrated on the nightstand.

18

Jonathan

Jonathan stood before the mirror, finally satisfied with his decision to wear the striped green shirt. He was running late for work and the shirts which hadn't made the cut lay in a pile on his bed. He spritzed himself with cologne and dashed out the door.

He sped to the campus. If he made it before nine, he'd have just enough time before his nine-forty-five class to meet Bree for breakfast. The traffic gods must have been on his side because he made it just in time to watch her saunter into her office. Only she could make a pair of track pants and windbreaker so appealing. He bolted into her office and shut the door behind him.

"Hey you!" she said before he swooped her up by the waist and planted her down on the desk.

"Hey yourself," he muttered as he nuzzled her neck, inhaling the subtle savor of jasmine in her hair. She wrapped her long legs around his waist as he began to unzip her jacket.

She stopped him. "What are you doing?"

"You have to ask?"

She grabbed his hand. "Not here, not now."

"It wouldn't be the first time," he said in between kisses.

"It's not even nine and there are people out there."

He reached behind her and clicked on her desk fan. "They won't hear a thing, I promise."

"You're so fresh. Stop." She playfully tapped the back of his hand. "I have a full plate today. I can't go around with your 'essence' all over me. Now I can't do lunch, but maybe we can have dinner later. I'll cook." She winked.

He slumped his shoulders with exaggeration. "Okay . . . okay. Later then, you tease." He zipped her jacket back up. "Got time to eat?"

"Nah, I have a meeting in ten." She pointed to the Herbalife shake on her desk. "That's my breakfast right there."

He squeezed her thigh. "And that protein is sure going to all the right places."

"Silly. I've got to go." She pushed him away. "So dinner tonight?"

Just as he was about to ask what time, his cell phone rang. He didn't need to look at it to know it was Lauryn. Her calls came like clockwork. She was probably calling to tell him she'd just gotten to the office and blah, blah, blah . . . Ah, and to remind him tonight was that awards dinner. Damn!

His face said it all.

"Tonight's no good, is it?" Bree said.

He shook his head. "Nah, I have this dinner thing. I'd forgotten all about it, I'm sorry—"

Her finger shot to his lips. "It's fine, you don't have to explain." He'd been around long enough to know *it's fine* meant anything but that.

"Another time." She hopped off the desk, grabbed her shake and gym bag and told him she'd talk to him later.

That evening, he sat beside Lauryn at a banquet table in a Long Island catering hall. Her boss' boss was the honoree of some award; so, three tables of his subordinates and their significant others were forced to celebrate by dining on bland reception food and house wine as they listened to a host of middle-aged men drone on about each other's accomplishments. His back ached and his tie, one of the three he owned, was making it hard to breathe. He fought the urge to loosen it.

As soon as the ego-stroking was done, his least favorite part of the evening began—the small talk and schmoozing hour. Cory's husband, Dean, who Jonathan had strategically avoided sitting next to, was in his element. He was engaged in a fervent discussion with another pint-sized loser about asset-backed securities. Before they could rope him into their debate on hi-yield bonds, Jonathan busied himself at the dessert bar.

"Tired are we?" He looked up to see Cory, who'd only recently returned to work from maternity leave.

He tried to bridle the look of disgust on his face. "What?"

"You just yawned three times in a row. You must be tired, I can only imagine how exhausting it must be playing *basketball* all day."

He turned his attention back to the petit fours on the table beside them.

"You know, you can go. We can drop Lauryn off." Cory's offer was a thinly veiled excuse to introduce Lauryn to one Dean's dull associates. Jonathan wouldn't have it.

"How kind of you," he sneered, "but no thanks."

She shot him an icy glare before turning to leave.

"Cory, wait," he called.

She turned around and stared at him impatiently as he chomped on a mini éclair. "What?"

"Tomorrow morning I'm teaching a bootcamp at the gym."

"And?"

"You should come, it'll be really good for losing that baby fat."

She presented him with her middle finger before stalking off.

Lauryn found him in the lobby later. "Babe, where've you been? Was looking for you."

"You ready to go yet?" he asked as he loosened his tie.

"Yeah, but what did you say to Cory? You know she's very sensitive about her weight right now."

"Fuck her."

On the way back to his apartment, she reminded him how he and Cory needed to get along since Lauryn was her best friend and the god-mother to Cory's son. All of this came before she questioned him about the pile of shirts on his bed and why he only recently started wearing the cologne she'd bought him over a year ago. While his answers satisfied Lauryn, they didn't satisfy his conscience. The following day he sent a dozen lilies to her job.

19

Elle

The brass buckle of her handbag clinked down on the glass table top, announcing Elle's arrival. She sat down across from Blair, pulled off her shades and leaned in. "Get to talking, lady. I got your little cryptic message. Now I want all the details." They were seated at a small iron-legged table at a new outdoor cafe.

"I ordered us some tea." Blair grinned widely as she poured Elle a cup.

"The trip. I want to hear about the trip."

"Well, I told you all about how he scooped me up from work and took me to the island—"

Elle rolled her wrist, gesturing impatience with Blair's preamble. "Yeah, yeah that I know. What happened then?"

Blair recapped the entire story.

"Renewed your vows? Let me see that." Elle examined Blair's

finger. The ring was exquisite. Just like everything else Blair owned. "Don't people usually add on to their original ring?"

"Vaughn said he considered that, but thought I should have a new ring to commemorate our new beginning. Isn't is gorgeous?" She extended her arm and rotated her wrist side to side, admiring the way it glistened under the afternoon sunshine.

"I know what you're going to say, but it just feels right. He was the same man I fell in love with back in college."

Elle's face hovered over her tea cup as she blew at its rising steam.

"Well, say something. I don't like the look on your face," Blair said.

"I'm still taking it in. Can't remember the last time you had anything positive to say about him." She took a tentative sip.

"I know. It's crazy, right? But something in my gut tells me it's for real."

Elle didn't want to be cynical, really she didn't, but she'd seen this song and dance before, sans the exotic trip and lavish diamond ring. The Vaughn-Blair roller coaster was full of twists and turns, dangerous drops and free falls. Blair would swear she was done, pack her stuff and leave and threaten divorce. But still she stayed, always there back in line, ticket in hand, waiting to get back on. Did Vaughn love Blair? Yes, that she believed, but not more than he loved himself and in Elle's eyes the best indicator of future behavior was past behavior. But what she couldn't deny was the euphoric look on her friend's face. Blair's skin was glowing and the dark circles under her eyes were gone. So she decided she wouldn't dampen it with skepticism. Rather, she'd throw caution to the wind and go with it.

"If it feels real, then it is. I'm happy for you, for both of you," she said with enthusiastic conviction.

"It's so good to hear you say that. I was worried you wouldn't approve or you'd try and talk me down," Blair said.

"If you're happy, then I'm happy. But you know my next question, right?"

A frown crossed Blair's face. "I know. Dylan."

"Uh, yeah. Dylan, the baby . . . "

"I haven't figured it all out yet, but I know two things. I have to have this baby and I cannot tell Vaughn it's not his."

Elle slammed her cup down, tiny beads of hot tea splashed on her face and neck. "You can't be serious!"

"Shhh!" Blair shot her a reprimanding look as her eyes shot around the cafe. There were only four other people out there, but their attention had been grasped.

"But you've hardly been sleeping with Vaughn," Elle whispered. "How's he going to believe that it's his? The man is not stupid. And even if he were, how could you live with yourself?"

Blair wiped the table with her napkin and spoke so faintly Elle had to lean in to hear her. "What option do I have? If I have an abortion, I may never be able to have children again. If I tell Vaughn—we're over." She shook her head pitifully. "I have no choice."

"You *always* have a choice. You may not like your choices, but you always have one. I mean Vaughn hasn't been a good husband. Seems he knows he was about to lose you. Maybe now is the time to tell him, while he's being all apologetic." Elle nodded, confirming the solution in her mind. "Yeah, this is probably the best time. He won't like it, but if he really loves you the way he says he does, he'll get past it. Hell, if he'd gotten some other woman pregnant, you would stay wouldn't you?"

Blair shook her head. "There's a difference between some random woman having his child and him having to watch me carry a baby which isn't his. He's coming around, but he's not that open minded. And I doubt he'll ever be. I know my husband."

"But could you live with yourself? That's a lie you'd have to take to your grave. You know that, right?" She pointed her fork towards Blair. "And Dylan. What about Dylan? How could you keep him from knowing he has a child?"

"You don't understand—"

"What's there to understand? It's wrong. No if, ands or buts about it. It's just wrong."

Blairs eyes were downcast. "I have no choice."

"Yes, you do."

"I've thought this through. A million different ways. There's no other way . . . "

"Of course there is."

"Elle, please. I need you to be on my side here. I really need your support."

"Do you know what you're asking me to do? To tell you it's okay to lie to two men about a baby. Blair, I love you, you know that, but c'mon. Think about this."

"And what do you think I've been doing? There's no other way. I don't have a choice—"

"Would you stop saying that? You have it a lot better than a lot of people Blair. You, of all people, have choices. If you plant this seed, there's no going back. I mean, you could never even tell the child. That's a really heavy cross to bear. Are you ready for that?"

"People grow up every day not knowing their fathers—"

"Yeah, and how did that make you and Norah feel? Is that what you want for your child?"

"That's different. My father not being there messed everything up. Maybe if he had been . . . " Blair cast a dismissive hand in the air. "Whatever, that's the past. And it's not the same thing. *This* child will never want for a thing, Elle. This baby is what Vaughn and I've wanted for years."

"And what about what *Dylan* wants?"

"He doesn't know. What he doesn't know can't hurt him."

"Isn't that the same credo Vaughn's been running on for years? You, of all people, should know how it *does* hurt."

Blair took a deep breath. "You don't have to agree with what I'm going to do, but I need you to be my friend and have my back."

"Have your back? What's that mean? You wan't me to lie—"

"No. I'm not asking you to lie about anything. Just be my friend and stand by me on this. And don't make me feel any worse than I already do . . ." Blair blinked back her tears. "*And* I need your word that you'll never repeat what I've just told you. Never."

The air crackled with tension.

"Elle?"

She looked away. She knew Blair well enough to know that face, to know her mind was made up and nothing she said could convince her otherwise.

"Well?" Blair's eyes pierced into her.

"I think you're wrong Blair, I'm going on record with that now. I wouldn't be a friend if I didn't tell you that." Elle took an even deeper breath. "But you have my word. I won't tell anybody."

Blair exhaled.

"But can you please just do me one favor? Can you at least sleep on it? Just one more night. Please. Just think this through a little bit more."

Blair slowly shook her head. "I have no other choice."

Elle couldn't help but wonder if she'd just lent her signature to a contract with the devil.

That night Blair told Vaughn about the baby. She fudged how far along she was so there was no question as to the date of conception. Luckily enough for her, there had been those few times she'd slept with him, albeit unenthusiastically, just to appease him. Because of those rare occasions, he didn't question his paternity and was ecstatic at the prospect of a baby. After she'd made what was easily the most difficult decision of her life, had told her best friend and lied to her husband, the hardest part was yet to come. It was time to tell Dylan it was over.

Their communication had been strained since she'd returned from her trip. They'd spoken via text and email, but had yet to see each another. It was by design she told Vaughn about the baby first, knowing that after which, there'd be no turning back. She needed that resolve before speaking with Dylan. Otherwise there was the chance she would change her mind—yet again.

A week later Blair was standing in Dylan's living room. Her body language only confirmed the tension he'd been sensing over the phone. Something was definitely awry. He somehow knew this visit, which he'd been waiting nearly a month for, was not going to be good.

"You look good," he said taking notice of her bronzed skin. She always looked especially beautiful when she was tanned. But this tan, she'd gotten on a tropical island—with *him*. He instantly regretted the compliment. He invited her to sit and offered her a drink. She declined both and stood near the door, subtly adjusting her linen frock so that it billowed out in front.

Her stomach had begun to swell and there was a hint of a bulge protruding from her petite frame. One which would be hardly discernible to anyone who had *not* seen her naked. They studied each other, each afraid to utter a word.

She gingerly stepped beyond the foyer and took a seat at the edge of his couch. "We have to talk," she finally said.

He knew those four words were coming. He'd feared them from the day he'd received her frantic messages from the airport. In actuality, he'd feared them since the day he first realized he was in love with her. He sat across from her.

"About?"

She stared down at the tip of her sandals. "I . . . I don't know how else to say this, except to just say it . . . we can't do this anymore."

There it was. Before the words even left her lips, the pain set in. An emotional kick to his chest. Although he knew exactly what she meant, he had to ask, hoping and praying maybe she meant something other than what he knew in his heart she did. "Can't do what, Blair?"

She inhaled. "This. Us. I just can't."

He looked away and took a deep breath. "What . . . what are you saying exactly?"

She looked up at him. "I love you, I do, but I can't leave him. I have to try and salvage my marriage, I just have to."

"*Salvage your marriage?*" His eyes grew wide. "What marriage? You call that a marriage?"

Her eyes dropped back down to the carpet beneath her feet. "Dylan, please—"

"No! It's the truth and you know it. All this time you've been saying how you want out and now you're talking about salvaging your marriage? What's come over you?" He sat with his elbows perched on his knees as he glared at her, trying to meet her eyes. "What happened on that island, Blair? What did he do to you?"

She refused to look at him. "He didn't do anything to me. I . . . I've just been thinking a lot lately. That's why you haven't heard from me. And I know now that I need to work this out. I've got to try."

"You've been *trying* for ten years. There's nothing left to try. You have to just let it go. Isn't that what we've been talking about since day one?"

"It was, but things have changed." She glanced up at his warm green eyes and teared up. It sounded clichéd, but the last thing she ever wanted to do was hurt him. If there was anyone who didn't deserve it, it was Dylan. Never in a million years had she thought she'd be sitting there, on the same couch she'd helped him select only months prior, telling him it was over. It was a speech she'd never rehearsed in her head, always believing somehow they'd end up together. The how's had never been worked out, but when it was all said and done, she believed it would be Dylan she lived out the rest of her days with. "Dylan, please . . . I'm sorry, I really am, but my mind is made up."

"*Dylan please*? What? So, I'm supposed to just say 'Okay, it's been real. Good luck with Vaughn'. What then, just shake your hand and say good-bye? What are you thinking?"

By now Blair's eyes were swimming with tears. "You have to understand, I'm trying to do the right thing. This is tearing me apart. I can't keep living two lives. I hate myself for what I'm doing to you and to him."

"Then don't." He knelt before her, wiping the tears from her cheeks, his hands mere inches from her stomach. "Just leave him—today. We'll hire someone to get your things and then file divorce papers. We can start over, just the two of us. C'mon, baby, just like we've always talked about. We can end all of this today. Just trust me."

His expression was pure, his eyes danced with hope as if he'd just arrived at the perfect solution. All she had to do was say yes. The vision played out in her mind. She'd call Vaughn and tell him she wasn't coming back. Before any movers could make it up the driveway, all of her stuff would be gone and all she'd be left with were the thousands of dollars worth of clothing on her back. Her car would sit in front of Dylan's house for only so long before it was repossessed, because even if Vaughn allowed her to keep it, she couldn't maintain the nine-hundred-dollar car note for long. She'd seek an attorney and he'd tell her what she already knew about their pre-nuptial agreement. And once Vaughn found out she was pregnant, he'd gladly sign the divorce papers and start anew. Probably even remarry before the ink was dry. *Insert new wife here.*

Just like that, all remnants of her would be gone and his new wife would reap the benefits of all her sacrifice and hard work. The new and improved Vaughn would be faithful to her. They wouldn't need years of therapy, expensive gifts and a trip to Turks & Caicos to build a new life together. Then Blair would have to call her family and everyone else who was subsidized by Vaughn and tell them to prepare themselves, for the well had run dry. She'd move into Dylan's three-bedroom townhouse and mill around all day while he worked. Hell, she couldn't even cook a decent meal for herself, let alone for Dylan *and* a baby. She surveyed his small living room and the even smaller galley kitchen she could see from where she sat. She couldn't picture herself sitting at his Target dining-room table, flipping through a checkbook ledger, trying to balance debits and credits. And bigger than all that was Vaughn. Despite everything, she still loved him. She'd fallen back in love with him during that trip. The way he talked to her, touched her, listened when she spoke now, it was what she'd always wanted, and now he was offering it up to her, all on a crystal platter.

She slowly shook her head. "I can't."

He clutched her limp hands. "Why not? You don't have any kids, it's a clean break. I know you're scared, baby, but I'm right here with you. We can do this together."

At the mention of kids, her tears flowed fast and furious. "It's too late, Dylan. You don't understand. It's just too late."

"Then make me understand."

"He's my husband—"

"Jesus Christ!" He jumped to his feet. "You're right, maybe I don't understand 'cause I can't wrap my mind around why you want to work things out with that guy. The same man who . . ." He went on to cite at least three deplorable examples of Vaughn's treatment of her, stories she now regretted ever telling him.

She tucked her purse beneath her arm and stood. "I didn't come here so you could tell me what a monster I'm married to. He has faults, but no one is perfect. Marriage is not just about the good times."

"No, but there's supposed to be more good than bad. And you don't even love him anymore. At least that's what you told me. Unless you've been lying all along. Is that it, Blair?" He waved at the space between them. "Is what we have some bullshit? Am . . . am I the asshole here?" She could tell the question was directed more towards himself than her.

"No!" She fought the urge to hold him just one last time. To feel his skin against hers. "You know how much I love you."

"Yeah? Were you loving me while you were all laid up with your husband on that island?" She responded with a pitiful stare. "So that's what I was, huh? A distraction for the poor, rich wife. Some play thing to make her feel better while Mr. Big Shot ran the streets with all his women." He slammed his fist into the wall. "I'm such an asshole!"

Blair jumped. She'd never seen him this angry before. But she wouldn't allow him to flip this back on her. She had never lied to him. He'd always known her situation.

"I came here to be honest with you. I never used you. I've always loved you and I still do but . . . " She hesitated before her next words for she knew they would sound cruel, but it had to be said, " . . . but in all fairness you knew about my situation from day one, so don't make it seem as if I pulled the wool over your eyes. What I'm doing is for the best. You can't see it now, but in time you will."

He looked at her as if her words had no meaning, as if she spoke a foreign language. Then he sat back on the couch and raked his fingers through his hair before looking back up her. An odd smirk crawled onto his face. After what felt like forever, he finally spoke.

"Seems like you've made up your mind. What else is there for me to say?" He stood. "Good luck with your *husband*. God knows you're going to need it. Let yourself out."

He turned and walked away.

"Dylan," she called, not knowing what she'd even say if he turned around. But he didn't.

20

Jonathan

"Well, it's about time, I'm on my second drink already," Elle barked as Jonathan made his way to the bar. He was over half an hour late.

"I'm sorry, traffic was crazy." He kissed her on the cheek and hopped on the stool beside her.

She caught the bartender's attention and pointed to the two empty martini glasses in front of her. "He's paying for those *and* the dirty martini I'm about to have next."

He raised a finger to the bartender. "Make that one more and make mine filthy." He flashed Elle his best you-know-you-can't-stay-angry-at-me smile.

"Don't try and make me laugh, I'm mad at you. You have me in here looking desperate. You know how many men I had to beat off, waiting on you?" The long bar, which spanned the length of the lounge, was full of men. A sprinkle of women lounged on the armless leather love-seats against the opposite wall, but because every flat-screen TV in the venue was tuned to the World Cup, it was an unofficial guy's night at their local hangout.

"Well, be sure and tell my man Luke I'm sorry I had his fiancée sitting here alone, looking like fresh meat for the taking." He laughed heartily at his own words.

She dipped her fingers in her water glass and flicked lemon-pulped water in his face. "You're such a fool. Now what's the story you couldn't tell me over the phone?"

He inched his stool closer to hers. "I met someone."

"What!"

"I did, and I really dig her. I don't know what to do." The bartender poured two cloudy mixtures in front of them. As soon as he walked away, Elle leaned in.

Her questions came in rapid fire. "Okay, give me some details. Who is she? How long ago? Where did you meet her and are you going to break up with Lauryn?"

He told her the story of how they'd met. He went on to explain how their compatibility extended way beyond the bedroom, nor was it limited to their professions, love of sports, or commitments to fitness. He loved her spontaneity; he could call her on a Sunday morning, invite her to go fishing, and she was game, never squealing at the sight of night crawlers. Nor had she complained about the paintball bruises on her thighs or the mosquitoes in their camping tent. When it started raining during their two-mile run, it was she who insisted they push on, with no concern for her hair getting wet. She was equally comfortable drinking beer and eating wings at Hooters as she was in a dress and sling-backs, was never offended when he cursed and didn't give lectures when he left the seat up. She knew her way around the kitchen *and* the basketball court and could easily rattle off NFL stats as she sat on the couch polishing her toe nails. She was a lady and a buddy, a lover and a friend all wrapped into one.

"And she knows about Lauryn." His smile waned. "Never really discussed it until the other night. Told me she understands my situation, but can't keep seeing me if there's no future."

"And you said?"

"Told her I don't want to stop seeing her, that my situation was complicated and I need some time to sort out my feelings. She said she understood, but we probably shouldn't talk until I did."

"Did what? Break up with Lauryn?" She strained to hear him as the lights dimmed and the background music rose several octaves.

"No, sort out my feelings."

"Have you?" she asked.

"Of course not. That's why I'm here drinking this dirty-ass martini with you." Two lonely olives sat at the base of his glass. He raised it to the bartender, gesturing for a refill.

Elle went into psychotherapist mode. "Okay, I need to know a few things first. Have you slept with her? Would you consider leaving Lauryn for her and are you sure the feelings are mutual?"

He nodded his head in response to all three questions. "What about everything else? I mean, how well do you know her, how long has this been going on?"

"About two months."

"Two months? And I'm just finding out now?"

"I know, I know, I just felt bad telling you after everything you went through with Marcus." He gnawed on the tip of his vodka-soaked toothpick. "I didn't want you to look at me like another no-good man."

She thought to tell him about Marcus's recent surface but decided against it. Mostly because it was Jonathan's night to vent, but also because he wouldn't understand her turmoil. He was a card-carrying member of Team Luke.

"You know I'd never look at you like that. You're not that guy, I mean you see how shocked I am. If you're driven to this, then there has to be something about her."

The room erupted with excitement. All eyes shot to the flat panels as Portugal scored a goal. Elle, who was probably the only person in the place not following the World Cup, turned her attention back to Jonathan who, for once, was also uninterested in a sporting event.

"There is. When I'm with Bree, I feel good, like I can just be myself. She gets me. None of that prim-and-proper crap like with Lauryn. I can eat a burger without getting a screw-face or some sermon about the perils of red meat. Being with Bree is just easy, if that makes any sense."

"Well, in her defense, look at her circle. They're all strait-laced snobs. 'You are the company you keep'. Just look at Cory and her mom. I almost feel sorry for them, they're so insulated, and to be honest, Jon, you just don't fit."

"And that's just it. I don't want to fit in." He scooped a handful of cracked peanuts from a glass bowl. "See, this is what they would call in bad taste."

"What? Eating peanuts?"

"Eating peanuts at a bar. If Lauryn were here, she would slap the back of my hand and then shoot off some statistic about the percentage of germs found in communal settings and how I don't know who else had their hands in here before me, blah, blah, blah . . . " He created a funnel with his hand and poured the nuts into his mouth.

Elle laughed. "Well, I doubt you'll get hepatitis from some nuts, but she has something of a point."

"I'm not tryna raise pretentious kids who go off to private

schools, playing tennis and polo and crap. I want my kids wearing sneakers and jeans, playing outside and eating junk food every now and then. Like I did."

"Hey. I went to private school. What are you trying to say?"

"C'mon, you're different. On the surface, you can pass for one of them, but we both know you curse like a dude and you're not afraid to eat ribs in public."

She shoved his arm. "Well, take it from someone who spent three years in a dorm with *them*, I don't think that's who she is, or at least not who she wants to be. Her mom and her friends, they have such a hold on her. I mean seriously, if she was just like them, she would never be with someone like you. No offense."

"If she could just relax, stop with the constant calling and texting. She's all over me. All the time. Sometimes I feel like I can't breathe." He pulled his buzzing cell phone from his waist. "See, this is her now."

Elle shrugged. "She's afraid of losing you. I can't blame her. A good man is hard to find. Believe me, I know."

He turned to face her. "But as much as she pisses me off, I feel horrible when I see her, I just feel so guilty. Ya know I've never cheated on her before. Thought about it, but never could bring myself to do it. As annoying as she can be, I know she loves me and would do anything for me. How many people can you say that about?"

It was true. That kind of love and commitment was rare. For all of Lauryn's faults, one thing was for sure—she adored Jonathan to no end. Her eyes still lit up whenever he entered a room. She went above and beyond to make sure all of his needs were met, all while enduring five years of grief from her friends and family for selecting someone of, as Roslyn would put it, questionable pedigree. Lauryn would have been the perfect wife for most men, but Jonathan wasn't most men.

"You know I love Lauryn, but you haven't really been happy for a while now. On the other hand, two months is hardly enough time to really know Bree. I guess it comes down to this. If you left Lauryn and things didn't pan out with Bree, would you be okay by yourself? Because that could be the reality of it. If you're okay with that, then you know what you need to do."

"That's the question." He waved to the bartender. "We'll need a couple more rounds tonight."

21

Elle

Luke and Elle planned a spur-of-the-minute trip to Florida. It turned out that their flight to Key West had a ridiculously long layover in Atlanta. So rather than sit in the airport for hours, Luke suggested they make a quick visit to his parents' house, which was just on the outskirts. Although he'd told his family of his engagement, the official 'meeting of the families' wasn't scheduled until the following month when his parents had planned to be in New York for a weekend before flying to Greece for their forty-fifth wedding anniversary. Elle was slightly jarred by the immediacy of an impromptu visit, but set aside her nerves, figuring it was as good a time as ever to meet her future in-laws. So off to Buckhead, Georgia, they went.

The cab driver followed Luke's directions and led them down a long, private road lined with enormous oak trees. Soon it emerged—a stately two-story, white brick colonial, adorned with six massive white columns. It was flanked by two brick chimneys, which stood like bookends. Full-length windows dressed with storybook black shutters dotted the face of the house and, at the top of the circular brick steps, was a set of onyx double entry doors. The lawn was a meticulously manicured lush shade of green. The cab maneuvered up the cobblestone driveway and came to a stop just behind a garden fountain, from which a forceful clear blue stream jutted into the air before cascading down into a pool of frothy, bubbling water.

Luke squeezed her hand. "I can't wait for them to meet you."

She met his excitement with a broad smile.

No sooner than the town car had slowed to a stop, a petite woman flew out from the front doors as fast as her three-inch heels would carry her. She bounded down the steps and ran into Luke's arms, then hugged him for what seemed like forever. Elle and the driver exchanged awkward glances as they stood aside, watching mother and son embrace. The driver asked her if they'd be requiring a return trip to the airport. Luke told him to come back around five. Elle looked at her watch; five o'clock seemed far away and by the looks of that hug, it would be a very long day.

"Well, let me take a look at you." Mrs. Cartright clutched both of her son's hands, stepped back and drank him in. "Are you eating? You look like you've lost some weight? Are you still keeping those crazy hours?" Her accent was thick. She reminded Elle of Blanche Devereaux from the "Golden Girls." She wore a linen, cornflower blue pantsuit and her flaxen blonde hair was perfectly coifed into an elegant, chin-length bob. She smelled of Chanel No.5.

"No, ma'am. I've been keeping pretty normal hours and eating quite a bit, probably more than I should." He patted his stomach for effect.

She told him she didn't see any weight and promised to fatten him up while he was home. He then introduced Elle.

"This is her," he said in a southern drawl which seemed to grow stronger the closer he got to his parent's home. "This is Elle."

His mother's blue, almond-shaped eyes flickered with something Elle couldn't quite identify. She extended a tiny hand, one which seemed way too delicate to support the weight of the huge diamonds and sapphires adorning her well-manicured fingers. "What a pretty name. How are you, my dear?"

Her hands were butter soft. It was easy to tell the woman had never worked a day in her life, probably never so much as washed a single dish.

"It's so nice to finally meet you, Mrs. Cartright. Luke has told me all about you and your family." Elle felt a bit like a teenager meeting her prom date's mother for the first time.

"Call me Olivia, dear. Mrs. Cartright was my mother-in-law, bless her soul." She made the sign of the cross on her chest.

"Let's get inside, why don't we? Can't wait to see Dad." Luke slid the strap of his duffle bag over his shoulder and held his arms out for the women to lead the way.

"Oh Luke, dear, he's not back from the club yet. You know how he gets when he's around his silly friends, but I hope you're both hungry. Elena is preparing lunch. He'll join us soon."

They stepped inside the two-story foyer. Elle's eyes were immediately drawn to the bridge balcony at the top of two classic curved staircases. The path towards the dining room was lined with elaborate oriental rugs. The walls were pale shades of lemon, sage and bisque. From them hung richly framed oil paintings. At the end of the hallway, white French doors opened to reveal a grand dining room replete with two crystal chandeliers hovering over an elaborately set table, one complemented by ivory, serpentine-backed chairs with carved legs. It was large enough for a party of twelve or more, but set for six. Sunlight cascaded through the French windows, reflecting off the table's silver candelabras.

As they took their places, a chubby middle-aged Hispanic woman dressed in a white uniform emerged. Her eyes registered a subtle flash of surprise when she rested them on Elle. Olivia sat directly across from her son, the head of the table was clearly reserved for her husband, who had yet to arrive. Luke sat to Elle's right.

"Where are those girls? I told them twelve o'clock sharp." Olivia looked disapprovingly at the grandfather clock in the corner. Its small hand neared the twelve and its large hand barely grazed the eight.

As if he read Elle's mind, Luke turned to Olivia. "Mom, it's not even a quarter to. No need to rush. We have plenty of time."

Her pretty face wrinkled with frustration. "I suppose. Why don't we adjourn next door for some tea as we wait for your sisters. Elena, would you be so kind as to bring us some."

As soon as they were seated in what was probably known to the average person as a den, but so eloquently described by Olivia as a sitting room, the questions began.

"So Elle, tell me all about yourself," Olivia asked, perched at the edge of a sage-green, French provincial chair. Elle sat across from her on a matching settee, which was far more beautiful than it was comfortable.

"Well, Luke and I met in his office. I was taking my god-daughter to an appointment and—"

"No dear, tell me about you." She waved a playful dismissive hand towards her son. "Not how you met *him*."

Elle told her she was born and raised mostly in New York, had gone to Georgetown, then grad school back in New York, and that she was an editor at a publishing firm in the city. It clearly wasn't enough because Olivia gave her a look as if to say go on.

"Now, why don't you tell us your biggest strengths and weakness?" Luke piped in. Olivia was temporarily amused, but it was obvious she sought more information and Elle wasn't quite sure what that could be. Just then they heard some voices in the hallway and in hurtled two petite blondes, both with striking resemblances to Olivia, only they were taller and younger. With them, they brought an infectious bubble of energy and excitement.

"Luke! My big brother is finally home!" Similar to her mother's animated affection, this sister embraced her brother as if she were seeing him for the first time in years. If Elle remembered correctly, Luke told her he'd just been home for Thanksgiving.

"Ashton, Madeleine, I'd like for you to meet Elle." Madeleine extended an eager hand. Ashton, however, hugged Elle tightly. Then they both oohed and aahed over her engagement ring, congratulating their big brother on his impeccable taste. Their southern twangs were even more pronounced than their mother's.

A whirlwind of excitement filled the sitting room. This was the kind of thing Elle had seen on TV and assumed was an exaggeration of Southern people, but low and behold, Southern belles really did exist. Just then Elena announced it was noon and lunch would be served. They took their places at the table and conversation flowed. Elle felt increasingly comfortable until Mr. Cartright suddenly appeared in the doorway. His entrance had been quiet, almost stealth-like, as if he appeared out of thin air. Olivia lightly clapped her tiny hands together. "Oh wonderful, you're here! We started without you, but I'll have Elena bring you a fresh plate."

He held his hand up. "No dear, I ate at the club." Luke's father was tall, about six-foot-three. He had a full head of appropriately placed salt and pepper hair. He wore a navy blue blazer and khaki slacks, a touch conservative for a Saturday afternoon, but something told Elle, for him this was considered casual. A handsome man by any measure, it was clear where Luke got his good looks. She estimated his age at around sixty-five, but surmised he might even be older because he was extremely fit and tanned and clearly took very good care of himself. There was a regal air about him which commanded the attention and respect from any room he entered. She could instantly tell he was admired by his children and adored by his wife. Olivia popped out of her seat like a schoolgirl at recess time and greeted her husband with a quick peck on his lips. Madeleine and Ashton followed suit and stood up to greet their father. He and Luke shook hands. It was apparent men did not hug in this household.

Again, Elle felt like something of an outsider as she witnessed more familial affection. She wasn't sure if she too should get up and approach Mr. Cartright or wait to be introduced. It had been a long time since she'd felt so socially awkward. Luke, however, who was exceptionally good at navigating uncomfortable situations, made the formal introduction.

Elle stood and extended her hand to the patriarch. "So nice to finally meet you, Mr. Cartright. Luke has told me so much about you all."

This time there was no invitation to call him by his first name. What she did get in return was a curt, 'How do you do?' delivered in a thick-yet-chilly Southern drawl. She could quickly tell that this man didn't desire a response and had no interest in learning anything about her. Elle quickly withdrew her hand and looked to Luke for a silent explanation. He, too, looked slightly confused. Ashton was the first break the silence.

"Well, Daddy, are you going to sit down and join us?" She plopped down in her seat and poured her father a glass of lemonade.

"I'm not hungry, I ate at the club. Need to freshen up, change and wrap up some business in my office. You all enjoy the rest of the afternoon. Luke, come see me before you leave, son." He retreated from the dining room as quickly as he appeared.

"Nathaniel . . . " Olivia followed after her husband.

Luke's sisters returned to their meals and resumed their light-hearted chatter. A frown flashed across Luke's face before he forced a smile, which Elle knew was for her benefit. "So, Madeleine," he said, "how's law school treating you?"

As soon as they had a moment alone, Elle began her line of questioning. She asked if she'd somehow offended his father. He assured her that she shouldn't be concerned and that his father was the strong silent type. And that it wasn't personal, it was just his way. He showed her the rest of their home, one with so many rooms, Elle quickly lost count. She learned their household staff consisted of a driver, a chef, grounds people, housekeepers, and two personal assistants—just to support the three of them who still lived there (Madeleine lived on campus). He also confirmed what Elle had already assumed, that his mother had never really worked, but was involved with a lot of charities. His father was retired for the most part, but still practiced law when he found a case particularly interesting. In his free time he consulted, hung out at 'the club', played golf, and sailed.

Luke never ceased to amaze her. How a man who grew up in such wealth could be so grounded was beyond her. She'd gotten the impression he came from money, but not to such a degree. There wasn't a pretentious bone in his body and at that moment, she found herself loving him that much more.

After the tour of the grounds and more time spent socializing with Olivia and Ashton (Madeleine left for an appointment), they settled out on the lanai, which overlooked a luscious Olympic-sized pool. Olivia was regaling them with tales of Luke's childhood antics when Elena appeared through the French doors to tell Luke his father had asked for him. Elle had never heard of such a thing—a father sending for his son. Why not just come out and get him or, better yet, join them all? Although Luke had chalked up his father's flimsy social skills to a stoic demeanor, there had to be more to the story. Luke excused himself.

When he still hadn't returned some fifteen minutes later, Elle excused herself to use the restroom. On her way she heard loud voices in the hallway. She slowed her pace and tip-toed until she was right outside of the doorway from which they came. She looked around, saw no one and leaned her ear towards the crack in the door. But she didn't have to strain as their voices were raised.

" . . . I see you're still that liberal, cockeyed optimist. And I applaud your efforts to uplift the oppressed and blur the lines of race, but this time you've taken it too far." She recognized the deep baritone drawl.

"Here we go . . . " she heard Luke say.

"Do you see me smiling? Should I find it funny that you've come in this house parading around with her?" Nathaniel's words were delivered in long, slow beats, drenched in a syrupy tone which was better suited for acclamation than for reprimand.

Luke struck back. "Do you know how ignorant you sound?"

"You think that damn medical degree you have gives you the right to insult me?" He paused. "Look now, I've worked hard to give you and your sisters everything you could ever want—"

She heard Luke sigh then say, "I should have known this speech was coming."

"You shut your mouth and listen. Don't forget who sent you to that damn medical school, who stood by you when you got divorced and has been there every step of the way." Elle could all but see him wagging a thick index finger in Luke's face. "And you thank me by arriving to my house with some nigger on your arm?"

Elle stopped breathing. She could not believe her ears. It was as if time had stopped. As if she was having an out-of-body experience, watching herself stand there with her body frozen and her mouth opened wide. Who were these people and how had she managed to come into their fold? What had she gotten herself into? In all of her thirty-two years, no one had ever called her that. Her emotions went from shock to anger to fear. She stood, unsure whether to stay and listen or head straight for the front door, for she could not go back out on the lanai and drink tea with that man's wife. Yes, Olivia had been warm and friendly, but her opinions could not be far removed from her husband's. Oh God, what was Luke going to say in response? The question terrified her. She thought she knew him, but never would have imagined this was the family he came from. Her entire life she'd received curious stares and people frequently asked what she was, but not once had she felt judged because her father was white and her mother was black. Luke knew her ethnicity and it seemed a complete non-issue. How did he not know his father would think otherwise?

"I can't believe you." Luke's voice was surprisingly calm. "You haven't changed a bit. I never wanted to believe what I always knew deep down, but you're just a racist. Plain and simple. You and Mom, with all of your philanthropy and charities. It's all bullshit because you still think you're better just because your skin is white." Elle exhaled a tiny bit of relief. Luke *was* the man she thought he was.

Nathaniel was unmoved by Luke's oration. "Say what you want, but I'm not apologizing for who I am. Be naïve and believe that civil rights crap if you want to. The fact still remains—whites and blacks have no business together. It's just not right, Luke. I'll give it to you, this one is pretty, looks like she's mixed with something, but she's still just a black girl. Shoot, take her to dinner, sleep with her if you want, I don't care, but don't you bring her in this house to meet your parents, to present her as your *fiancée*. What the hell are you thinking, boy? Now you already screwed up once, you better get it right the next time and marry somebody who's good for you so you can finally settle your ass down."

There was silence. Elle hated herself for eavesdropping, she'd gotten way more than she bargained for.

Nathaniel went on. "Now you know your mother and sisters will show hospitality to damn near anyone, but your mother doesn't want to see you with her. Good Lord, can you imagine you coming in here with some mixed-breed kids. Can't even fathom such a thing. Better yet, don't sleep with her. We don't want any accidents smearing the Cartright name. Now, take your little friend back to New York and we'll forget this whole thing ever happened. Maybe Madeline can introduce you to one of her little friends in law school." His tone was trivial and dismissive, as if he'd just found the perfect solution to the problem which had recently entered his home. "So, now that we've squared that away, how's your practice coming along?"

"You disgust me. I'm out of here," she heard Luke say. Elle then spun on her heels and dashed back to the bathroom. She quietly closed the door behind her. Her reflection in the mirror was telling; her cheeks were flushed and her forehead was beaded with sweat. She wanted to climb out of the window, make a run to the nearest bus stop and take a Greyhound straight back to New York. How could she face them? How could she pretend she hadn't just heard that? As she mulled over her options, she heard someone rapping lightly on the door. She splashed her face with cold water and gave herself a quick pep talk. She could not hide in the bathroom forever. Then she slowly turned the knob, unsure of what to expect on the other side of the door. It was Luke.

"Umm, it's time to go. We're leaving." His firm tone left no room for questioning and it was exactly what she wanted to hear.

Within a moment, they were back out front, a mere three hours from the time they'd arrived. A car pulled up, as if out of nowhere; they scrambled into the backseat and were on their way. They sat in silence. She would not be the first to bring it up. Finally Luke turned to her.

"I'm sure you're wondering why we left like that. It's hard to explain," he stammered. "My father and I had something of an argument and I just couldn't stand to be there any longer, I'm sorry." He turned and faced the window.

Although she'd heard most of their conversation, she couldn't help but wonder why Luke would have even brought her there, knowing what his father was. Was she, in fact, an exotic turn off his beaten path? Or a product of his sowing his post-divorce oats? Or maybe even a bullet point on his bucket list that went too far. Her mind raced with questions and fears. It wasn't until they had landed in Key West and were checked into their suite when they addressed the elephant in the room.

"Look," Elle said, "I'm going to be honest. I overheard your conversation with your father. I heard what he said about me. I know why you stormed out of there."

He stopped unpacking his bag. "You heard us? From the bathroom?"

"No," she admitted, "I heard you both yelling when I was on my way to the bathroom and was curious, so I was listening by the door. I'm sorry, but I was concerned. I've never heard you raise your voice before, I thought something was wrong."

A wave of embarrassment cast across his face. "So, you heard everything?"

"Um, maybe not everything, but enough."

He shook his head apologetically. "I'm sorry you had to hear that. I hope you don't think that's how we are. My father is—"

"Luke, I have to be honest, I've never been more offended in my life. Does your mother feel the same way?"

There was disappointment in his eyes. "My mom thinks whatever my father thinks, unfortunately. She just doesn't have it in her to be cold like him. You saw, she's a sweetheart, but not as open-minded as I or my sisters. Believe me, if I had any idea he would have acted like that or said those things, I never would have brought you there. You have to know that."

"But how could you not know your father's a racist?" She instantly regretted her choice of words. As much as she now despised Nathaniel, he was still Luke's father. The words stung, she could tell.

"I don't know. I mean, growing up I would hear him say off-color remarks, but the older I got, it seemed he grew more tolerant. I know this is going to sound clichéd, but he has black friends, or associates, I should say. He's invited them to the house. Race never seemed to come up." He shrugged. "Of course these were attorneys at his firm, special clients and the like. I've never heard him speak the way he did today. Never." His hazel eyes flickered, taking on a shade of green under the artificial light of the amber sconces. "I can tell you don't believe me, but what you have to understand is people from the South, people who run in the high-end circles like my parents, are all about social status and posturing. Image is everything, so they're the most polite and gracious people you'll ever meet. But underneath the surface, it's often a whole other story. So, just because I've never heard my father say such things means nothing. He's just as prejudiced as his father and grandfather before him. As much as folks don't like to admit it, this part of the country is still very segregated and a lot of these people are stuck in their ways. It's part of the reason I left."

His words made sense, but they failed to stem the bad taste in her mouth. Despite all of her accomplishments, her sparkling personality and the love she had for his son, no amount of persuading would ever convince Nathaniel she was good enough, and she wasn't sure it was a battle she wanted to take on. She loved Luke intensely, but questioned if he, if they, were worthy of such a crusade.

Back in New York the days turned into weeks and their lives eventually fell back in line. What happened in Georgia was never discussed again. That elephant sat quietly in the corner minding its own business while Luke and Elle stepped over him, moved around him and avoided his eye contact.

22

Jonathan

"Where are you going?" Jonathan was lying in Bree's bed, watching as she tugged on her jeans.

"I have some things I need to do and you need to leave," she said.

He sat up. "What's the problem?"

Since the time she'd called an end to their relationship, he'd managed to somehow lure her back into his life. He'd believed all was running smoothly, up until that morning.

She stopped dressing and stared at him. "I can't do this anymore. I can't have you come over here, sleep with me and then walk out that door and go back to her every night. I thought I could, but I can't."

He pushed aside the covers and scooted to the edge of the bed. "But I thought we talked about this, I told you I just need a little more time.

"Time? Time for what Jonathan? To make up your mind? To figure out if this is where you want to be?"

"I know where I want to be."

"And where is that?"

"With you."

"So, why is she still in the damn picture?"

"I told you, it's hard."

"How many times do I have to keep telling you? *Life* is hard! We *all* have hard decisions to make, Jonathan."

"I know," he said.

"Do you really though? Because since I've known you, I have yet to see you make one."

"What's that supposed to mean?"

"It means that all you do is waffle back and forth. You're always hanging in the balance, waiting for things to resolve themselves. Well that's not the way the real world works."

"Look, I know how the real world works—"

"I don't know that you do. I watch you do it at work and I see you doing it now—with us. Would you grow a damn pair already?"

That fiery spirit of Bree's is part of what had drawn Jonathan to her, but when it was directed at him he second guessed its appeal. She had a way of slicing through him with her words.

"At work?" he said. "Don't act as if you know anything about what I do at work." She had better not go there. If there was one thing Jonathan was confident about, it was his team and his talent as a coach.

"But I do," she said. "You coddle those boys. Take Shawn Garrett for example. You let him stay on the team, even after that DWI. He should have been kicked off. You should have reported it—"

"He's a good kid, Bree."

"A good kid who drinks and drives?"

"He made a mistake, it was just that one time. He was stressed about his girlfriend—"

"Excuses. There you go again making excuses for people."

"He's not people. He's a good kid. He just needed some direction. If I kicked him off, he would have lost his scholarship, then what?" Jonathan said. "Everybody makes mistakes."

"And what if he kills somebody the next time he decides to handle his *stress*, by drinking before he gets on the road."

"That's not going to happen."

"How do you know?"

"Because I won't let it."

"What are you going to do? Follow him around twenty-four seven? Whatever. Shawn Garrett is not the issue."

"Well then what is it? You brought him up."

"It's your inability to toe the line. Your inability to tell people no, to hurt people's feelings."

"Who wants to go around hurting people's feelings?"

"Nobody *wants* to, but sometimes it has to be done. How long have you been promising me you're going to break it off with her? How long, Jonathan?"

"But we talked about this Bree. I can't leave when her father just died. She needs me."

Bree clenched her fists. "See! This is that shit. You make me feel like a monster for putting my feelings before hers. What am I supposed to say? That I don't care? If I do, then I'm the bitch—"

"Nobody thinks you're a bitch."

"That's not the point. I've been patient, but I can't do it anymore. Not going to keep sleeping with someone else's man, I deserve more than that." She raked a brush through her hair before twirling it into a disheveled bun. "I love you, I do, but I won't share you. Not anymore."

"Is this an ultimatum?"

"No, it's a choice. It's me and just me or you choose her and forget all about me."

"Bree, you expect me to go to this woman two weeks after her father died and tell her I'm leaving her? Hell, she's waiting on an engagement ring. That's where her head's at. As a woman, can't you understand that?"

She shook her head. "You just don't get it." She slipped on her rain boots. "I don't need this. Make sure you're gone by the time I get home. Leave my keys on the table."

"Bree . . . "

―――――

The mood in the Lewis home was somber. Ed's passing left them all shells of their former selves. He'd been the pulse of the family. His positive energy and warm personality endeared everyone he came in contact with—he was the calm amidst the storm that was Roslyn. Lauryn's sister and brother had been staying at the house to keep their mother company, although she barely left her room. Family came and went, but no one could get more than a sentence from her.

Lauryn and her father had been exceptionally close. She relied on Jonathan's support and he complied. He understood Bree's position, more so after speaking with Elle, but even she agreed leaving Lauryn now would be cruel. This was his time for sacrifice. He'd have to be there for her as long as she needed. His happiness would have to wait until the time was right. He only prayed Bree would still be around when the right time came.

He'd left Bree's keys as she'd demanded, but she consumed his thoughts. She was cordial when he saw her at work, but gave him the silent treatment everywhere else. She ignored all his calls and messages. For him there were many sleepless nights, unfinished meals and moments of staring into space over the next several weeks.

Gloom was all about him. Lauryn was understandably sad and withdrawn, his team was having a losing streak, and going to work brought about a mixed bag of emotions. He'd glimpse Bree's face and instantly get excited, just to be let down when he'd see the anger in her dark brown eyes. The only good thing to come of it all was the five pounds of muscle he'd put on from excessive hours at the gym. When he couldn't take it anymore, he drove to Bree's house without so much as a clue of what he planned to say.

He spent an hour sitting double-parked in front of her building until he was shooed away by a local patrol car. The next half hour he paced back and forth in her lobby until he received disapproving glances from an elderly couple as they retrieved their mail. After which he sat on a tiny bench in front of her building. Finally she appeared from around the corner carrying two Macy's shopping bags and engrossed in a conversation on her cell phone.

"Bree," he called as soon as she neared him.

He called her name again and she shot around. Her expression shifted from fear to surprise to annoyance. "What the hell are you doing here?"

He approached tentatively. His hands suddenly felt empty and he wished he'd brought some candy or flowers or something. "I didn't meant to scare you. It's just that you won't take my calls or anything. You ignore me at school and I didn't know what else to do."

She didn't break stride. "I told you already. If she was your choice, then you need to forget about me."

He followed her to the elevator. "Can we just talk for a minute?"

"About what? There's nothing else to say." She told the person on the phone she'd call them back. "I don't hate you, Jon, but we can't be friends, so let's just leave well enough alone."

The elevator door opened. He started to follow her, but she raised her hand, blocking his entrance. "Don't. Just let it go."

The door attempted to close, but he stopped it with his foot. "Just hear me out, would you?" She rested her shopping bags down and jabbed at the button, as if in doing so the door would close faster. A young delivery man zipped into the elevator carrying two bags of Chinese food, leaving Jonathan no choice but to move his foot. The door closed in his face. He watched the numbers illuminate as they ascended to the sixth floor.

He was at a crossroads. He could walk away, go back to Lauryn and resume the unfulfilled life he'd known, or he could fight for Bree, for the love between them and the future he wanted to see with her. He recalled Bree's words about making hard decisions. She was right. He *had* lived his life tip-toeing around people's feelings and sacrificing his own needs for everyone around him.

When he was eighteen, it wasn't his choice to stay at home and attend a local college. But he had, because his mother had expressed in not-so-many-words that she needed her only son close by, not only to watch over his younger sister, but to keep her company after her ugly divorce from his father. So, Jonathan turned down his prized scholarship to Louisiana State University and stood by to watch as his friends moved out of New Jersey and registered at colleges in exciting new places. Meanwhile he enrolled in a community college a mere six miles from his house and took a part-time job at local hardware store —for his mother. He also hadn't been happy with the person Lauryn had morphed into over the past few years. There was a stark difference between the fun-loving, confident woman he'd met (at a wedding ironically enough) five years ago and the woman she was today. It wasn't a relationship he wanted anymore, it hadn't been for years. But he'd stayed—for her. It was time he made a decision for Jonathan.

In lightning speed, he hurtled up the six flights of stairs and pressed on her bell. He pleaded again for Bree to hear him out and open the door, a request she ignored at first then responded to with a curt, 'Just go away'.

Before he realized what he was saying, the words flew out of his mouth. "Bree, just open the door. I've made my decision—I want you. I'll tell her it's over tonight. Just open the door."

He heard the locks turning. She cracked open the door and gave him a pensive stare. "Are you serious?"

"I am." He shook his head, feeling a sudden rush of adrenaline coupled with the ardent belief he could do it. He was ready.

She, however, was skeptical. "And what's changed? Why now?"

"I miss you," he said.

"You miss me?" She surveyed him. "Just realizing now that you miss me?"

"Been missing you since the day you kicked me out."

"I didn't kick you out, Jon."

"You know what I mean. I can't be without you. It's killing me to look at you every day and know I can't have you." This was the closest he'd gotten to her in weeks. Small details, like the beauty mark on her chin and the dimple in her left cheek, drew him in all over again. She had to take him back. He wouldn't know what to do with himself if she didn't.

"You mean it? You'll tell her tonight?"

"I will."

She stared at him a moment, he knew it was more for effect than out of contemplation. He shifted on his feet and reassured her she wouldn't regret it. She slowly opened the door and let him in.

Now he just had to live up to his end of the bargain. It was going to be a long night.

———————

Six hours later, he was seated on Lauryn's couch. As luck would have it, she was in good spirits that day. Jonathan, however, was despondent. He'd found a dozen or so reasons to postpone their talk, but then would picture Bree's face and knew he couldn't disappoint her. It had to be done. For everyone's sake—his, Bree's and Lauryn's. He just didn't love her the way she deserved. They both deserved more and he'd wasted her time for way too long. She would find someone else soon, for she was beautiful, smart and good-hearted. Now she could move on and have all of those children she dreamed of. She'd be sad for now, but would one day thank Jonathan for releasing her. She'd come to understand and maybe they could even be friends one day. Yes, he was doing the right thing—for the both of them. He loved Lauryn and wanted her to be happy.

His heart began to pound when she asked what was wrong. He patted the seat beside him, asked her to sit, and told her they needed to talk.

With much trepidation, she sat. "What about?"

"Us." He took a deep breath. "You know I love you, but we haven't been happy for a long time and you deserve to be happy. We both do." He took an even deeper breath. "So I think we need to move on, for both of our sakes." Whew. He'd gotten it out. The sentence he'd rehearsed the entire ride over finally took leave from his mouth. The worst was over.

"Move on?" Her head whipped from side to side. "What does that mean? Are you breaking up with me?"

He had to be strong, he could not waver. He nodded. "Yeah."

"Are you freakin' kidding me? You're breaking up with me after five years and not even two months after my dad died?" Tears began streaming down her cheeks.

"Lauryn, calm down. I know this is going to sound bad, but there's never a good time to break up. Please don't make this more difficult than it has to be and listen to what I'm saying. We're *not* happy. Haven't been for a long time." He pulled a package of tissues from his pocket; he'd grabbed them as an afterthought at the gas station, knowing that waterworks were guaranteed.

She snatched a tissue and blew her nose. "I *am* happy and I thought you were too."

"You think you are, but let's be real. You've wanted me to be somebody I'm not for a long time. We just aren't right for each other." He couldn't bear to look at her. "I know it hurts, but you have to be honest with yourself. This . . . this isn't the relationship you want."

"I can't believe this." She started wheezing. "I can't believe you're doing this to me. I need some water." She started for the kitchen.

He gritted his teeth. The dramatics were an unexpected twist. If he ignored them, he'd be deemed an insensitive ass. If he indulged them, she'd run with it.

"I can't breathe." She held one arm against the wall, the other clutched her chest. "I . . . I can't believe you're doing this."

What the hell was going on? Tears he'd expected, but not this. Her face took on a bluish tint and her breathing was labored. He was quickly convinced it wasn't an act. He jumped from his seat.

"Lauryn! You've gotta calm down, come sit." He led her back to the couch. But before she reached it, she collapsed to the floor with a loud thud.

"Oh my God! Can you hear me?" He ran to the kitchen for a glass of tap water, then splashed it in her face. Her eyes rolled back in her head and she wouldn't respond. He called 911. She remained unconscious until the EMS arrived. Eventually she came to, but her face was drained of its color, she was disoriented and mumbling things no one understood. In the ambulance, he sat beside her, gripping her clammy hand. How had his life become so complicated? He'd always done the right thing and played by the rules; all he wanted was to be happy and here he was on his way to the hospital.

After an hour of waiting in the emergency room, amongst crying babies, coughing adults and a man bleeding far too much to have been waiting so long, a young dark-haired doctor in scrubs entered.

"Mr. Moore?" he called.

Jonathan sprang to his feet. "Yeah, that's me. How is she?"

"I'm Dr. Clark." He shook his hand. "Lauryn is okay, but she must have struck her head when she fell. She has a contusion on her temple. It's not a huge deal, it'll heal. We're more concerned about any internal damage she may have suffered."

"Internal damage?"

"Yeah, initially it appeared she just passed out from a minor panic attack, but she's still disoriented and we're concerned there may have been some residual trauma." He removed his glasses and rubbed his eyes with the back of his hand. "We want to keep her overnight under observation, just as a precaution."

"Disoriented how? You mean she has memory loss?"

"I doubt it, but she's showing some cognitive delays which I find concerning. But I believe she'll be fine. Like I said, we're just keeping her as a precaution. She'll most likely be able to go home tomorrow."

Jonathan sighed a breath of relief. The doctor's prognosis eased both his tension and his guilt. A little. "Can I see her?"

"Of course. She's in the second room to the right." He glanced down at his chart. "Oh, pardon me, I failed to mention the most important thing. The baby is fine. No harm done at all." He turned to walk away.

Jonathan grabbed his arm. "Whoa, wait a minute. The baby? What are you talking about?"

Dr. Clark shot him a reprimanding look. Jonathan released him and apologized. "She's pregnant?"

"I assumed you knew. But yes, about eight weeks."

Jonathan ran his palm down his face. "Sorry doctor, it's . . . it's just been a crazy day. Can I go see her now?"

Jonathan approached Lauryn's bed. Her body was swathed in stiff, white sheets. An IV line was taped to the back of her left hand. Her honey-brown hair fanned out over the pillow. Her skin was pallid, revealing tiny hints of blue veins beneath the surface and her lips had a purplish hue. Only the light fluttering of her eyelids revealed any vitality. She looked eerily beautiful. His thoughts jumped to the doctor's word. *The baby is fine.* Why hadn't she told him? For the next four hours his mind raced until he was numb—nearly twelve hours ago he was making love to the woman he adored. Fast forward and he was in the hospital with a woman he loved, but didn't want to be with and had just learned he might be a father.

His cell phone vibrated in his pocket. He had a slew of messages and missed calls. Bree was the last person he wanted to speak to. Her first text was inquisitive: *I hope all is going well. I know this will be hard for u. Sorry it has to be like this, but I love u and can't wait until it's just the 2 of us.*

The second message had come six hours later: *I guess no news is good news. Please call me when u get home.*

The last read: *It's almost 3 am and I still haven't heard from u. I don't even know what to think. U need to call me.*

He ignored the voicemail message.

"Jonathan?" Lauryn's voice was hoarse.

He propped up then leaned over her. "Hey, how are you feeling?"

"My head is killing me." She gently pressed the heel of her palm against her temple then ran her fingers across the gauzed bandage on her forehead.

He reached for her hand. "I know. You hit the floor pretty hard. But the doctor says you're going to be just fine."

"How long have I been here?" She glanced around the small gray room.

"A few hours. They want you to spend the night. I can take you back home in the morning."

She squinted at him. "Did you really break up with me or was that just a bad dream?"

He looked away. "Let's not talk about that now, okay? Just get some rest."

"No! I want to know. Did you? You did, didn't you? Jonathan, you couldn't have meant that. You can't leave me."

He grabbed a tissue off the nightstand and dabbed at her eyes. "Lauryn, please stop. Let's talk later, okay? You need to get your rest." As she sobbed silently, he could hear his cell phone vibrating on his waist.

She pleaded with him to reconsider, but he continued to deflect the topic. Not once did she mention being pregnant and that's when he realized she didn't know. The doctor had most likely told her, but she must not have been coherent enough to absorb the news. He thought back. Yup, it had been about eight weeks since Ed had died. He recalled the night of the funeral. They'd had sex. In fact it was the last time he'd slept with her. The pieces fell into place. She was pregnant and it was his.

23

Blair

Pregnancy was agreeing with Blair. She was glowing and no longer had any of the symptoms which had plagued her during her first trimester. Her gynecologist assured her all was progressing well and she was likely out of the miscarriage-danger zone they'd feared early on. She and Vaughn were excited to learn they were expecting a girl. He attended all of her doctor appointments and each week came home with something new for the baby. They furnished their daughter's bedroom suite and its decoration became Blair's newest project.

Vaughn remained true to his promise and worked hard to redeem himself. He not only resorted to what was familiar, showering her with expensive things, but also took interest in matters closer to her heart. Simple things like agreeing to watch the movies she liked, spending less time with his friends, and listening when she spoke. Before, her words had never seemed to hold his attention longer than a moment. Happiness had finally found her. But every so often a dark cloud would eclipse her sunshine—Dylan. She hadn't spoken to him since the day she'd called it quits. All of her apologetic emails went unreturned. It was for the best, that she knew, but it still hurt all the same. She tried to remain busy so as not to be forced to think about him or the way she'd hurt him and especially not the fact that she was carrying his child. It was a truth she hadn't mentioned aloud to a soul since the day she'd told Elle of her decision. She'd tucked it away, deep down in a crevice of her memory, never to be revisited.

And there it remained until the evening she and Vaughn attended a National Urban League awards dinner at the Marriott Marquis in Manhattan. Vaughn was being recognized for a non-profit organization he'd spearheaded for inner city youth, one of many of his philanthropic endeavors. They spent a majority of the evening mingling amongst their peers while receiving countless congratulations and well wishes. When she casually flipped through the program she stumbled upon the name and photo of a man she knew all too well. There, second to last in the list of honored guests, it read:

Recipient of the Inroads in Education Award
Dylan Stewart, Professor, Drexel University

Her stomach sank. Not only was he in the same room with them, but he was being honored as well, which meant he'd be sitting on the dais alongside Vaughn. This would also be the first time he'd see her pregnant. She had to get out of there. Blair only heard snippets of what the woman standing across from her was saying, something about looking for board members and how Blair would be perfect. Blair's eye darted around the room. Where was he? It was damn near impossible to find him in the sea of dark suits and tuxedos. She just had to find him before he found her. She told the charity lady she'd be in touch and hastened away. As she weaved through the crowd, she concocted the story she'd tell Vaughn, how she was sick to her stomach and they needed to leave right away. Just as her get-away plan was hatched, she turned to see her husband standing a few feet away, engaged in a conversation. She took several quick steps towards him then stopped cold in her tracks. Across from Vaughn stood a familiar figure. He was clad in a dark suit and nodding enthusiastically at Vaughn's words. Then he turned slightly to the left and his profile came into full view. A sharp, handsome profile which Blair knew all too well.

She turned towards the door, ready to bee-line out of the ballroom, when she heard her name. The room began to spin. *No, the baby.* She couldn't allow herself to faint. It might save her for the moment, but she couldn't risk it. Instead she stopped, her heels frozen in their place.

"Ah, there you are, honey. Been looking for you," Vaughn called, his arms outreached. "I want to introduce you to somebody." Her husband and ex-lover were making their way towards her. Her stomach twisted into knots. "Blair, this is Dylan Stewart. He's an honoree as well. Dylan, I'd like for you to meet my wife."

24

Elle

Despite his parent's refusal to acknowledge their impending nuptials, Luke was thrilled to be planning what would be his second wedding. Elle, however, didn't share his enthusiasm. Having been raised an only child, she never quite felt the comfort of a tight-knit family. She spent a lot of her adolescence away at school and away from her parents. She'd eventually gotten used to it, which was why she wasn't big on holidays, but a major part of her missed it. She craved large family gatherings where cousins, grandparents, and aunts and uncles would wrap around a huge kitchen table to eat and share stories. Most of her Christmases past the age of ten had been spent with the families of close friends, where she would sit on the sidelines and watch them exchange presents. It wasn't so much about the gifts, as she always had a load of expensive ones at home. Rather, it was about the experience—the intimacy and closeness displayed by people sitting around in their pajamas, swapping colorful boxes and waiting to see the sparkle in each others' eyes when they opened the perfect gift.

Her father's diplomatic duties kept him traveling and her mother preferred to vacation over the holidays. To some, her globetrotting childhood sounded chic and cosmopolitan, yet to Elle, Thanksgivings in European restaurants left a lot to be desired. Family was important to her and she'd always imagined recreating what she had missed with her husband's family. The thought of uncomfortable visits and separate holidays troubled her. Could she live her life with a man whose parents would never accept her?

When she raised her concerns to Luke, he'd tell her his parents' feelings were of little consequence. He would ask her if he made her happy. To which she'd answer yes and he'd say, 'Then that's all that matters.'

He took the reins in planning all of the details. Not one thing, not the catering, nor flowers, nor deejay selection escaped him. Elle had never seen a man so involved in his own wedding planning.

Then came the weekend for her to select her gown. For weeks she'd perused countless magazines and websites, looking for just the right dress, until she arrived at a Manhattan boutique with several pictures in hand. Only her mother, who could barely contain her excitement, accompanied her. Each dress she tried on was more striking than the one before and the decision became exceedingly difficult. That was until she found the one. An ivory silk sheath with subtle lace detailing. It fit nearly perfect, in it she felt beautiful. Her mother offered a silent nod, indicating their search was over.

As she modeled in front of the three-way mirror, she imagined herself standing at the altar next to Luke while he recited his vows. However, when it was her turn, she couldn't find the words. Everything in the scene was absolutely perfect, everything except the feelings. She loved Luke, that she was certain of, but why did her thoughts keep reverting back to Marcus? It was his face which flashed in front of her when

Luke had proposed and there had even been times she fought to erase thoughts of him as she and Luke made love. Today, as she tried on gowns and imagined the ceremony, it was Marcus's voice she heard in her head. It was driving her insane. All she wanted to do was move on with her life, but at every significant turn, there he loomed—Marcus. Arrogant, deceitful, selfish Marcus. Not Luke, not her handsome, perfect Luke. This was no way to begin a life with someone. She wished for a lobotomy of sorts, something which could erase the memory of Marcus, so she could finally move on because until he was completely out of her mind, she could not. As much as she tried to recall Blair's warning that she was getting in her own way and Jonathan's advice to move on, her heart wouldn't allow it. It stubbornly refused to budge from its place. It clung to Marcus's ankle the way a child does the first time her mother leaves. It wanted no parts of a future without him, even though it knew deep down he would likely shatter it again. It craved the high he gave it, even if just for a little while. It felt alive, desired and impassioned when it was under his will. Something it hadn't felt with Luke. While Luke made it feel loved and secure, Marcus cast it under a spell, one she didn't know how to break.

It was at that moment she knew she couldn't go forward with the wedding. She could not ruin Luke's life by letting him marry a woman who was unable to love him the way he loved her. Three days later, as they drove home from dinner, she blurted it out.

"So, what do you think about "*Everything*"? Luke asked.

"What?"

"*Everything*", by Michael Bublé. For the first dance. I've always loved that song."

"I can't do this." She hadn't planned to say it there and then, but it laid heavily on her mind all throughout dinner. Every time he'd make mention of a wedding detail, she cringed inside. And when he placed his hand over hers, gently running his thumb over her ring, she felt a stab to her core. She had to tell him.

"You can't do what?" He still had a smile on his face. He had no clue how his life was about to change.

She turned towards him and took a deep breath. "Get married."

Immediately he pulled the car to the side of the road. A horn sounded behind them. "What are you talking about?"

She slowly shook her head. "I can't marry you, I'm sorry."

The reality of her words struck him and she watched his awkward smile dissolve. A pained expression took its place. "Wait, wait. Where's this coming from? What happened?"

"I don't know," she said, although she did. But she wouldn't add injury to insult by admitting it had to do with another man.

He rested his elbow on the armrest between them, then stroked his temple and forehead as if he were searching for the answer to a complex math equation. "What is this? Cold feet? Is that what you have? You're just nervous, that's normal. I felt that way before Tricia and I got married." He laughed nervously. "Well, maybe that's not a good example, but you get what I'm saying."

"It's not cold feet." *Or was it*, she thought. Was she simply afraid of getting married? No. Nothing about marriage scared her. Not the commitment or living together or even the end to her single life. She welcomed it all, but what kind of wife would she be when she still pined over another man? That was no way to begin a new life. Luke had already committed to one woman and she'd let him down. Elle refused to do the same thing to him.

His face was incredulous. "But I don't understand how things changed overnight. Just yesterday we were talking about the invitations." He took a deep breath. "You're scared, I get that. But it's just fears. It happens to everybody."

Maybe it was fear, a fear she wasn't even aware of that clouded her mind. But would those fears go away once she said 'I do'? Possibly, but she would never know until it was too late. The thought of having to tell him six months or even a year from now that she wanted out was too much to handle. He'd be humiliated. His parents would berate him and tell him they told him so. No, she couldn't subject him to that. He deserved so much better. She knew what it felt like to have someone trample all over her world simply because they didn't know what they wanted. She loved Luke too much to do that to him. So, she shook her head.

"It's not just nerves, it's more than that." She searched for the right words. He deserved some kind of explanation. It simply wasn't enough to say she'd changed her mind. As much as she sought to avoid the tried and true, it's-me-not-you speech, she knew that is exactly how it was coming across. "I've thought this through, Luke. I have and . . . and you deserve better. You do. I can't be the kind of wife you deserve, I just can't."

"What does that mean, Elle? I don't understand. Is it something I did? Is it because of my parents? Is that it? If it is, you have to let that go." He reached over, and gently guided her chin towards him so their eyes met. "I don't care what they have to say or what they think. I want to spend my life with *you*. I'm in love with *you*, that's all that matters."

Tears pooled in the corners of her eyes. God, he was making it so hard. She took a deep breath and several swallows before she could bring any more words to the surface.

"Luke, I just can't." She wiped her cheeks with the back of her hand. "I just can't. I'm not giving you everything you deserve. I want to, believe me I do, but I just can't. It wouldn't be fair to you."

She knew she hadn't shed any light on her decision. She didn't want to lie and make him believe it was him, but at the same time, the truth was ugly. The truth of it disgusted even her. She hated herself at that moment and wished she could open the door and fling herself into oncoming traffic. Anything to avoid breaking this man's heart. Although she knew she already had.

His mouth opened to protest, but nothing came out. Instead, he turned his head to his window. For the next few minutes, no one said a word. In befitting timing, rain began to fall, tapping on the windshield and providing a welcome break to the silence.

He turned back towards her. "You're sure this is what you want?"

"Yes," she said quickly before she could change her mind.

He wiped away her tears with his thumb. "Why don't we just sleep on this? Can you do that for me? Can you just take the night and really think this through?"

Her first instinct was to accept his offer. However, she knew in her heart that another twelve hours would make no difference. She needed to let this man go. There would always be a part of her that wanted to be with Marcus and until she was over it, she couldn't move on. She'd been mistaken to believe she could.

Her head shook in response. "Luke, I already know—"

As if reading her mind, he asked, "Is this about your ex?"

Another reason she loved him. He was so intuitive. He had a way of seeing that which couldn't be seen.

"You're not really over him are you?" he asked.

As the tears streamed down her cheeks, she looked away and whispered, "No."

He sighed heavily. "You know, I kind of already knew that. Well, I thought I did and I'll be honest, it was the one reason, the only reason, I hesitated in proposing to you." He ran his palm down his face and stared straight ahead. "I guess I should have listened to my gut."

There were no words to describe the emptiness she felt. It was beyond pain. It was somewhere in the realm of numbness, which was far worse than pain because it was so raw and there was absolutely nothing that could be done to alleviate it. Neither shouting nor crying nor sleep could abate it. It was like an albatross drawn tightly about the neck, a constant reminder of one's misery.

All she could think to say was, "I'm sorry, I never should have said yes . . . never should have let all this planning move forward. I'll pay you back for all of the deposits." She began to remove the ring.

He extended his hand. "No, don't."

"I can't keep it," she said. Her gesture wasn't a manufactured attempt to appear noble. She really didn't want to keep it, for it would be a constant reminder of what had been and of him. She knew she'd likely never forget him, but the ring would only anchor her to the memory.

"Don't." He leaned over, kissed her lightly on her lips and squeezed her left hand.

The weeks and months following their break up were difficult. Luke told her it was too painful for them to speak and all communication ceased. She questioned her decision on a daily basis. To say she was heartbroken would have been an understatement. However, she respected his wishes and kept her distance. It was the second time in one year she'd been forced to walk away from a man she loved.

25

Jonathan

"Well?" Bree perched at the edge of the seat in his office. It was the first time they'd seen each other face to face since the night he'd spent in the hospital with Lauryn.

"Can you close the door?"

She swung it shut with her foot. "Well?"

"Well, you know we ended up in the emergency room." He twisted the cap of his pen. "After I told her it was over, she passed out."

Bree rolled her eyes. "Are you kidding me?"

He went on to explain that the doctor said she had a panic attack and needed to stay overnight for observation.

"And let me guess, the only thing that made her feel better was having you bedside holding her hand, right? She's such an actress."

"Listen, I was there. It was for real. I guess the stress of her father's death played a part and she just couldn't handle it all." Telling the story aloud troubled his conscience. What kind of bastard did he sound like? What man breaks up with his ex on the heels of her father's death? An ex who was pregnant, no less. He no longer wanted to discuss it, but Bree insisted. She wanted more details and he felt obligated to comply. Maybe she'd feel bad, too, and have sympathy for the woman whose man she now had. A woman who'd just suffered two losses. Maybe Bree would be compassionate. But she wasn't, as was evidenced by what she said next.

"Listen, things happen. None of us has had it easy, but sometimes you just have to pick up the pieces, suck it up and keep it moving."

He looked at her as if she had two heads. Was she really that cold? That's when he decided he couldn't tell her about the baby. She wasn't ready.

The following few weeks were awkward between Lauryn and him. Her spirits lifted upon learning she was with child and she spared not a moment in telling all of her family and friends. The news did wonders for her mother, inspiring her to end her self-imposed isolation. The fact that they weren't married, which would've been quite the quandary a year ago, now seemed a non-issue. No one brought it up, surprisingly, not even Lauryn. He'd tried, on more than one occasion, to revisit the talk they'd been having when she passed out. He told her he had every intention of being a good father to their child, but he still didn't want to be in the relationship. The first few times she'd cried and begged him not to break up their family. She wanted to know what it was she'd done and promised to fix it. She asked if there was someone else, he said there wasn't.

Their last discussion about the matter took an unexpected turn.

It was her idea to meet in Central Park and take advantage of the Indian-summer weather. He hesitated at first, as Central Park had become his special place with Bree, it was where they'd had their first date and where they took their Sunday afternoon jogs. In an odd turn of events, he felt like he was cheating on Bree by being there with Lauryn.

She didn't waste much time in presenting her agenda. As they strolled along the perimeter of the Wollman Rink, he offered her some of his jumbo pretzel. She took a small piece and rubbed away the large grains of salt with her thumb before putting it in her mouth. She began to plead her case again.

"Do you really want me here with you just because of the baby? Think about it. Is that really what you want?" he asked.

She shook her head.

"Then think about what you're asking me to do." He gestured towards an empty bench positioned under a large cluster of trees, offering the perfect amount of shade.

They sat down. "It's not just about this baby. I want you, I've always wanted you."

"Lauryn."

"I know, I know you're not happy and I kinda always knew you stayed because you felt safe with me and because we've been together for so long. I know, and as much as I should be offended by that, I'm not, because I just want to be with you. Maybe that makes me weak—"

"I don't think you're weak," he said, more so out of kindness than honesty.

She turned to face him. For the first time, he recognized the early signs of her pregnancy. Her face appeared a bit fuller and he saw a slight swell to her bosom.

"Maybe I am. I don't always like what I see when I look in the mirror, but this is who I am and I don't know how to be anyone else. To answer your question, no, I don't want you to stay with me out of obligation, but if that's what it has to be for now, I'll take it. You know, all I've ever wanted was to be your wife and to have your children. And now I will be, well—at least your child's mother." She placed her hand over his. "Jonathan, I never tried to trap you, which I could have. I figured eventually you'd come around. You didn't, but God blessed us with this baby and we have to trust His will that it happened for a reason."

Her lack of self-worth was troubling. Yet, a part of him applauded her honesty, for she was laying her cards on the table, as pitiful as they may seem.

"And I know about Bree," she continued. "I've known for quite some time now. It broke my heart. Still does to be honest, but I know that no matter what it is you feel for her, she'll never be there for you the way I have. She'll never love you the way I do." She took his hand and pressed it against the tiny bulge of her belly. "This is our chance to start over. We used to be so in love. We can get there again. I know we can if you would just meet me halfway."

He was floored. How in the world did she know about Bree? Who'd told her? Elle would never betray his confidence and no one else knew. Had she seen them together, followed him even? And why was she so freaking calm? It was all too much to digest. He was ashamed. This was not who he was.

"I need some time," he eventually said.

26

Blair

Dylan extended his hand. The warmth of his palm and familiarity of his touch sent a shiver down Blair's spine. She quickly released it.

"Dylan is a professor at Drexel," Vaughn told her. "He started an exchange program for students in Kenya."

Blair remembered Dylan telling her about his plans for such a program. Seemed such a long time ago. She couldn't help but feel proud of him. Dylan, who was always so humble, shrugged as if to say, *it's no big deal.* She marveled at how handsome he looked in a dark suit. She'd never seen him in anything dressier than a pair of cords and an oxford shirt. The flecks of olive green in his tie brought out the color in his eyes. She surveyed them as they stood side by side, each handsome and striking in his own way. Vaughn was easily six inches taller and way more brawny, but Dylan, with his slim physique, stood out in a low-key, unassuming way. Behind those horn-rimmed frames, something in his eyes flickered. There was something about the gentle, unobtrusive way he moved about that had intrigued Blair when they first met. It was the same something which made her want to learn more about him, to engage him in conversation and look at the world, even for a moment, through his eyes.

"It's nice to meet you," she finally said after she'd found her voice. Then she began to study the look on his face. What was that? It wasn't sadness or even anger. Rather it was indifference. He no longer cared. She hadn't expected it to hurt the way it did. Only moments ago she'd wanted nothing more than to avoid him. Now that he was standing before her, she wanted something. She searched his face for a flicker of acknowledgment that he missed her, possibly even still loved her. But there was no such recognition. Then his vacant gaze lowered to her bulging stomach. His brow furrowed and his jaw clenched. His eyes shot from her stomach to her face, then to Vaughn's before he quickly regained his composure and said, "I guess I should be telling you congratulations. Looks like you two have a bundle on the way."

"Thank you." Vaughn offered him a firm handshake. "We're very excited. Can't wait until November to see her little face. Right, baby?" Vaughn placed his arm over Blair's shoulder and pulled her close. Dylan winced. Her voice abandoned her again.

She could tell he was doing the math in his head. "November? How nice, just in time for the holidays." He was putting the pieces of the puzzle together and thinking one of two things. Either she'd been sleeping with them both at the same time, something she'd always feared he would believe, or even worse, that the child was his.

"Yup," Vaughn said, "she's given me the best Christmas present any man can ask for. Listen, in case I don't catch up with you before this is over, let's exchange info. I have some ideas for my non-profit that may tie in well with what you're doing over at Drexel."

Business cards were exchanged. Dylan pulled out the monogrammed card holder Blair had bought him for his last birthday.

"Well, I see somebody I need to go speak with. Vaughn, we'll be in touch. And Blair—" He tilted his head to the side. "It is Blair, right?"

She held her breath and nodded.

"It was very nice to meet you," he said before vanishing into the crowd.

———

It had been nearly a month since the awards dinner when Blair received the call.

"Is there something you need to tell me?" Dylan's words bore through her. The goblet in her hand slipped from her grip and crashed to the kitchen floor. Shards of glass scattered about her feet and cranberry juice splashed everywhere.

Rosa came rushing to the kitchen. "Miss Blair, everything okay?"

Blair pressed the phone to her chest. "It . . . it just slipped. Leave it, I'll clean it up." As soon as Rosa left, she brought the phone back to her ear. "What do you want?"

"Something I should know about your *Christmas gift?*" His voice dripped with contempt.

"I don't know what you're talking about," she whispered.

"You sure? I'll give you a moment to reconsider." His tone was unnerving. Dylan had never raised his voice with her or been in the least bit harsh. Well, at least not until that last day, and even then he was more hurt than anything else. What she was hearing now was a voice she barely recognized.

"I said, I don't know what you're talking about."

"Really?"

"Yes, really."

"You've never been a good liar. I see things haven't changed."

"Dylan, what do you want? I haven't heard from you in months. You ignored all of my messages and now, out of the blue, you call me?" She knew Vaughn wouldn't be home for hours, but she couldn't help but dart her eyes all about the kitchen, fearful he'd appear in the doorway at any moment.

"And just what was I supposed to call you back to say, Blair? That I'm happy for you and your husband? Huh? Is that what you wanted from me?"

"No, just acknowledgement that you—"

"That I what?"

He was right. She'd called him to ease her own conscience, she couldn't stand the thought of him hating her, although she knew he had every right to.

"Maybe I shouldn't have called. I just felt so bad and I didn't know what else to do," she confessed.

"How about stick to the plan, Blair? How about doing what you said were going to do?"

"It wasn't that simple. You know that."

"Nothing in life is simple. If I was who you wanted to be with, you could've set the wheels in motion, but you wouldn't. And now I know why—because you're weak." His words cut through her. *Weak*? After everything she'd been through, all that she'd dealt with. There was nothing weak about her. Nothing.

"I'm not—"

"Yes you are. You're weak. For all of Vaughn's bullshit, he's created quite a comfortable life for you. You could never be woman enough to throw it all away. You need it. You say you don't. You say it's not worth what he's put you through, but it is. He knows it. You know it. I was the only one too stupid to see it—"

She snapped the phone shut. Her hands wouldn't stop trembling. Theoiiii, phone vibrated and she hurled it against the wall. Tomorrow she'd buy a new one and change her number. Fuck him! What the hell did he know about her life? He was just bitter and angry. Jealous of the fact that Vaughn had won. What a bastard he was. He'd known the deal from day one. He knew there was always the possibility she would go back to her husband and he would lose, yet he still chose to play. She refused to pity him. After all, she was the one left holding the bag. It was she, who had to lie to her husband and bear the weight of her guilt, not him. He could go on with his life, meet someone new and start over and none would be the wiser. How she envied, loved and hated him at the same time.

An hour later, after she had calmed, she retrieved her phone from the corner. It buzzed softly. There was one text message and it read, *And I know that baby is mine. What are you going to do when Vaughn finds out?*

27

Elle

"You need to talk to your cousin. Her head is all over the place. I told her a thousand times to forget about that fool and get on with her life. I keep trying to get her to move down to North Carolina, even told her she can stay with me until she gets on her feet."

Elle nodded and sipped sweet no-frills juice from a six-ounce paper cup. All about them, kids ran wild, jumping to snatch balloons from drooping streamers and popping them in each other's ears. A six-foot Barney in a nappy purple costume pranced about with a trail of six-year-olds on his heels.

"She keeps on with some nonsense about Simone missing her father. He hardly sees her as is. What good is a father if he's barely around?" Vivian, Elle's maternal aunt, was seated beside her on a metal folding chair. She sat crossing and uncrossing her panty-hosed legs, as she used a stiff, purple napkin to blot the grease off of a slice of pizza.

Elle nodded again as she folded her slice in half and chomped away, reassuring herself she'd burn it off the next day during Bikram yoga.

"Do you talk to her? Are you guys still spending a lot of time together? If not, please make an effort to. She needs you," Vivian implored. "I keep telling Michelle that she can learn a lot from you. You have your stuff together. Speaking of which, how's that gorgeous doctor of yours?"

Elle released an exasperated sigh before giving her aunt an abridged version of her recent break-up with Luke.

Vivian offered a sympathetic look, then squeezed Elle's hand. "Oh, I didn't know. Your mother never said anything."

Elle nodded as if to say, *it is what it is,* as she stared down into her paper cup and wished it were a glass of wine. It became easier day by day to live with her decision, but a part of her wondered if she'd done the right thing. It was a doubt she kept to herself. All of her friends remained tight lipped, keeping their opinions to themselves about what she'd reported —that she and Luke decided to slow down and rethink their relationship. Only Jonathan and Blair knew the truth. Blair's opinion wavered from week to week as she fretted over the advantages of a whirlwind marriage to a man as steady and too-good-to-be-true as Luke versus the disadvantages of what was possibly just a rebound romance. Jonathan's stance, however, was clear—Luke was the man for her and Marcus should remain a remnant of Elle's past. Elle sat at the center of her friends' seesaw, sliding in alternating directions from day to day. She had let go of the prospect of Luke in hopes of resolving old feelings for Marcus, but was in no way closer to doing so. All she had to show for her uncertainty was an empty Marlboro carton in her garage.

As quickly as her aunt's sorrowful face had arrived, it departed. Then she said, "Who needs a man anyway, when you have a career, a nice house to come home to and money in the bank. Men are just accessories. Take them out the drawer every so often, wear them and when you're done, put them back where they belong." Vivian mimed the placement of a piece of jewelry into a drawer. "They're not good for much else."

Something about the faraway look in her aunt's eyes told Elle she didn't believe her own words. Had her high-powered VP position really been a substitute for her three failed marriages? Did those three-thousand-square-feet she lived in, alone, keep her warm at night? There was no denying her aunt was a sight to behold; her flawless make-up, Chanel suit and six-hundred-dollar pumps begged noticing—a stark contrast to her daughter's Old Navy jeans and Skechers. But there was an authentic smile on Michelle's face as she cut her daughter's birthday cake. And no doubt it would still be there later when she drove home in her ten-year-old Civic and turned the key in her humble two-bedroom walk-up.

"First sign of nonsense from Michelle's dad and I up and left, you know. If I hadn't, I'd still be up here, working for Con Edison, living check to check. The way she is now."

"Well, she'll get it together soon enough," was all Elle could think to say.

"When?" Vivian snatched up her trench coat just in time to avoid the sticky fingers of a little boy who made a point of bouncing his ball against every chair in the room. His mother had shot him a disapproving glance, but it did little to deter him. "Look at this. Having my granddaughter's birthday party in the basement of some old run-down church. It's embarrassing. If we were in Charlotte, we could all be spread out in my backyard. Did she tell you my property sits on three acres?" She clicked through her cell phone and showed Elle picture after picture of a sprawling, meticulously landscaped yard.

"Very nice, Aunt V, I have to get down there and see it real soon."

She patted Elle's knee. "I know, dear, but you're busy with your job. Out there making those big bucks just like your aunt." She smiled warmly for the first time that day. "I always said you're just like me, my little carbon copy."

Her aunt's words rang in her ears the entire drive home. *Just like me. My carbon copy.* Was that how everyone saw her? She had to admit she'd always been in awe of her mother's older sister. After all, Aunt V had been the one to buy Elle her first designer handbag when she was nine. The same aunt who'd rented her and her friends a flat in Barcelona the summer of her senior year in high school. And it was her aunt who she'd called first to tell her of her acceptance to Georgetown early admission. Aunt V. She had it all together in so many ways, but beneath that tough exterior was a sad woman who painted on smiles with thirty-dollar lipstick and armored herself with expensive clothing to shield a fragile heart. One which had been hurt one time too many. When she wasn't at work or busy criticizing Michelle's choices, she was at home reading true-crime books and dining on expensive chef-inspired meals by herself. *Her carbon copy. Sigh.*

28

Jonathan

On Bree's thirtieth birthday, Jonathan took her to Foxwoods Casino in Connecticut. They stopped in Mystic to visit the aquarium and stroll the streets of Olde Mistick Village. He was at ease, and although the time away was temporary, it was just what the two of them needed. There'd been no mention of Lauryn since he told Bree about the ER incident. Jonathan took advantage of this fact as he mulled over the best way to tell her about the baby. Each day it grew harder, for each day he fell more in love and more afraid of losing her.

In the casino, Jonathan sat at the Texas Hold Em' table. He'd just won the last two hands and was counting his winnings when he spied a familiar face. The dealer dished out the next set of cards and Jonathan peeled up the corner of his hand to see if his luck had run out. When he looked up again, he quickly realized it had. There, standing two feet away, was Cory.

"Well, well, well. If it isn't Mr. Jonathan Moore. What a surprise running into you here." Her face wore its signature sneer.

"Cory. What's up?" he said flatly, his eyes glued to his cards.

"So, what are you doing here?" she asked. Her arms were folded and her mouth was twisted into a crooked line.

He folded his hand and rose from the table. "I *was* playing poker."

Just at that moment, Bree approached them. Cory scanned her. "Looks like that's not all you were playing."

Bree said nothing, but her glare sent a clear message to Jonathan that an explanation was in order. A small part of him wanted to see them go at it. As a man, he could never handle Cory the way he wanted to, but Bree was just the one to do it. The women sized each other up until Cory whipped out her cell phone, then tapped the keys and brought it to her ear. "Lauryn, it's me. You would never guess who I've run into up here at Foxwoods . . . Jonathan of all people. Him and his friend . . . " She turned to Bree. "Um, what did you say your name was?"

Bree's nostrils flared. Cory flicked her hand in response and resumed her conversation with Lauryn's voicemail.

"I'm going upstairs to *our* room," Bree told Jonathan. "When you're done with this nonsense, we'll talk?" It was phrased as a question, but clearly an order. Bree shot Cory one final dagger before walking away.

"Where's your friend going? It wasn't something I said, was it?"

"Cory, this isn't a game," he cautioned. "You need to mind your business."

"Oh, this is my business." She stepped forward, creating only inches between them. "My best friend is at home pregnant with your child and you're up here playing cards with some chick?"

He stepped back. "I don't know what Lauryn told you, but we're going through some things right now."

"I don't care what you're going through," she spat, her red fingernail wagging only inches from his face. "You're making her look like a fool."

He looked around and noticed several sets of eyes glancing their way. He lowered his volume. "You don't know what the hell you're talking about and you're really overstepping your boundaries."

Cory wasn't intimidated. "I'm not going to let you embarrass her like this. I've always known you were a self-serving bastard, but this takes the cake. She should have left your ass a long time ago."

He turned to walk away. She grabbed his forearm.

"Don't you walk away from me, you smug son-of-a-bitch. I'm not done with you."

"Get your hands off of me! Are you crazy?" A table of gamblers turned to stare. Even the dealer froze mid-shuffle.

She released his arm, but maintained her stance. "No, but you must be."

"This conversation is over," he said, "and if you know what's good for you, you'll get out of my face."

He stomped away. What the hell was he going to tell Bree? It wasn't time to tell her about the baby. Not yet. Damn, why was Lauryn such a coward? Why did she have her friends and family still believing they were together? Of course he looked like a heel. Not that it gave Cory the right to do what she did, for she was completely out of line. But that was Cory, she'd never had a filter and now she had a cause to fuel her fury. She'd probably been waiting years for this day, the day when she could finally sink her claws into him and tell Lauryn that she'd told her so. But this wasn't about Cory, it was about Lauryn's inability to face the truth.

Three elevators came and went, but he couldn't step foot inside. What the hell was he going to tell Bree? Two men exited the elevator, each carrying a bottle of Miller Lite. A drink. Yes, that's what he needed to help him think. He headed straight for the lobby bar.

One hour and four cocktails later, he was no closer to a resolution. Then his cell phone rang.

"Is it true?" Lauryn's voice was shrill.

"What?"

"Are you really up there in Foxwoods—with *her*." The day Lauryn admitted that she knew about Bree was the last time she ever referred to her by name.

He downed what was left in his rocks glass. "Obviously you know I am."

"I thought we had an understanding," she hissed.

"What understanding?"

"That until we worked this out, we wouldn't let people know we're not together. How can you be running around town with her? Do you know how this makes us look?"

"I never promised I wouldn't say anything. What I said was, I needed time." He gnawed on the tip of a toothpick.

"Do you know how this makes me look?"

"People break up every day Lauryn, it's not that huge a deal."

"But I'm carrying your child. Doesn't that mean anything to you?"

"Of course it does, but we already discussed this. A baby is not a reason to stay together." Two women, seated a few stools away, looked at him, then each other and shook their heads. He lowered his voice.

"How can you say that? Of course it is."

"Oh God, this is ridiculous. We keep having the same conversation over and over. I told you— I need time!"

"Time for what? To see if it works out with her? You just met her. How can she mean that much to you already? We've been together for years and here she comes out of the blue and now you need time?" He could all but see the tears streaming down her face. "What kind of woman wants to be with a man who's having a baby with someone else? What's wrong with her? Is she that desperate or is she just stupid?"

"Stop," he warned.

"Is she? What kind of stupid woman are you dealing with? What's wrong with you—"

"I'm getting off the phone."

"No, you're not! You're going to hear me out this time. I'm tired of waiting on you to come around. It's time to grow up and handle your responsibilities, I've been patient long enough. Now tell that girl it's over and let's move on with our lives!" The Lauryn he knew would never say such things or make such demands. It was that damn Cory. She'd planted the battery in Lauryn's back.

"Lauryn, I'm done. I'm getting off the phone. We'll talk when you've calmed down."

"Don't you hang up this phone on me."

"Good night."

He hesitated before sliding the keycard in the hotel door. He owed Lauryn a lot and didn't want to see her hurt or embarrassed, but when was it time to think about what he wanted. *Who* he wanted. He hadn't planned any of this, he hadn't looked for Bree. She walked smack dab into his life. How was he supposed to walk away from her? It just wasn't fair.

He quietly inched open the door. The lights were out and Bree was lying motionless in the middle of the bed. He slipped between the sheets and spooned her until he fell asleep.

Hours later, he was roused by the sound of steady rapping on the door. He stumbled towards it feeling the effects of a mild hangover. "Come back later," he called.

The knocking persisted, only louder. He squinted through the peephole, but couldn't make out the face without his contacts, so he cracked open the door ready to tell the chambermaid to come back later. But it wasn't housekeeping. His life took a turn from bad to worse.

29

Blair

For the next few weeks, Blair walked on eggshells, unsure of what to expect from Dylan. His text message was a clear threat. Only question was, now that he had direct access to Vaughn, when would he strike? The Dylan she knew wasn't spiteful or vengeful, but everything was different now.

She listened closely to Vaughn's business calls and casually asked about his non-profit venture to get a sense of whether or not they'd spoken. She had no such indication. Calling Dylan back was way too risky. It was best to just lie low. Besides, there was no way he could prove the child was his, at least not until after she was born, and Blair would never allow a paternity test.

She rid herself of all evidence of their relationship. That was the easy part. Ridding him from her thoughts was not. It was a constant struggle. She vacillated between hating him and missing him. She'd catch herself wondering about her daughter and if she would look like Dylan or have his personality. It saddened her to think he would never know his child. It was sad, but necessary. Maybe Elle had been right and she wasn't built for this. Each day the cross grew heavier to bear. Many nights she'd lie awake in bed and think of Dylan, sometimes even allowing herself to miss him. A tiny smile crept to her face as she recalled the day they first met.

Drexel University was a client of her public relations firm and she'd gone to the campus to interview one of their newest professors, one who was launching a Kenyan exchange program. Their initial meeting in his office extended to lunch at a nearby restaurant. The steakhouse would come to be their regular spot, not only for its sentimental value, but also for its seclusion. During the meeting she discovered he was the antithesis of her husband: humble and compassionate, scholarly and open minded and not in the least bit judgmental. He shared her interests in culture and history and indulged her appreciation of the arts, whereas Vaughn often mocked it or deprecatingly believed it could be satisfied with Broadway tickets. When she and Vaughn vacationed in Europe, she was forced to sightsee alone or with a group of strangers while he stayed in their suite watching TV or luxuriating on hotel amenities. He'd only leave the hotel to dine on five-star meals or shop for expensive souvenirs he didn't really appreciate or want. When Blair would return to their room hours later with accounts of her adventures or pictures from historical sites, he'd listen half-heartedly and offer distracted smiles. She was grateful to have the means to travel, but having no one to share it with diminished the experience.

Dylan, on the other hand, had seen considerably less of the world, but saw it with appreciative eyes, and the two of them would spend hours comparing notes on the world's treasures they'd both seen and make unfulfilled plans to track their footprints over the rest of the globe.

She couldn't help but smile even as she recalled their rough patches, jealous rages (hers) and heated arguments. On a night when she'd stolen a few hours to be alone with him and he had failed to return her string of calls, she found herself waiting on the steps of his townhouse, watching for his headlights to come around the bend. Her anger subsided each time a car approached, then rose again each time it drove past. When he finally did show, she laid into him for not answering his phone, for unknowingly wasting their precious hours and for arriving home near midnight when his last class had ended at four. He told her he'd left his phone in the car. When he confessed he'd been on a date, all hell broke loose. Tears and hateful slurs filled the room. She likened him to Vaughn and called an end to their relationship. That's when his calm demeanor took flight. Before she could storm out the door, he grabbed her by the arm.

"Blair, stop."

"Get off of me!" she spat. "Call back your *date*. Maybe she'll come over when I leave."

"Hey!" He gripped her by both of her arms and spun her around to face him. "You've a lot of nerve, you know that? You show up here on my doorstep unannounced and start questioning me about where I've been and with whom and then accuse me of being a liar. Blair, you are married! Have you forgotten that? 'Cause I sure haven't. You have a husband who you go home to every night."

She opened her mouth in protest, but nothing came out.

"How do you think that shit makes me feel? To know the woman I love wakes up in bed with another man every day. So, you need to put yourself in my shoes before you start pointing fingers and making accusations. I'm being honest with you, which is much more than you can say about that husband of yours."

Blair was stunned, but he was right. She was in no position to question him, but the thought of him with another woman drove her insane. Despite her situation, she expected him to be faithful. As crazy as it sounded, it's what she expected. She selfishly wanted Dylan all to herself. And eventually that's what he gave her because his efforts to move on or at least spread his eggs beyond one basket failed—Blair was all he wanted.

That argument had sparked a topic they'd danced around on several occasions—her divorce. In an effort to prove to Dylan (and herself) that he wasn't just a fling, rather someone she wished to spend her life with, she consulted an attorney for the first time in her entire marriage.

Preston James came highly recommended. His track record was remarkable; he was known for striding into courthouses and effecting results. She wanted him on her side. As she explained her situation he sat behind his leather-topped, cherry-stained desk, slowly rocking back and forth in his stately executive chair with his hands clasped behind his head. She explained she'd been married nearly ten years, had no children, and wanted out on the grounds of infidelity (his not hers). Preston's face encouraged her until she told him she'd signed a pre-nuptial agreement; she lowered her head in shame when she had to admit she knew not what it said. His question, as to how she managed to sign something of such significance without reading it, made her feel stupid and justifiably so, for she had been. Although only twenty-two at the time, she was old enough to know better, especially since Vaughn's inability to be monogamous had become apparent years before they even walked down the aisle. She should have been smarter, she should have known better, but back then her eyes were veiled with rose-colored lenses. Preston told her he couldn't offer any counsel until he'd seen the pre-nup, so she went home and searched through Vaughn's documents. It read:

Except as otherwise provided in this Agreement, each party specifically agrees that neither shall make any claim for or be entitled to receive any money or property from the other as alimony, spousal support, or maintenance in the event of separation, annulment, dissolution or any other domestic relations proceeding of any kind or nature, and each of the parties waives and relinquishes any claim for alimony, spousal support or maintenance, including, but not limited to, any claims for services rendered, work performed, and labor expended by either of the parties during any period of cohabitation prior to the marriage and during the entire length of the marriage. The waiver of spousal support shall apply to claims both pre and post-judgment.

Blair needed no legal training to understand that single paragraph was her undoing. Preston confirmed her fears by advising it was ironclad. She left his office deflated, feeling hopeless and stuck. She'd either stay and deal with his ways or leave penniless. Dylan, however, didn't understand her plight.

"So, you can't get a divorce because of a prenup? Is that what you're telling me?" His voice teetered on anger. They were eating dinner at the same steakhouse where they'd shared their first meal.

"No, of course I can get a divorce. It's just that I'd be walking away with nothing and I can't do that," she said in a hush, her eye on the couple sitting in the booth across from them.

His face was incredulous. "And that's the issue? Seriously?"

"Of course it is. I have nothing, Dylan. Nothing!"

"I can't believe you just said that." His anger was thawing into hurt. "You have me."

"That's not what I meant."

"What else could you possibly mean?"

"Dylan, I have no money, no savings, no property. It's *all* in his name. If I walk away, I'm a thirty-one-year-old woman with a bullshit PR job, no home of my own. Hell, even my car is in his name. How do I start over?"

He reached over the table and clasped both of her hands. "You start over with me, that's how. You'll stay with me. We'll get you a better job. A car, whatever you need. No, I don't have an estate or millions in the bank, but I have enough. We'll be okay together, I promise you."

She pulled her hands away and lowered her eyes to the napkin spread across her lap. "Dylan, you don't understand, I can't live off of you."

He sighed. "Why not? You're living off him."

"But he has it. It's nothing to him. I can't come into your world and expect you to do all those things for me. Especially not—" She quickly caught the words before they left her lips.

"Not on my salary? Is that what you were going to say?"

She shook her head. "No, what I meant was—"

"Forget it, Blair. Don't bother, I understand. You'd rather live miserably with him as long as the big house and black card comes with it. I see."

He'd left her sitting there that night and they stopped speaking for weeks. It became their pattern. They would fight, time would pass, and they would reconcile.

Vaughn stirred in the bed next to her, then draped his heavy arm over her stomach, gently stroking her hard belly. She forced the memories of Dylan out of her mind, then placed her hand over Vaughn's and went to sleep.

30

Jonathan

There Lauryn stood, in a pair of wrinkled khaki pants and a hooded sweatshirt, with her arms folded and her face full of rage. Her hair was slicked back into a ponytail, drawing attention to her peaked complexion and red-rimmed eyes.

"You can't be serious?" He looked back at Bree, she was still sleeping. He stepped into the hall and closed the door behind him. "What the hell are you doing here?"

"You hung up on me."

"And you drove three hours to tell me that?"

"We need to talk, and since you aren't man enough to handle this on the phone, we'll do it face to face." Cory lurked in the background, silently maneuvering Lauryn's puppet strings.

"Are you crazy? What's gotten into you?" He pointed to Cory. "It's this one here. I know she's the mastermind of this. When are you gonna stop letting her run you?"

"You're the only one trying to run her," Cory said. "Did you really think I wasn't going to tell her what I saw?"

"You didn't see shit, and what the hell is wrong with you? Don't you have a kid at home? Why are you so obsessed with me and what I'm doing?"

"Yeah, I do." She gestured towards Lauryn's stomach. "Just like you're about to. Does Sleeping Beauty in there know that? She ought to."

"Cory's right," Lauryn said. "She should know. We're all adults here and if she's going to be a part of your life, then I need to know her, so we can all—"

"So we can all what? Bree doesn't have anything to do with this." He pointed to Cory. "And neither does she. Don't do this, Lauryn. I know she put you up to it, but it's not who you are. Don't let her get all up in your head. Tomorrow, I'll come by and we'll talk, but don't do this. Seriously."

Her expression softened until she turned to Cory, whose icy glare urged her to press on.

"I gave you a chance to talk last night and you hung up on me," she spat.

"I didn't hang up on you. I told you I'd come by and we'd talk. C'mon now."

He thought he heard movement in the room, stuck his head inside and saw Bree stirring. God, he couldn't let her wake up to this scene. He had to tell her on his terms, when he was ready. Not like this. He looked back at the two sets of determined eyes and knew they wouldn't relent.

"Okay, okay, meet us downstairs in half an hour. We've gotta get dressed."

We've gotta get dressed. Lauryn flinched. *We.* She and Jonathan used to be a *we*. Now she was an unmarried pregnant woman, standing outside the door of the man she loved as he struggled to protect the woman sleeping inside. Begrudgingly, she and Cory agreed and left.

Jonathan tugged at the sheets. "Baby, wake up. We've got to go."

"What?" Bree squinted and blocked her eyes from the rays of sun piercing through the blinds. "What's the matter?"

"We need to get up and get out of here. I'll explain why later." He pulled on his jeans.

She sat up and rubbed her eyes. "Does this have to do with that woman in the casino last night?"

"Yeah, it kinda does," he said as he buttoned his shirt.

She searched in between the sheets for the television remote. "So, what's the story? She's friends with your ex, I take it." She yawned as she clicked through the stations.

He went to the bathroom to brush his teeth and grab the rest of his things. "Yeah, and she's trying to make waves. It's already complicated enough. I just don't want any more issues."

She muted the television. "What's complicated about it? You broke up. It is what it is."

"Yeah, but she hasn't told all of her friends. So Cory, the girl from last night, thought Lauryn and I were still together and that I was up here cheating."

Bree laughed. "Ha, that explains her attitude, I guess I can understand that. She's still a bitch for eyeing me up and down, but I guess I can see where she was coming from. But what does that have to do with us leaving?"

Jonathan instantly regretted the lie he was about to tell. "The thing is, Cory and lot of their friends are all staying here for some sorority convention or something. They're gonna be everywhere and I don't want us to spend your birthday weekend dodging them. You know how catty you'll women can be. Let's just get out of here. I called the MGM and they've got a nice suite available." His delivery was light-hearted and casual, but he made a point to avoid her eyes as he laced up his sneakers.

Bree didn't budge. "You have to be kidding me."

"Huh?"

"You can't believe that I'd agree to moving to another hotel just because of some women." She gave him a careful appraisal. "What aren't you telling me?"

"Nothing, I told you why." It sounded like a lie and he knew it.

"You know I couldn't care less about some random chicks looking at me. And I would think you wouldn't either. Jonathan, don't lie to me. There's more to this story, I know there is."

He stood at a crossroads. Again. It was the ideal time to tell her the whole story. She was asking, and Lauryn and Cory were downstairs waiting to expose him. If he told her now, it would all be out in the open. His conscience would be eased. Maybe he'd sleep through the night for the first time in months. He should just tell her. Just blurt it out and tell her.

"What aren't you telling me?" she repeated.

He said nothing.

"Are you two still together? Is that it?" Her eyes grew large. "Have you been lying to me this whole time?"

His mind raced. *Tell her Jonathan. Tell her now. Maybe she'll understand. The lying has to stop. It's not fair to her.* But it's her birthday. No, he can't tell her today. As soon as they get back home. Yes, then he'll tell her everything.

"No, baby, I didn't lie. It's over. I told her. Truth is, she doesn't want to accept it, but I told her." That part was the truth.

Her eyes narrowed. "*She doesn't want to accept it?* What's that supposed to mean?"

"Just means she hasn't told her friends or family yet. She thinks I'll change my mind." That too was true.

"And she knows about us?" she asked.

"Yes." It didn't matter if he wasn't the one who had told her. The truth was that Lauryn knew.

"And she still thinks you're going back?"

He shrugged his shoulders. "I guess."

"What do you mean *you guess?* Don't stand here and act like you don't know what's going on. Why does she think you're going back?"

For the second time an opportunity to confess presented itself. "I guess because we've been together so long." For the second time he lied.

"Just because you've been together so long?" Her brows lowered.

"Bree, I can't get inside of her head. Yes, it's irrational, but that's what she believes." He milled around the room collecting the rest of his things.

She snatched the shaving kit from his hand. "Stop it! What aren't you telling me?"

She deserved the truth, but he couldn't bring himself to reveal that one crucial piece of information. As much as he wanted the weight off his shoulders, with the truth came a hoard of issues he wasn't prepared to handle. So he cupped her face in his hands, kissed her on the lips and said, "Bree, I love you. You have to trust me on this. I'm gonna handle it, so that it's never an issue again. I promise you that. It's your birthday and I want it to be all about you. I'm not running from anything. I planned for this to be the perfect weekend and whatever I have to do to make that happen, I will. So let me just get you away from this nonsense and we can get back to celebrating you, because that's why we're here."

She watched his brown eyes twinkle with sincerity. She fought the urge to protest because what she saw in his face was love, and at that moment it was enough for her.

Moments later they were out front waiting for the valet to bring his pick-up around. No sooner than he'd pulled off, he had a sudden urge to turn back. He told her he'd left his watch in the room's safe and would be right back. He headed straight to the coffee shop. True to their threat, there they were. Lauryn and Cory were seated in the corner wearing their game faces, prepared for an ambush. Cory managed to look even angrier when she noticed he was alone. Lauryn, on the other hand, looked relieved.

He told Cory, without so much as looking in her direction, that he needed to speak with Lauryn alone. She, of course, protested and told him she was abreast of all the dirty details of his ménage à trois and wasn't going anywhere. To his surprise, Lauryn put her foot down and told Cory to leave. It was the first time she'd used such a firm voice with her best friend. Lauryn was fed up and tired of being dictated to. She hadn't wanted to drive up to Connecticut or show up at his room, or demand he come downstairs with Bree, but Cory had insisted. Lauryn was a mixed bag of anger, sadness and resentment.

Jonathan sat down across from her. "Listen, I'm not even going to tell you how I feel about your coming up here. I know that's not you. You've always been influenced by Cory so I know where it came from, but I'm disappointed you weren't strong enough to stand up to her, to tell her to mind her business."

She nodded. "I don't know what I was thinking. Not that it's an excuse, but I'm just an emotional mess right now."

"I know." He placed his hand over hers. "I understand, but you've gotta know that nothing I'm doing is to hurt you. I love you and always will, no matter what happens between us. Just because we aren't in a good place right now doesn't mean we should try and hurt each other."

"I know."

"I see where you're coming from, I do, but please try and see my point of view too. Right now, I just don't want to be in a relationship with you. I'll support you one hundred percent as far as the baby is concerned, but right now, I don't want anything more than to be a good father. Can you understand that?"

To his surprise, she nodded. "I thought about it and you were right. We haven't been happy for a while. I refused to see it for a long time, but I know it was true. I want to be with you, but it has to be your decision. As for the baby, we'll figure it out as we go along, I guess."

He breathed a heavy sigh of relief as several pounds of stress rolled off of his shoulders. *Ah, catastrophe averted*, he thought. *For now.*

31

Elle

Elle was tucked away in the corner, nestled in her usual spot at her favorite Starbucks. When she glanced up from her laptop, she spied a familiar face. Were her eyes deceiving her? No. It really was Marcus standing at the counter, pouring way too much brown sugar into his espresso. Her heart skipped a beat. The butterflies in her stomach still managed to flutter whenever she heard his voice or saw his face. Today was no different. She slouched down in her armchair, hoping he wouldn't look in her direction. If she got up to leave, he would definitely see her. A small part of her wished he would, so he could come over and plead his case for forgiveness—again. It had been several months since the night he'd showed up at her house intoxicated. A day later he'd left her a sheepish voicemail, followed by the delivery of a purple orchid and an apologetic, handwritten card. While she hadn't responded to either, she was disappointed that he'd actually done what she had kept asking him to do—to keep his distance. The sporadic calls she'd grown accustomed to ceased. She always knew a day would come when he'd stop altogether. It had come.

Just when she thought he was going to leave, he sat at a table near the door. Damn it. Now she was stuck until he finished his coffee. She quickly took stock of the situation. Was she being silly? Why was she avoiding him? What was the worst that could happen? It might be a bit awkward, but maybe the sight of her would restore his interest. Perhaps he'd be encouraged to make another plea. But what if he didn't? What if he really was over her and bumping into her was a non-issue. The thought of it troubled her, but the prospect of it actually happening completely unnerved her. Knowing in the back of her mind that her ex was over her was one thing, but experiencing it first hand was another. She watched him tap away on his Blackberry as she weighed her options. A voice within told her to act her age and be mature. In a city as large and small as New York, this wasn't likely to be the last time she saw him. *Act like an adult*, she told her herself. So she collected her things and prepared to walk his way.

She didn't expect what happened next. An attractive auburn-haired woman appeared and sat across from him. Elle quickly sunk back into her seat. Oh God, is he on a date? Of all the Starbucks on the west side, she had to be in the exact one he'd chosen for a Saturday afternoon date. Ugh! She could tell by the way the woman placed her hand over his when he spoke that they weren't just friends. From the looks of it, they may even have been intimate.

For the next forty-five minutes, Marcus and his lady friend remained, drinking and chatting up a storm. Elle's cup, however, was empty. Her laptop battery was all but dead and she was desperate to leave, but she couldn't. She'd wait as long as it took to avoid seeing him. Seeing *them*.

Another twenty minutes passed before the woman, who she was now convinced was sleeping with her ex, got up to place another order. More coffee? They couldn't be serious. She refused to sit through another hour of this. It was voyeuristic. Enough was enough. She had no choice but to be a woman about it. She'd acknowledge them, politely say hello, and saunter out the door. She collected her belongings, gave herself a quick once-over in her compact, and headed towards the exit. By now, Marcus's companion had returned to her seat.

Elle strode towards the door with her eyes glued to the screen of her Blackberry. When she reached their table, she feigned a double take and smiled widely. "Hey!"

Marcus, who was in fact surprised, popped up from his seat. "Elle? Hey!"

She saw genuine delight on his face. Elle glanced at his companion, searching for traces of something, anything, which would shed light on the nature of their relationship. Did she think Elle was merely an acquaintance or maybe a colleague or just a good friend? Her brown eyes registered nothing. She simply smiled and patiently awaited an introduction.

"How are you?" Marcus asked. His voice was warm.

"Good." She gestured towards her laptop. "Just getting some work done, as usual."

"It's good to see you. Really."

"You too." She extended her hand to his companion. "How are you? I'm Elle."

Ah, there it was. Upon hearing those four letters, that one syllable, his lady friend's expression changed. Her smile faded. She stood and returned a firm handshake and a terse greeting. "Evelyn. Nice to meet you."

Marcus stood between the two women, revealing no sign of awkwardness or discomfort. But Marcus never would. He was way too much of a cool-under-pressure kind of man, unless he'd just been caught in an interstate love triangle. *Stop it Elle, that's in the past,* she quickly reminded herself.

"Well, I have to be going. Nice to meet you, Evelyn. Take care Marcus."

Evelyn nodded and Marcus reached for Elle's hand, which he gently squeezed. "It's really good seeing you. Don't be a stranger."

She smiled, then left. As soon as she was back in her car, she was able to breathe again. Who was this Evelyn to him? It sure looked like a date and Evelyn clearly knew who she was. The look on her face upon hearing Elle's name was telltale. But how much did she know about her? Had Marcus told her everything? No. No, Marcus would never lay all of his cards on the table. He wouldn't admit to being the bad guy. That wasn't his way. Evelyn wasn't just a friend, that much she knew, yet how close were they? Marcus had unashamedly asked her to stay in touch and had squeezed her hand, in the same way he'd always touched her. So, what was his deal with Evelyn that he could do that in front of her? Ugh! Why did she even care? She couldn't have expected him to remain single forever, especially since she'd made it clear that they were over. But she did care. The thought of him in love, or even just in like with another woman, ate away at her. It shouldn't, but it did.

Just then her cell phone rang. "I hope you know she's no replacement for you."

"Marcus?"

"Yeah, I'm seeing her, but she doesn't hold a candle to you or what we had. I'm trying to move on with my life, like you told me I should, but no one compares to you. You know that, right?"

Her heart smiled. A wide grin reflected in her rearview mirror. Her voice, however, remained stoic. "I don't know what to say."

"You don't have to say anything. Just wanted you to know. Not that it even matters. I know you're starting a whole new life and all, but I just wanted you to know how I feel. That's all."

There was an awkward silence.

"It means a lot to me to hear you say that."

"Glad to hear it, Ellie. You take care of yourself, okay?"

Ellie. No one had called her that in a long time. Just then a Sade song came on the radio and, although it had always been one of her favorites, she'd never quite listened to the words. Today, the lyrics spoke to her. *Love is stronger than pride* took on new meaning. Love *was* stronger than pride. At least it should be. She thought back. Where had her pride gotten her? Yes, it had often protected her heart and at times massaged her ego, but when it was all said and done, it had left her alone. Sad, incomplete and alone.

Was this all a sign? Had the chance encounter and hearing the song on the radio all been by design? She sat in her car and cried. For the first time in a long time, she really just let it all out. For so long she'd been trying to remain strong, but she couldn't any longer. The barrels of frustration and sadness and anger had been pent up inside of her for way too long. It was time. Time to let it all out. So she did. For the next thirty minutes, she cried. Cried until her eyes were bone dry. Cried until her chest felt lighter. The load she'd been carrying lifted. That angry haze she'd been viewing the world through began to evaporate. It became clear to her that what she'd been grappling with the most was fear. Not just the fear of getting hurt again, but fear of playing the fool twice. She didn't want to end up like Aunt V, a woman who had everything yet no one to share it with. That's not what she saw for herself, but it's who she was becoming. No, she wouldn't allow it. Her feelings toward Marcus had not changed. He'd relentlessly professed his love and worn his heart on his sleeve. She believed he was sorry and she missed him. She knew it was time to forgive, so she did.

32

Jonathan

"Jon? Jonathan Moore. Is that you?"

Jonathan and Bree strolled hand in hand through the cobblestone streets of lower Manhattan. They'd just left the Body Exhibit at South Street Seaport when he heard someone call his name. Jonathan whipped around to find his friend Mitch, whom he hadn't seen in years. They embraced and quickly brought each other up to speed. Jonathan asked about Mitch's family and Mitch opened Pandora's box when he asked Jonathan about his.

"So, I hear you're joining the club." He offered Jonathan a firm handshake and congratulatory pat on the back.

Jonathan was puzzled. "Huh?"

"The dad club. Spoke to Jeff last week. He told me you and your lady were expecting. So funny I should run into you now." He turned to Bree. "Mazel tov. When are you guys due?"

Bree looked to Jonathan. His face blanched.

Mitch quickly appraised their reactions, then brought the heel of his palm to his forehead. "Man, what am I talking about? It wasn't you, it was . . . it was Joe he was telling me about. Yeah, Joe's got a little one on the way."

Bree's pupils grew dark.

Jonathan laughed nervously. "Yeah man, you and your memory. This dude was always mixing up his stories, even way back in the day. You need to start taking some ginkoba or something."

"Must be that old age creeping up on me." Mitch gestured towards his receding hairline. "Apparently this ain't all I'm losing." He glimpsed his watch. "Well, let me get going. Gotta meet up with some people across town. Jon, we'll catch up real soon. Was nice meeting you, Bree."

As quickly as he'd appeared, he vanished into the bustling Manhattan crowd.

"That guy is something else." Jonathan laughed uncomfortably. "So, what do you feel like for dinner? There's a really good Cuban restaurant somewhere around here." He reached for Bree's hand, it was a limp participant.

She stared at him for a moment, then broke away from his hold before walking off without direction, stopping only when she'd reached the end of the pier. There she leaned against the railing, her eyes fixated on the rough, murky waters of the East River. At that moment he knew that she knew. Mitch hadn't said much, but the little he had said, verified what she'd already suspected.

There'd been random events, which in and of themselves weren't significant, but coupled with Mitch's blunder, were all the confirmation she needed. Things like the afternoons he left work early to take Lauryn to her doctor appointments, the late night texts (one of which made him bolt from bed at two a.m. to drive her to the ER for what turned out to be just a scare), the lock he now kept on his cell phone, and the general uneasiness she felt whenever she asked if he'd heard from Lauryn. At best, Bree had believed Jonathan to be a weak man who was unable to cut off communication with his ex-girlfriend. She reasoned that a man who was sensitive to a woman's feelings, even those of an ex, was not a terrible thing. It was something she could live with, given his other redeeming qualities. At worst, she believed he was still sleeping with her. The possibility crept into her thoughts from time to time, but she managed to push it away and file it in the what-I-don't-know-won't-hurt-me drawer, because in every other way, Jonathan was a stand-up man. But then there were those times when she felt as if everyone knew something she didn't.

"So, what's the story, Jonathan?" She leaned towards the railing, her palms resting flat against the chipped iron rung.

"Story?"

"What was Mike talking about?" she asked, refusing to look in his direction.

"Mike?"

"Your friend! Whatever his name was. What was he talking about?"

"Oh, Mitch?" He made a dismissive gesture. "Don't mind him, he's always mixing people up."

Bree turned to face him. The intensity of her glare forced him to look away. His inclination was to lie, yet he couldn't find the words. But he didn't need to because Bree already had them.

"Lauryn's pregnant isn't she?"

He stared up at the overcast sky, willing the clouds to swallow him up, anything to avoid this conversation. The day had been coming and bearing down on him for months. He still wasn't ready, but he nodded.

"And it's yours?"

He was tempted to say he didn't know for sure, but it would just be a weak attempt to buy him more time. Time for what? The child was his, that he knew. So again, he nodded.

She inhaled deeply. "When is she due?"

He looked down. "About nine weeks."

"Nine weeks?" Her hand flew to her throat. "And when were you going to tell me?"

He stood with his hands crammed into his pockets studying the pebbles beneath his feet. "I . . . "

"Or did you ever plan to tell me?"

"Of course I was."

"When, then? After the baby came?"

"No."

"So when, Jonathan? Tomorrow or next week or next month? When?"

"I don't know exactly. I wanted to, but I didn't know how you'd react. This is really hard for me—"

"Are you still with her?"

"No, no. Not at all." He shook his head earnestly.

She squinted, as if seeing him for the first time. "Are you still sleeping with her?"

"No, I'm not," he said. "It was a mistake, Bree, and I'm sorry. The last thing I ever wanted to do was hurt you."

"*Last thing you wanted to do . . .*" she mocked. "Doesn't that sound familiar."

"Don't do that. Don't lump me in with those other guys you used to deal with. I'm not like them."

She jabbed her finger into his chest. "You're right. You're nothing like them because they never got anyone pregnant while we were together."

"Bree—" He reached for her arm. She smacked his hand away.

"Don't Bree me."

219

"Can we just go home and talk about this?" he pleaded. "People are staring."

"I don't give a damn about these people."

"Bree, please, lower your voice. Let's just go home and I'll tell you everything. C'mon, please."

The skies opened up. There was a solid clap of thunder. It was followed by a warm and light drizzle, which, in an instant, was replaced with heavy, angry raindrops. All about them people scattered, seeking shelter, but Bree wouldn't budge. The rain beat down, plastering her bangs to her forehead. Her t-shirt and jeans clung to her body. Still she didn't move. Rather she stood with her feet cemented to the ground, her arms folded and her eyes piercing into Jonathan's.

"Babe, let's go, it's really coming down. We can talk about this at home." He reached for her wrist. This time she allowed him to touch her and lead her back to the car. They drove home in complete silence, but as soon as he closed the door behind them, she laid into him.

She slammed her keys down on the table. "So, when's the last time you had sex with her?"

"Can we get out of these wet clothes first?" He undressed near the front door and hung his jeans and shirt over the closet door.

She peeled off her jacket and kicked off her sneakers, leaving them in a damp pile. "Answer me! When?"

He grabbed a towel from his linen closet and patted himself down. When he handed her one, she tossed it aside. "When?"

"The time she got pregnant."

"How do you know for sure?" She followed him into the bedroom.

"Because it was only that one time after she and I broke up." He sat on his bed and looked up at her, preparing for the inquisition he knew had only just begun.

"And why should I believe that?"

"Because." He inhaled sharply. "Because it was around the time her father died—"

She threw her hands in the air. "Oh God! Here we go again. You're going to sit here and use her dead father as an excuse?"

"It's not an excuse, Bree. I'm just trying to explain why she and I were even together—because of the funeral. She was upset and I was trying to comfort her and . . . and well one thing led to another."

"The night of the funeral? It happened that night?" Her eyes grew wide.

"Bree, it doesn't matter what day it was—"

"No, it does. Was it that night? Is that when you slept with her?"

He nodded.

"I remember that night." There was a faraway look in her eye. "It was raining and you told me you couldn't come over because you had to drive her aunt home, back to Southampton, the same night you didn't answer your phone when I called you. I remember worrying because it was raining so hard and your wipers were bad. Remember, just the week before I'd told you to replace them, but you didn't and I was worried . . . "

"Wipers? Bree, don't start racking your brain over the how's and when's. It doesn't matter—"

"No! It matters because there I was at home worrying about you, while you were fucking your ex." Her hand delivered a sharp, deliberate slap across his face.

His hand rushed to his mouth. He could already taste the blood seeping from the corner of his lip. He eyed the bright red droplets on his fingers then looked at Bree in astonishment. There was no remorse on her face. Rather, she stared down at him, daring him with her eyes to react. He brushed past her towards the bathroom where he pressed a washcloth to his lip.

She followed.

Although he stared at her in disbelief, part of him wasn't at all surprised. Bree's temper was vicious and he'd committed the worst crime any man could. He tried to reconcile with the pain as he rationalized her behavior. As much as he knew he probably deserved it, he needed a moment to regroup, but she wouldn't allow it. When he tried to close the bathroom door, she stopped it with her foot.

"We're not done."

He made a gesture of helplessness. "What else is there to say, Bree?"

"So, did you make her feel all better after the funeral? Did your dick take the pain away?" Her words sliced through him.

"Stop it."

"Well, did it? That's what you do now? Run around town fucking bereaved women?" She stood in the doorway blocking his exit. Her long arms stretched to either side of the frame.

He'd heard enough. He met her glare. "You asked me to be honest and I am. What would you rather hear? That she threw herself on me and all I could do was think of you the whole time? Well, that's not what happened! Ed's passing is not an excuse, but death brings people closer together, Bree, it just does. I loved that man too. It was hard for the both of us. We leaned on each other and, like I said, one thing led to another."

"You leaned on each other, all right."

"And truth be told, it doesn't really make any difference how it happened. The fact of the matter is, she's pregnant now and we have to deal with it. I understand you're hurt and I'm sorry. So, if you wanna cry or throw things, then do it. But don't stand here and try to dissect it as if it's ever gonna make sense to you."

She glowered, but softened her tone. "Well, are you even positive it's yours?"

"Yeah."

"How?" She crossed her arms. "You can't take a test until the baby is here."

"'Cause I just know."

"How could you?" she pressed.

"I just do."

"That's not good enough. How?"

"Because she's not like that." The thought had never crossed his mind. He didn't doubt for one second the child Lauryn was carrying was anyone's but his.

Her arms flailed wildly. "*She's not like that*? What the hell's that supposed to mean?"

"It means she doesn't sleep around."

"Yeah, she's a fucking saint, right? A saint who sleeps with other women's men."

He laughed.

"Oh, you find this funny?"

He shook his head.

"Oh, I see what you're getting at. Because I was seeing you when you were still with her? Is that it? Well, that's different," she said.

"Is it really, though?"

She pointed an accusatory finger at him. "You have a lot of nerve. Don't make me out to be the bad guy. You're the one who betrayed the both of us."

"I made a mistake—"

"*A mistake*? This is more than a mistake. Things will never be the same. Don't you see that?" Her voice vacillated between wounded and irate. "Who else knows about this situation?"

Situation? Yes, she had every right to be upset, but did she have to refer to his unborn child as a situation? He admitted his mother and sister knew, and after more prodding, that a few of his friends did as well. When she asked about Elle, he considered lying, but didn't. "Is that why she's been acting funny around me lately?" she asked, her voice now settled on hurt.

He hesitated. "Probably. She kept telling me to tell you before—"

"Before I found out like this?"

He nodded.

"Everybody must think I'm a damn fool. I must be the laughing stock of New York. How do you know people at work don't know? Your friend, Mike or Matt or whatever, he knew and you haven't seen him in forever. I must look like such an asshole!" The tears she'd been struggling to hold back streamed down her cheeks. "How could you do this to me?"

It was the first time he'd ever seen her cry. Anger he'd seen, but never tears. It was different than watching Lauryn, who sobbed at the drop of a dime; Bree had never shown any weakness and here it was on display and it was all because of him.

33

Elle

Elle hesitated to admit to her friends and her family—the same friends and family to whom she'd vehemently declared she would never take him back—that she had done exactly that. Her parents took it well. Her father even admitted he was happy to hear it and always thought Marcus was a fine young man. (Of course he did not know the whole story. Details of messy breakups were not typical father-daughter subject matter.) Her mother, the least judgmental person she knew, subscribed to the as-long-as-you're-happy-I'm-happy, school of thought. Blair also jumped on the as long as you're happy . . . bandwagon. Jonathan begrudgingly did so as well, but Elle knew that if he wasn't so enthralled in his own drama, he'd have put up a stronger case for her to leave Marcus alone.

Elle found peace in her decision. She and Marcus never discussed the reason her engagement ended. If Marcus had even an inkling of the truth, he never let on. While she'd come to terms with choosing him over Luke, there were times she second-guessed herself, especially on the days when Marcus's behavior called his commitment into question.

"What are you doing on Saturday?" Marcus asked as he reclined on Elle's brand new chaise lounge. She cringed as she noticed his loafered feet creeping close to the edge of its pristine, blush fabric. She mumbled a distracted, 'Nothing' as she considered scolding him for putting his feet up on her new chair. But she didn't want to sully their reunion with chastisement, so she bit her lip and watched his feet closely. He flipped through several TV stations before settling on ESPN.

"There are a couple of properties I want to look at," he said. "I'd like your opinion."

Ironically, Vaughn Hill was one of the three ESPN panelists recapping highlights from last weekend's football games. Although Elle had resolved to accept Vaughn and Blair's reconciliation, she couldn't help but feel annoyance at the sound of his voice.

"My opinion?" she asked.

"Yeah, with rates so low, I figure now is as good a time as ever to buy. My agent has four or five houses she wants me to see."

She looked up from her laptop. "You're looking for a house? Since when?"

"That's a flag!" he yelled at the television.

"Marcus?" she repeated, tension rising in her voice.

"Huh, hold a sec. Let me see this replay."

She grabbed the remote and clicked it off.

His hands flew up. "What the hell?"

She snapped her laptop shut. "I'm trying to have a conversation with you."

He sat erect. "I was just watching one little replay. What's your problem?"

"So, you're buying a house? By yourself?" she asked.

"Yeah, that's the plan." He reached for the remote.

She held it behind her back. "You never even discussed it with me."

"I *just* told you."

"Exactly, you *told* me."

He shook his head. "What are you getting at? What? Was I supposed to get your permission to buy myself a house? I'm lost here."

"We just got back together. How is it that you're ready to make such a huge decision without factoring me into it?"

"I asked you to come with me, didn't I?"

"For my opinion, you said, just for my opinion."

"Yeah, I figure since you'll be spending time there, I'd like your input." He smiled, proud of his reply.

"Spending time?" Her voice began to whine. She quickly tempered her tone. "Marcus, we aren't some couple in our twenties who are just dating. I'd think at this stage we should be making decisions about our future together."

"And what does *our* future have to do with *my* house?"

"That's just it, *your* house. At this stage shouldn't we be thinking along the lines of *our* house?" This wasn't the way their future was supposed to be discussed. Her telling him how he should feel and his itching to watch a football game.

"So . . . what? You want to move in?"

She dropped the remote in his lap. "Here, go back to your game."

"What, Elle, what's the problem?" He made a gesture of helplessness. "What did I say?"

She was about to tell him to forget it, but decided against it. She had to speak her piece. If she didn't, he'd run on the do-you-expect-me-to-read-your-mind platform, to which men always defaulted.

"No, I don't want to move into your house. What I'm saying is, shouldn't we be looking to make moves as a couple? Isn't the plan to get married and build together?"

"Married?"

"Yeah, married."

"You want to get married?" He removed his glasses and rubbed the bridge of his nose.

"You don't?" she asked, fearful of his response.

He stood up, went to the kitchen and uncorked a bottle of wine. He carefully selected a glass from the cabinet, held it up by its stem and examined it before filling it a quarter of the way with Cabernet. He swirled it clockwise, then raised it to his nose for a sniff. "Um yeah, eventually. Doesn't everybody?"

She followed him. "I'm not concerned about everybody. What I want to know is if *Marcus* wants to get married."

He offered her a glass before taking a sip. "Yeah, I do. Just not sure I want to do it right now."

"I don't mean right now as in tomorrow, but within the next year or two," she said, indulging the concept as she spoke. She had no set date in time. She hadn't even given it a lot of thought, but upon realizing he had given it even less thought, it became an urgent matter in her mind.

"Um, Elle, you know I love you. But I'm not sure I see the point in getting married so soon. I mean, we just got back together."

Just got back together? Wasn't this what he'd pled and begged for, for months on end? What happened to all of the flowery emails and apologetic voicemail messages, to his professions of love and commitment, and to his tales of not being able to sleep or think straight without her in his life? And now he was presenting her with *we just got back together* as if she were some new employee on probation, waiting for her benefits to kick in.

"Yeah, we just got back together, but after three and a half years. I mean, you know who I am already. Nothing is going to change three or four years from now. So either I'm the one or I'm not."

He studied her for a moment. "Can I give this some thought?"

Was he serious? She couldn't believe her ears. She hated herself for even having to say the words, for having to bring it up. Was she that woman, the one who either hinted her man to death for a proposal or, even worse, the one who stomped her feet and demanded a ring while mentally drafting an ultimatum. A woman like Lauryn, who set aside her pride and self respect for the promise of a lace veil, tiered cake, and the first dance. No, that wasn't who she was. She wouldn't allow it. She wouldn't try and coerce a man—a man who'd already proven himself weak—to walk down the aisle. No.

"You want to give it some thought? What exactly is it you want to give some thought, Marcus?" She anchored her elbows on the island and rested her chin in her palm. "Do you need to figure out if you want to get married at all? Or if you want to marry me?"

He took a deliberate sip of his wine. "That's not it."

"So tell me what it is."

His head swayed from side to side. "I just need a little time to make sure it's what I want."

"It?"

"Meaning marriage," he said.

Her eyes narrowed. "But you know you want to be with me. Just not sure you want to *marry* me. Is that what you're saying?"

He nodded, then poured more wine into his glass. "Something like that."

A long silence elapsed before Elle released a scornful laugh.

"What's so funny?"

She stood up straight, a smirk curled onto her face. "I'll tell you what's funny. What's funny and ironic and sad is that after all this time, you still aren't sure. After the good years we had together, after the time we spent apart, after you broke my heart and begged for months on end for me to forgive you—you still aren't sure. That's what's funny." Her gaze rose to the ceiling and back. "And you know what's even funnier, Marcus? That a man who only knew me for a few months, a man who comes from a *completely* different world than me, was willing to set aside his own parents to be with me. To *marry me*. But you. You still aren't sure."

He placed the glass down. "Don't you compare me to him."

"Oh, you don't have to worry about that, because there's no comparison."

"What's that supposed to mean?"

"I think I'll have a glass after all."

She reached for the wine bottle. He snatched it away before slamming it down on the counter.

She shot him a look. "These countertops were very expensive."

"To hell with the counter. What are you trying to say?"

"It's okay now. I understand. *Now*, I get it." She left him in the kitchen and headed upstairs.

"Hey! I'm talking to you!" He was on her heels. "Would you stop acting like a child and answer me?"

She stopped in the doorway of her bedroom and faced him. "Ya know, it's funny, you never even asked me why Luke and I broke up. Thought it was strange, but now I know why—because you didn't care. Just like you never cared about anything that wasn't about you."

"What? Why should I care about that guy?"

"Not about him. About me. About why I let him go. About why I took you back. You never even cared because you always assumed this is where I'd end up. Here, with you. Never even thought there was a possibility I could meet someone else."

He rolled his eyes.

"Well, you want to know what happened? I told him I couldn't marry him because I was still in love with someone else. Broke his heart, but he understood and told me he wished me well and that he'd always love me."

"C'mon now." He waved his hand. "I don't want to hear about that."

She went on. "And he did love me, because after knowing me only a few months he knew he could spend the rest of his life with me. A few months, Marcus!" Her voice grew hoarse. "And I let him go so that I could be here with you. You, who needs to give it some thought."

"I didn't say I didn't want to marry you—"

"No, but you said exactly what I needed to hear." She appraised him with new eyes. "I think you should leave."

"So what are you saying, it's over?" He sighed. "Again?"

"Just go. I'll make sure and get all of your stuff to you before the week is out."

"Just like that? So what, now you're going to go running back to that guy just because he told you he wanted to marry you?"

"I'm not running back to anyone. It's over, Marcus. Let's not fuss and fight. Just let it go. I'm done. We're done." She patted him on his chest. "Good luck on your house hunt."

"Elle, you can't be serious."

She stared into his eyes and it all became clear. "Oh, but I am. Very. You should leave now."

34

Jonathan

Everyday Jonathan expected to turn the key in his door and find Bree gone. But she didn't leave. Rather, she did the exact opposite; she moved most of her belongings into his apartment and spent all of her free time with him. They slept in the same bed, ate their meals together and resumed a level of normalcy. There was no mention of Lauryn or the baby. Jonathan wasn't naïve enough to believe he'd been forgiven, but was too afraid to ask. Instead he pretended not to notice the chill in the air, which was most evident during sex. It had become purely physical between them, void of all emotion. He wished she would rant and rave or lash out, anything so he knew where he stood, but she gave him no such satisfaction. She was there, but she wasn't there.

On the evening Lauryn called, the uneasiness of it all came to a head. He and Bree were seated on opposite ends of his couch watching television when his cell phone vibrated on the coffee table. Before he could snatch it up, Lauryn's name blinked brightly in neon green. Up until that point, he'd been lucky enough to limit most of his conversations with her to text, and when he did speak to her over the phone, he'd always been alone. Bree could easily ignore the buzzing of the call, but could not ignore Jonathan's marked angst. Her eyes remained fixated on the TV as he answered on the fourth ring. He watched Bree from the corner of his eye as he used as few words as possible to tell Lauryn he'd pick her up in the morning and take her to her doctor's appointment. After he hung up, he sidled closer to Bree and rested his hand on her thigh. She inhaled sharply then sprang up from her seat and left the room.

"Bree," he called.

It was no surprise to him that she didn't respond. Part of him knew he should go after her, to try and soothe her, yet another part of him was not up for the emotional ride. Besides, what else was there for him to say but that he was sorry. Maybe he should just give her some space, some time alone with her thoughts. But if he remained on the couch and continued to watch CSI, while she cried in the next room, he would be the bad guy—again.

He rapped lightly on his bedroom door. "Bree?"

Slowly, he entered the room and found her lying face down, diagonally across the bed.

He sat beside her. The sheets were damp, her face was pink and her eyes were puffy. "What's wrong?"

"What do you think?" Her voice cracked. "I can't do this anymore."

"Do what?"

"This. All of this. She's what matters in your life now and I'm not going to take second place. I won't."

"Look at me." He gently lifted her chin from the pillow.

"She's not what matters. You are. You and my child are the two most important things to me now. And there's enough room in my life and heart for the both of you."

Was there? It was the appropriate thing to say, but he didn't know for sure it was true.

Her face took on a crazed look. "I hate it when she calls you. I hate that she needs you and that you have to be there for her and I hate the way this makes me feel. I'm just so mad. I try not to be, I do, but I can't help it. It's all I can think about and it's eating me up inside."

He told her she had every right to be angry and apologized for what felt like the thousandth time. When he asked her what, if anything, he could do to make her feel better she told him, nothing. Nothing short of turning back the hands of time. A small internal voice urged him to let her go, that she'd never be able to get over it. That he should set her free, because he couldn't make her happy, not anymore. But he pushed the voice aside. He couldn't lose her.

The next day they showered and dressed in silence. Before he left, he leaned over the breakfast bar, kissed her goodbye and told her he'd see her at work. He pretended not to notice the violent way she scraped the burnt coating from her bagel. She knew why they weren't commuting together that morning and it took everything in her to offer up a weak smile as she watched Matt Lauer deliver the morning news.

As Jonathan got into his car, something told him to look up. There stood Bree in his window frame, with a coffee cup in hand and sadness in her eyes, as she watched him drive off to his child's mother.

In the thirty minutes it took to reach Lauryn's house, he somehow managed to switch his mental gears and compartmentalize the memory of Bree's sad face. It was

Jonathan, the father to be—not Jonathan the unfaithful heel Bree had woken up to—who greeted Lauryn at her door.

Lauryn opened her front door with a wide smile, one which she quickly tempered. Pregnancy was agreeing with her. She looked normal all except for her bulging belly. Her skin was rosy. She had none of the quintessential pregnancy side effects, no swollen ankles, widened nose, or adult acne. From behind one wouldn't even know she was with child. How she managed to look so good considering how sad she was, was a mystery. All about him were unhappy women.

———————

Since their talk at Foxwoods, Lauryn had stayed true to her word that she'd let Jonathan sort out his feelings for himself. She no longer questioned him or pressured him to make a decision. It was clear that she still wanted to be with him, but she accepted that it had to be a decision he came to on his own for she knew that pressuring him would only push him further away. She also needed to maintain a strong front for her family and friends who were inclined to pity her, regarding her as a single, rejected baby's mother. So she stopped short of saying negative things about him out of fear they'd later hold it against him when they were back together. Most of them remained neutral or at least had kept their feelings to themselves—all except Cory and Lauryn's brother, Brandon. Cory was Jonathan's worst critic and gave Lauryn her opinion every chance she had. But it was Brandon's confrontation with Jonathan which left a weighty impact. Part of the reason Jonathan barely stepped inside Lauryn's house now was due to a confrontation between them from weeks prior.

Brandon had goaded Jonathan on by implying he didn't spend enough time with his sister. To which Jonathan responded by saying he'd been busy with work, but saw Lauryn as often as he could. Brandon scoffed, insisting that it wasn't work which kept him away; rather, it was Bree. Lauryn looked away to avoid the glare Jonathan shot her way for having told Brandon the whole story. If Brandon knew, it meant Roslyn and the rest of the family knew. They were probably sitting around the coffee table exchanging disapproving nods and congratulating themselves for having seen it all along. Roslyn, with her pinched face, would sit cross-legged at the helm, reminding them all how she'd told Lauryn so, that the man did not come from good stock. And how she'd predicted it was only a matter of time before he pulled such a stunt. Then in private, she'd admonish Lauryn for being too stupid to see what they'd all seen—that he was not good enough.

Lauryn could see where the exchange was heading and as much as she didn't want to see Jonathan leave, she remained silent and allowed her brother to lay into him. Brandon would say the things she wanted to, but never had the nerve to. So, rather than intervene, she stood back, munched on her imaginary popcorn and watched the scene unfold.

"What's going on between Lauryn and I is not your business." Jonathan had said. "I don't have to explain anything to you. If she wants to fill you in after I leave, that's on her, but I'm not gonna stand here and be chastised like a child."

Jonathan's authoritative tone did little to intimidate Brandon. "As long as it concerns my sister and my niece or nephew, it will always be my business," Brandon spat. "And if I have to be here and watch her cry her eyes out every night because you want to be out there running the streets, then it is my business. She might fall for all of your fast talking bullshit 'cause she loves you, but I see you for what you are. "

They locked horns. The three stood in a triangle. Lauryn's eyes darted back and forth between the two of them. The tension brimmed until Jonathan eventually threw his hands up and said, "What do you want from me?"

A question Brandon easily answered. "You know what I want? I want you to either do right by my sister and be a father to this baby or stay the hell out of her life. All this back and forth has got to stop. You keep giving her the impression there's still a chance, getting her hopes all up, and then when it gets to be too much, you run back to that girl and hide behind the fact that there's someone else." Brandon sliced the air with his words. "Oh, I see the game you're playing. You're still trying to figure out if your girl on the side is the one. If she's not, you'll always have my sister here as a back-up, knowing she'll take you back on a whim. And she can't even move on 'cause she's pregnant. You have her stuck between a rock and a hard place and you know it."

As much as Jonathan wanted to dismiss Brandon's words as the rant of a protective little brother, he couldn't. Was he in fact using Lauryn as a back-up? Yes, Lauryn would probably take him back in a heartbeat and she'd never make him pay for all he'd put her through. She was, in fact, a safe bet. And as much as he loved Bree, she was an enigma. She loved him, but he sometimes questioned her loyalty. Had he in fact been hedging his bets by keeping the news of the baby from Bree while telling Lauryn he still needed time? The answer frightened him. It wasn't the kind of man he wanted to be. He was better than that. Or was he?

35

Elle

This time around, Marcus respected Elle's wishes. He didn't call or write. No letters on her doorstep or flowers at her desk. She heard no more from him after she'd delivered all of his belongings, along with a terse note telling him he could toss whatever she'd left behind at his house.

She wasn't sad or angry for he'd been honest. He wasn't ready, or at the very least wasn't ready to marry her. It was a tough pill to swallow, but it needed to happen that way. If it hadn't, she never would have gotten over him. She would have continued to pine for what had been and could be, when in fact they'd reached their peak well over a year ago, even way before the confrontation in Maryland. That incident was just a symptom of what had been wrong in their relationship. It had been a union based on image and expectations. Marcus was the man she was *supposed* to be with. The man her parents adored, her single friends envied and the world thought was her perfect other half. He'd fit the bill in all categories, all except the one that mattered. He just wasn't right for her. It was a reality she'd grown to accept. Her greatest regret had nothing to do with Marcus, but rather with Luke. That Luke had been a casualty of it all. Albeit short-lived, what they had was genuine and she now saw that they could have been happy with each other, despite even his parent's objections. If only her emotions hadn't been clouded by unfinished business.

The weeks following their break-up grew into months, proving the adage that 'time heals all wounds'. As the seasons changed, she turned her focus back to work and eventually reconciled to being alone—again.

On a random Wednesday night, as she was ending a phone call with Michelle, she learned news which changed everything.

"Oh wait," Michelle said, "before I let you go, can you ask around at work, see if anyone can recommend a good pediatrician for Simone?"

"Sure, I'll see tomorrow," Elle answered mindlessly as she stirred a pot of spaghetti sauce.

"Cool, thanks. Her doctor's relocating so I need a new one."

Just then it struck her. "Wait! Luke is leaving his practice?" She dropped the spoon, splashing boiling sauce everywhere. "Ow! Shit. Hold on!"

As she suspended her right wrist under a stream of cold water, she pressed the phone to her ear with her other hand.

"Oh damn," Michelle said. "I completely forgot about that. Oh yeah, you and Dr. Cartright. I got a card from his office saying his practice was closing and he was relocating. Doesn't say where to."

"I have to go."

As soon as she hung up, she clumsily scrolled through her cell for Luke's number. It was listed immediately before

Marcus's, another number she hadn't dialed in months. After tapping send, she felt an instant wave of indecision, so she hung up. What would she say after all of this time? She sat at her kitchen table and played out several scenarios in her mind. She could just call to say she'd heard he was relocating and was just checking up on him. That was safe enough. Or she could pretend she had no clue about his move and it was just by chance she'd called. Either could work, but then what? So he moved. Great, *then* what would she say?

It's not that she hadn't wanted to call. There were times she picked up the phone, gone so far as to dial his number, but would always hang up before she had the guts to press send. Her fears restrained her, but not a day went by when she wasn't riddled with what-ifs. Had Michelle's phone call been a sign? Elle had never placed much stock in serendipity, but there was something mystical about it all. Her need to speak with him was suddenly overwhelming. She couldn't let him leave without telling him how she felt. So, this time she dialed with confidence. Her heart flip-flopped with each ring. Twice. Three times. She could hear it beat through her chest.

"Hi there!" His familiar chipper voice sounded through the airwaves.

She gulped. "Luke. Hi, it's me—"

Her rehearsed intro was interrupted. " . . . I can't get to the phone right now but if you'll kindly leave me a message, I'll get right back to you. Have a great day!"

Oh Elle, you fool, she thought. Unprepared to leave a message, she hung up.

A few sips of red wine later, she redialed. The liquid courage helped.

Hi Luke, it's me, Elle. Been a while since we last spoke. Just wanted to let you know I was thinking about you and would love to hear your voice, so give me a ring when you get a chance.

She quickly rattled off her phone number for good measure.

Now came the part she loathed. Waiting for the return call. Although he'd handled their break-up well, extremely well, she still didn't know what to expect. He'd most likely call back if for no other reason than it was the proper thing to do. Luke was all about good manners and etiquette; Olivia had taught him well. But when he called, what would he say? The question kept her up most of the night.

Promptly at noon the following day, her cell phone rang. She was on a conference call, one which she'd grown uninterested in seconds after it began, so she welcomed any distraction. When she saw those four letters light up on her screen, her heart pitter-pattered.

Her hand hovered over the phone, she was itching to press her ear to it and hear his voice, but she still had no idea what she was going to say. Today, without a wine-induced moxie, she felt a fool. It stopped ringing. She waited with bated breath for that little envelope to appear in the top right corner of her phone. This was actually better. She could gauge his feelings from his message. She'd be better prepared. But thirty minutes later, there still was no message. Now both irritated and nervous, she excused herself from the conference call, closed her office door and paced the small room, checking her voicemail every few minutes.

Nothing. Had she missed her one opportunity to speak to him? Should she employ the old did-I-just-miss-your-call line? But if he'd wanted her to call him back, he would have left a message.

Damn, Damn, Damn! How did she end up back there, all caught up with the voices in her head. Yesterday at that time she'd been just fine—lonely, but fine. Her office phone rang. She sprang up. Was he calling her at work? Yes, that made sense. If she didn't answer her cell, he'd call her desk. That's what he used to do. She exhaled and was filled with an odd mixture of relief and anxiety. She cradled the receiver and answered in an upbeat and professional-yet-inviting voice. But it wasn't him, it was just her assistant calling to ask if she could leave early.

Why had she called him? Why hadn't she just left well enough alone? Why had her stupid cousin even called her in the first place? How was it that Michelle didn't remember Elle had been engaged to the man? What a freaking airhead!

She had to get out of the office. She needed fresh air, maybe even a wet lunch to calm her nerves. Just as she'd logged off her computer and grabbed her Cole Haan bag, she heard her phone vibrate from within. She thrust her hand inside and quickly drew it back out, howling in pain, from the burn she'd all but forgotten about. She fished the phone out with her left hand, just as it pulsed one final time.

"Hey!" she exclaimed in a high-pitched, unrehearsed voice.

"Elle?"

"Yeah, it's me. Hi!"

"Hey, I tried you about ten minutes ago, but it went straight to your voicemail." It had been more like an hour ago, forty-eight minutes to be exact, she thought.

"I was in a meeting." She eased back into her chair. "How are you?"

"Good. And yourself?" His voice was warm.

"I'm okay. I heard you closed your practice." Her plan to play it cool went out of the window. She was already grabbing at straws.

"Yup."

"Why?"

"I'm moving out of New York."

Her heart sank. "Why?"

"It's just time."

"Where are you going?"

"Back to Georgia. Joining a practice in Buckhead."

Georgia—right in his parent's backyard. Right where they always wanted him. What else had he compromised on to please his parents? Was there a sweet southern white girl from the right side of the tracks in Buckhead too? A girl whose father played golf with Nathaniel, who belonged to the same sorority as Ashton and whose mother was on the board of a local charity with Olivia? Was that girl there in Buckhead, too?

"Back home, huh?"

"Yeah, Ryan is leaving for college soon. He was the main reason I stayed up here, so I could be close to him. He'll be at Chapel Hill in the fall, so he won't be too far away."

She muttered a congratulations.

"Yeah, I'm proud of him. So, how's everything with you?"

His tone was obligatorily polite. Did he even really care how she was? Her pride told her no, so she replied with a flat, "Everything is good."

There was a long pause.

"So, when are you leaving?" She had to get the question out of the way, as it was weighing heavily on her mind.

"Next week. Packing as we speak."

Sadness flooded over her. "Need some help?"

"No thanks, I'm pretty much done." He hesitated. "Besides . . ."

"Besides what?"

"Nothing. Forget it."

"No, what were you going to say?"

"Nothing, really. Listen, I have another call. It was great hearing from you. I'll give you a ring once I've settled in, okay? Take care, Elle."

Before she could protest, he was gone.

Ten minutes later she found herself in her car, battling eastbound traffic on the Long Island Expressway. Not sure what had come over her, all she knew was that as soon as Luke hung up, something told her to go to him. To go and see him in person to say good-bye. The feeling was urgent and she was unable to talk herself out of it.

Over an hour later, as tiny snowflakes danced on her windshield, she slowly turned onto his block. His silver Camry was parked in the driveway, she pulled in behind it and uttered a quick prayer. A second later she was ringing his doorbell. After what felt like forever, he came to the door.

"Elle? What are you doing here?"

She hadn't seen his face in so long she couldn't help but stare. His chestnut-brown hair was longer and his temples were a bit grayer than she remembered. A light fuzz shadowed his face; she almost forgot how sexy he was with a beard. He looked like he'd lost a little weight, or maybe not. It was hard to tell under his bulky UNC sweatshirt.

"I know you didn't want to talk to me today, but I just needed to see you before you left," she blurted out.

He gestured for her to come inside, then offered to take her coat. As he slid it from her shoulders, she looked around to see that all of his furniture was gone; the living room was speckled with boxes.

"Sorry there's no place to sit," he said before dragging a large duct-taped box from the corner and gesturing for her to sit down.

She shook her head. "Luke, I'm just going to cut to the chase. I made a huge mistake—"

"Elle, you don't have to—"

"Please, let me finish. I never should have let you go. I was stupid. My head was clouded, I hadn't worked through all of my issues with my ex. When you asked me that day after the movies if I was open to a relationship, I should have been honest. I thought I was but . . . anyway you deserved better than what I gave you and all of this time I stayed away because I didn't know how to say what I'm saying now. I miss you and I want you back in my life." There—she'd said it. Not as eloquently as she'd rehearsed, but there it was, out in the universe. She held her breath waiting for his response.

He stepped backwards and sat on the box, gently massaging the stubble on his chin.

She stepped towards him. "Aren't you going to say something?"

He looked up at her. "I don't know what to say. This is all coming out of left field. I never expected to hear this from you, especially not now. I mean, so much time has passed."

"Have you met someone else?" Again she held her breath.

"No, that's not it. I just thought this chapter was closed. So I filed it away so I wouldn't have to think about it again."

She knelt down before him resting her hand on his knee. "I know and I'm so sorry to have put you through that. Believe me when I tell you."

"Stop apologizing. You were honest with me." He placed his hand on top of hers. "I can't be angry with you for that."

"So, you're not mad at me?"

"No, not *mad*."

"Does that mean you'd be willing to give us another chance?" She looked up at him and watched as his brows furrowed. She knew that expression.

"Elle, I don't know." He stood up. "So much time has passed and I . . . I still think you're wonderful and all, but I don't want to be in a relationship."

She rose slowly. "In any relationship or one with me?"

"I know we weren't together a long time, but I trusted my gut when it told me you were the one for me. It felt right, so I went out on a limb and proposed. And the way I saw it, if you said yes, then it was meant to be and my instincts had been right." He raked his fingers through his hair. "But if you said no, then it was God's way of telling me it wasn't right. That's why I wasn't angry. Disappointed yes, but not angry. If it wasn't meant to be, it was better we knew then, rather than later."

A knot formed in her throat. "But . . . but sometimes things are just a little bit messy, doesn't mean it's not meant to be. The timing is just off." His spiritual theory was a hard one to argue with, but she had to convince him they belonged together. "Luke, you always used to say everything happens for a reason, right?"

He offered a half-hearted nod.

"Well then, isn't it possible this is the way things are supposed to work for us? Maybe we needed a break to realize what we had and now we can pick up where we left off?"

"A break? I didn't need a break, Elle. I knew exactly what I wanted. *You* were the one who was confused." He studied her for a moment. "What if you decide a month or a year from now that you still aren't sure what you want? Would you expect me to understand that too? I'm forty-two years old, I don't have the luxury of playing games anymore. I want a wife, someone to walk through life with, not . . . "

"What?" Did she even want to know what he was about to say?

"Nothing. Let's just let it go. I care about you and I don't want this to turn into an argument when it really doesn't even matter anymore."

She winced.

"I don't mean it like that, I just don't want rehash the whole thing."

The rejection stung. How foolish she'd been thinking she could waltz back into his life and pick up where they left off. She could feel the bruise swelling on her ego, but it was way more than that. There was an inexplicable emptiness building inside of her. One which she doubted could be filled by any man besides Luke. As her mind barreled back through all of the memories they'd shared and all they'd experienced in the short time they were together it became that more apparent that Luke was the one man, the *only* man for her. How was it that she'd failed to see that before? She took one final glance about the room and imagined how different it all would have been if she hadn't ended their relationship. The now empty, barren space was a reflection of how she felt—the perfect backdrop for her emotions. She was unable to tell if the sadness in Luke's eyes was evidence of his own pain or of his embarrassment for her. She decided it was a little bit of both then muttered the most appropriate and mature words she could.

"I . . . I understand. I told myself before I came over, whatever the outcome, I'd respect your feelings. So, I guess that's what I need to do."

He shook his head. "This isn't easy for me, either."

"My coat? Would you mind grabbing my coat?" It was all she could think to say.

He offered one final 'I'm sorry' as he held out her jacket for her. She felt a rush of sadness knowing this would likely be the last time he'd offer her such a gesture.

"Don't be." She kissed him lightly on his cheek and closed the door behind her.

36

Jonathan

The call came on a bleak night in the dead of winter. Bree and Jonathan were having dinner in downtown Brooklyn. Shortly after the seared ahi tuna appetizer had arrived, but before the petite filets could make it to their table, his cell phone sounded.

Cory's voice, light with excitement for once, delivered the words he'd been both anticipating and fearing for the past several months. *Lauryn is in labor.*

Bree didn't share his excitement, but a baby's impending birth was news she felt one needed to show enthusiasm for, even when they didn't care. Even when they wished it wasn't so. So, she mustered the most enthusiastic 'Oh, wow' she could, realizing even at her best, it was plain to see, that she was crushed.

Again he pretended not to notice and said, "I guess I better get down there."

Bree's face fell flat when he summoned the waiter for the check. "I'm sorry, baby." He squeezed her hand. "We didn't get a chance to eat or anything. We can have them wrap it up." He knew her downcast face had nothing to do with uneaten steak, but he didn't feel it appropriate to apologize for anything more.

"It's okay, you go ahead. I'll take a cab home." No sooner than the words left her mouth did she want to take them back, because if he left her there to find her way home, she'd be devastated.

"No, you take the truck, I'll catch a cab." He tucked a few bills under the pepper shaker. "I'll call you as soon as I know something. Love you." He leaned over and tapped her on her lips, then he was gone. Less than an hour later, Jonathan was in the lobby of New York-Presbyterian Hospital, where he was directed to the seventh floor to change into scrubs and make his way into the delivery suite. The guilty thoughts, which had racked his brain on the entire cab ride over, quickly faded away.

Six hours later, there was no baby. Only an exhausted Lauryn who was ready to concede to the Caesarean-section they warned she may need. Her doctor implored her to try and push one last time; she did, and to the delight of everyone in the room, successfully delivered a little boy. Jonathan, full of trepidation, cut the umbilical cord and watched closely as they prepared his son to be held by Lauryn, who by this point was sobbing. So was Roslyn, who, to Jonathan's surprise and delight, took the day off from belittling him. He held his son for the first time, quickly understanding what people meant when they said having a baby changes everything. The problems, which had racked his brain for the last year all seemed so insignificant, tiny specks on the canvas which was his life. Nothing else mattered.

A couple of hours later, he was in the nursery with Elle, who'd bolted to the hospital as soon as she received the call. She and Jonathan pressed their faces to the window and stared at

Zoe McKnight

eight sleeping babies swathed in fuzzy pink and blue blankets. Lauryn, wrapped in the lavender, ankle-length cashmere robe Roslyn had bought her specifically 'for receiving guests', joined them. She looked and walked as though she were still pregnant, but had regained her ruddy complexion. The sparkle in her eyes sent a clear message to the world that she was overjoyed.

———

When Elle prepared to leave with Jonathan, who'd agreed to make a run to a local sushi bar to satisfy Lauryn's sudden craving for California rolls, Lauryn stopped her and urged her to stay behind.

As soon as Jonathan left, Lauryn revealed her purpose. "I need to talk to you,"

"Okay . . . " Elle said.

"Let's go for a walk." She looped her arm through Elle's and they walked towards the elevator. "You have to help me."

"Help you with what?"

Lauryn stopped to face her and squeezed both of Elle's hands. "You have to talk to Jonathan. He listens to you."

Elle cocked her head to the side. "Talk to him about what?"

"About his family. He needs to realize he has a family now and we need to be together."

"Lauryn . . . "

"Elle, you have to. If it comes from you—"

She'd been ambushed. The sushi run was a ruse. "Um, I can't tell him what to do. Or how to think. He has to come to that on his own."

Lauryn nodded eagerly. "But you can nudge him in the right direction. Tell him his place is with me and his son. Because it is."

"Maybe you need to tell him that. Who am I to?"

250

"You're his best friend. He respects you. Your opinion holds a lot of weight with him, you know that."

Elle bit her lip. "Lauryn, this is really awkward—"

"Do you like her?"

"Like who?"

"Bree. Do you like her? I know you've met her. Do you think she's better for him than me?" Lauryn's questions came like rapid fire.

Elle shrugged and looked down the hall in both directions, willing Jonathan to return, or anyone for that matter. "Yeah, I've met her, but I don't really know her."

"But he talks about her to you, doesn't he?"

Elle gave a half-committed nod.

"So, based on what he's told you, do you like her?"

"She seems like a nice enough girl, I guess."

"Better for him than I am?"

"No, I wouldn't say better. I think you and Bree are just different and Jonathan loves different things about you both." She instantly regretted her choice of words.

"Loves? He told you he loves her?" Lauryn's face crumbled.

"No. No, he didn't. That was a poor choice of words. I meant to say he's *attracted* to different things about each of you."

She studied Lauryn's face to determine if her recant was successful. It was.

"But how is she different than me? I mean, what do you think it is about her that he likes?"

"Lauryn, I really can't say . . . I don't know."

"You can tell. Just tell me. I can take it," she persisted.

Elle mulled over her answer. She wanted to be honest, but at the same time remain sensitive to the emotions of a woman who'd just given birth. "I don't know for sure but I think he likes that she's strong, self reliant. She doesn't need him, she's not clingy."

"So, he wants a strong independent woman, then?"

Elle made a gesture of ignorance. "I don't know what he wants per se, I just think that's what attracted him to her."

"Hmmm, interesting."

Elle had said enough. Lauryn would have to digest it and make whatever sense from it she could.

"What else about her?"

"I don't know. You need to ask him. Better yet, why do you even care what he sees in her? You should focus on your son and *your* relationship with Jonathan."

Lauryn chewed her fingernail. "I know, but I just didn't see this all coming. I have to wonder what it is about this woman that keeps him from me. I just don't get it, I've seen her and she's not that pretty."

Elle sighed. She now saw firsthand what it was Jonathan complained about for so many years.

————

Before Jonathan turned the key in his front door, he took a deep breath, preparing for the argument which awaited him. Not only had he left Bree at the restaurant, but he hadn't called her since. It wasn't intentional. It just had been a jam-packed day and he didn't have the energy to coddle her. Similar to the way it was when he used to break curfew as a kid, if he was in trouble anyway, he may as well stay out all night. He opened the door. All of the lights were out and it was quiet. *Ah. Some time to be alone,* he thought. Just what he needed. She was most likely back at her apartment brooding. He'd deal with her later. He needed sleep.

It wasn't until he awoke hours later that he realized something was awry. None of Bree's shoes were in their usual spot near the front door. Nor were any of her clothes in the closet. Her toothbrush, blow dryer and contact solution were all gone. He checked his phones and saw that there were no messages. Then he made the first of what would be several unanswered calls. He considered going to her apartment, but decided against it. He'd let her have her space. When she was ready, she would call.

He learned the truth of the matter days later when he went back to work. He found her office bare, all of her credenzas were empty and only a blank monitor sat atop the dusty desk. All traces of Bree were gone.

"Her last day was Monday." He turned to find Rita Newman, an administrative assistant, staring at him from across the aisle. "It all happened so fast. We didn't get a chance to have a cake or anything. She said she had a personal matter back home and had to leave."

"A personal matter?" He approached Rita's desk. "Did she say what?"

"No, she never said much, ya know. Kept to herself, mostly." She peered at him over the rim of her black, cat-eye frames. "Can't say I knew a lot about her, but it's strange she would just up and leave. And with only a day's notice."

"Did you see her on Monday? Was she upset?"

"Only for a few minutes. I tried to talk to her, but she went in there, closed the door and before I knew it, was all packed up and out of here." Rita peeked over the walls of her cubicle, then lowered her voice. She gestured for him to come closer. Jonathan leaned in.

"Personally, I think it had something to do with a man," she said.

"A man?"

"Yeah, I remember her saying she didn't know anybody in New York when she first moved here, then I would hear her on the phone giggling like a school girl. She seemed really happy for a little while, but I have to say for the last few months I saw a change in her. She was moody, hardly smiled anymore. The only thing that can take a woman from high to low that fast is a man." She rolled her eyes to the ceiling. "Take it from me, I know."

He left Rita and dialed Bree's number several times over. Now her voicemail was full. He sent text messages. There were no replies. An hour later he was too distracted to work so he asked his assistant to take over the afternoon practice and bolted out of the door. He sped to Bree's apartment. There was no answer, only confirmation of Rita's news from the woman next door, who told him she'd moved out two days prior. He walked back to his pick-up truck in a daze. She was gone. She really was gone. Just like that. He'd only wanted to give her time to cool off. Never imagined she'd just walk away, with not so much as a word.

The days turned into weeks and none of his messages were returned. He busied himself with work and his new full-time job of being a father. Each day he fell more in love with his son and couldn't imagine a life without him. Christopher's birth was the catalyst to change; everyone was in high spirits. Roslyn's contempt for him thawed, for he'd finally given her a grandchild. The hostility between him and Brandon and Cory even managed to simmer. Everyone now channeled their energies and emotions into Christopher. But no one was in her glory more than Lauryn. Between motherhood and the attention from Jonathan, she was elated.

Besides Elle, he'd told no one of Bree's disappearance. He missed her enormously, but grew to appreciate the time it allowed him to bond with his son. No longer was there a need to split his time and attention between her and Lauryn. And as he awed at each stage of Christopher's growth and development, his life took on new meaning. The small, trivial matters which he once fixated on became just that—small and trivial. He was seeing life through new eyes. And those eyes even began to look at Lauryn differently. Watching her with their son shed light on a side of her which he'd never seen. She was more mature and focused, much less needy and insecure. He looked forward to their time together with just the three of them; it was reminiscent of how things had been when they first dated, before the pressure of marriage and babies reared its ugly head. Every so often he'd find himself staring at her as she fed Christopher or rocked him to sleep. Was he falling in love with her all over again? No, that couldn't be it. It must just be his emotions. After all, he still loved Bree. She was the woman he wanted to be with. He and Lauryn weren't right for each other. It's what he kept telling Lauryn *and* himself. It was the truth. Or was it?

He'd soon find out.

———————

Six weeks to the day of Christopher's birth, they were nestled on Lauryn's couch. She was stretched out, her feet resting on Jonathan's lap. A black and white movie hummed in the background, providing the only illumination in the room.

"A penny for your thoughts," Lauryn said.

"Just a penny?" he asked, as he rubbed the arches of her feet, in the same way he used to.

"What's on your mind? You've been real quiet today." No sooner than the question left her mouth did she regret it, afraid she'd opened the door for him to tell her bad news. There'd been no mention of Bree in a while and she didn't know what to make of it.

"I miss you," he finally said.

Her heart leapt. She'd been waiting to hear those words for what seemed like forever. She struggled to contain her excitement. "You miss me?"

"I do."

The movie ended and credits slowly crawled down the black screen. Although partially shadowed from the scant light of the television, she recognized the look on his face. It was one she hadn't seen in years, not since way before Bree had entered the picture. "But you see me every day."

"Not like that. What I mean is, I miss *us*. Miss what we used to be," he admitted sheepishly.

She didn't think it possible for her heart to race any faster, but it did. "Really?"

"Yeah Lauryn, really. What are we doing?"

She shrugged and shook her head as if to say, *I don't know.*

"What about you? Do you miss us too?"

Did she miss him? Was he crazy? He was all she ever thought about. Being with him and having a family was all she ever wanted. It was what she prayed for each night. But should she admit this? No. No, she had to play this hand perfectly if she were to get what she wanted.

"Not like that, I don't." Her voice was flat.

"Oh, I thought . . . "

Her chest flooded with regret. It was so hard to be cold towards him, but she had to behave detached. She could not make this easy for him. He'd made her wait entirely too long. Yes, she wanted him back, but this time it would be on her terms.

"Jonathan, it's been so long and I've gotten used to us being apart."

"I'm sorry, I guess I read into some things . . . I just thought . . . " He looked away, then at the floor before hastily lacing up his sneakers and grabbing his sweatshirt.

Please don't leave, Lauryn thought. *Stay. Stay and convince me that we should be together. Please do not walk out that door. Don't go back to her. Don't!*

She muzzled her thoughts. Refusing to revert back into the spineless sap she'd always been, she stood her ground and said nothing. He would be back. He had to come back. She needed time to figure out what to do next to get him back where she wanted him.

———————

There was so much he wanted to say, but his ego wouldn't allow it. He had to get out of there. He zipped up his sweatshirt, grabbed his coat and headed for the front door. Before he unlocked it, he looked back at her. Their eyes met. His silently told hers that he was sorry for all he'd put her through and he wanted another chance. Hers replied that nothing in the world would make her happier. But their eyes couldn't speak, so their thoughts remained just that, and he closed the door behind him.

37

Elle

Amid the pile of bills crammed into Elle's mailbox were several brightly covered envelopes that she knew had to be birthday cards. She smiled as she opened cards from her parents, goddaughter, Aunt V and a couple of long-distance friends. Just when she thought she'd seen them all, a blush-colored envelope with choppy handwriting caught her attention. Her heart leapt when she saw the return address—Atlanta, Georgia. She ripped it open to find a textured ivory card which simply stated, *Wishing you the best on your special day. Love, Luke.* The card said nothing, yet it said everything. Without hesitation, she picked up the phone and called him.

He answered on the first ring. "Elle? Hey!"

His reception warmed her heart. "Just received your card. Thank you so much for remembering."

"How could I forget?"

"I knew you wouldn't. I just didn't expect a card." She studied the words. *Love, Luke.* Not sincerely or fondly or any of the other standard salutations people used to indicate literary affection.

Their conversation flowed as if they'd just spoken the day before.

After nearly an hour of catching up, she blurted it out. "I really miss you, Luke."

He was quiet for a second. "Not more than I miss you. I was really hoping you'd call."

She did a happy dance in her kitchen. "I thought you didn't want to hear from me."

"Not want to hear from you?" He laughed. "I wanted to marry you."

She started to say she was sorry, but he stopped her.

"What did I tell you about apologizing? It's just really good to hear your voice. If you're ever in or around Atlanta, I'd love to see you."

"I think that can be arranged."

That night Elle went to sleep a year older and a world happier.

38

Jonathan

As he approached his building, a familiar figure strode towards him. A flash of heat shot across his face and the hairs on the back of his neck stood.

"Jonathan."

He instantly recognized the low raspy voice. "Bree?" He squinted, although she was in full sight. Her willowy frame stood a mere six feet away. "What are you doing here?"

"Here to see you," she said. There was a silly, uncomfortable smile on her face. "Can we talk?"

He paused and her scent wafted past him. God how he used to love that smell. The memory made him angry. He kept walking. "We've got nothing to talk about."

"Baby, please, let me explain." She followed him.

"Don't call me that."

"Just hear me out please, I can explain," she said.

He stopped abruptly and turned towards her, causing her to nearly crash into him. "Explain what, Bree? It's been four months. Four months! It's too late for any explanation."

She drew back, her words caught in her throat. "I . . . I just needed some time."

"Some time? C'mon, man." He made a dismissive gesture then entered his lobby.

She was close at his heels. "I didn't know what else to do—"

"You talk, Bree. That's what adults do. They don't just up and leave."

"Can we go upstairs and talk please?" she whispered.

He slammed the elevator button in response and they stood in silence. Moments later, she was tentatively stepping inside his apartment. Her stomach caved. There was a playpen in the living room and baby bottles and formula strewn across the kitchen counter. Whose house was this? Not the one they'd created so many memories in. Rather it was the home of a stranger, a father with a whole new set of priorities. Where, if anywhere, could she fit in?

Awkwardly she removed her coat and gently placed it over the arm of his leather love-seat, a seat they had in fact once made love on. Now it was draped with a baby blue receiving blanket. He made no effort to ease her comfort. Rather he removed his coat, grabbed a beer from the refrigerator and leaned against the sink with his arms folded.

"Okay, so you wanna talk? The floor is yours," he said.

She drew her eyes away from the blanket and looked to him. "I just needed time," she repeated. "There was so much going on and I couldn't . . . I just couldn't handle it."

His deadpan expression was her cue to continue.

"It all happened so fast. We met and fell in love so quickly and then she was pregnant and then the baby. I just couldn't—"

"Couldn't what? You knew about my son. You knew he was coming. What happened that you felt the need to up and run out of here without so much as a single word, not even a damn note—nothing."

"Jonathan, I—"   ♦

"Not a fuckin' word, Bree? After everything we'd been through, I had to go to work and find your office empty? What the fuck is that?" He couldn't stop cursing. He had to get a hold of himself. Was he really still this angry, after all of this time? Why wasn't he over it yet? "I called you, I don't even know how many times. I sent messages and emails, I damn near flew to Florida to go and find you and you couldn't give me the courtesy, the respect, to tell me it was over to my face? What kind of person does that, Bree?" He shook his head with disgust. "I thought so much better of you. But you're not the woman I thought you were."

"I was wrong, I know that now. I was just so angry at the whole situation and then with myself for getting all caught up in it. When the call came that night, I saw a glimpse of our future and . . . and all I could see was night after night of you running off to her and your—" She couldn't bring herself to utter the word 'son'.

"But we talked about that. I told you point blank I never would have put her before you. I promised you." He took a swig of his Corona. "But I guess my word meant nothing."

"But that night it was different. I knew from that moment on our lives would never be the same and I couldn't bear to see it happen. So I left. I'm sorry, but I didn't know what else to do."

Despite his steely expression, she sidled towards him, calculating his reaction with each step. He still loved her, she could tell; she was hopeful their reconciliation would be a quick one. Having pined over this day and conversation for weeks, she was relieved it was finally over. Now they could move on with their lives. In an instant she was a mere foot away, staring up at him, confident he'd be drawn into her apologetic brown eyes. He had to give in, just as she had so many times in the past. Once he saw her face to face, he wouldn't be able to resist; it was the mantra she'd clung to the entire way back to New York.

His expression softened. She moved closer. His scowl waned, yet his arms remained folded and his fist remained gripped around the bottle. She slowly wrapped her arms around his waist and leaned into him.

He looked away. "Bree, stop."

She held him closer, tilted her head slightly, and kissed him on his lips—they were stiff and unresponsive.

"Baby, stop being like that. I said I'm sorry. We can get past this." She removed the bottle from his grasp and unfurled his arms. "Just hold me. Everything will be okay."

"Bree, stop it."

"I know you're upset, but come on. I've forgiven you before." She hadn't wanted to play that card so early, but he was unrelenting.

He shook his head. "You don't get it."

"Don't get what? I said I'm sorry. No, I shouldn't have left, but I'm back now. Let's just pick up where we left off. "

"We can't."

Hints of frustration leaked from her voice. "Why not?"

"Because—"

"Because what?"

"Because I'm getting married."

39

Elle

"So, what's the big news?" Blair asked as she polished off the last bite of the bourbon pecan pie the server had promised her would be absolutely divine. "I know you, and you have something to tell me."

Elle offered a sly smile. She'd wanted to wait until they'd finished their meals to share her big news. She was prepared to tell her over the phone, but when Blair invited her to the Four Seasons for lunch, she figured the timing was perfect.

"Well?" Blair said, as their server refilled their coffee cups.

"Luke and I are back together!"

"What?" Blair dropped her fork, it fell against her plate with a loud clink. "Shut up! When did this happen?"

Elle leaned in. "This past weekend. We had a long talk and we just realized we don't want to be without each other."

Blair's hands met in a series of tiny, silent claps. "Oh God, I'm so happy for you! But wait, didn't he move back to Alabama?"

"Georgia."

"Same difference," Blair said. "So, he's moving back to New York?"

Elle took a deep breath. "No, I'm moving to Atlanta."

"What!"

"Yeah," Elle said, acknowledging that telling even her parents had been easier than telling her best friend. After all, her parents were used to having distance between them due to the summers she spent abroad, her stint at that New England private school and of course her college years in Maryland. Yet over the last decade, she and Blair had never lived farther than a thirty-minute commute.

"Why do you have to move? Can't you just do the long distance thing and see what happens?"

"We could, but why? I want to be with him every day. Long weekends and hours on the phone aren't going to cut it," Elle said, realizing for the first time that she hadn't even considered a long-distance relationship. Moving just seemed like the only thing to do.

As was usually the case, Blair's face revealed her feelings. "Don't you think it's kind of a big move for a man you barely know?"

"*Barely know*? I more than barely know him. We were in a relationship. Hell, we were engaged."

"And how long were you together before you got engaged?" Blair dabbed her lips with a napkin. "A few months?"

"Yeah, and I clearly remember somebody trying to convince me to marry him after only a few months."

"That's different. You weren't thinking of moving to another state."

265

"Wait, it's okay to marry the man, but not move to be with him? You're not making any sense." The conversation was taking a turn. Elle wished she could hit the pause button or, better yet, hit rewind before it completely went off course. A sentiment Blair clearly didn't share, because she went on.

"What I'm saying is, I don't see why you would uproot your life and move someplace where you don't know anyone, just for a man. I mean what if you had moved somewhere to be with Marcus? Look what happened to that, and you knew him for years."

Elle looked away, deliberately focusing her gaze on the metal beaded curtains at the far end of the room. She refused to meet Blair's eyes. "This is not Marcus we're talking about and Luke would *never* treat me like that."

"How do you know that?" Blair cocked her head to the side with the condescension of a mother whose daughter had just told her, 'But he loves me'.

"How do we know anything? You just have to trust your heart. Nothing is guaranteed."

"So if that's the case, how come you didn't marry him when you had the chance—if you *knew* he was the one."

"Because I was confused. I needed to make sure I was over Marcus." Elle's voice began to crack. A lump formed in her throat, not only from her frustration in not being able to come up with a more concrete explanation, but because she even had to give an explanation—and to Blair of all people.

"Elle, I'm not trying to burst your bubble. I just want you to think about this. Your job is here, your friends, your family. What are you going to do down there? Be a doctor's wife? That's not you. You have a great career, a beautiful house. How are you going to give that all up for a man?"

"If anybody should understand, it should be you."

Blair's eyes narrowed. "What's that supposed to mean?"

Elle ran her finger across the prongs of her fork. "I'm just saying."

"What, Elle, what are you *just* saying?"

Hell, if Blair had no trouble giving her opinion, then she'd be equally as honest. "Let's be real here. You've made a lot of concessions to be with Vaughn, okay? I just find it odd that you can't understand how I feel."

Blair downed what was left of her water and angrily chomped on the ice. The sound of it created the only noise between them.

"Can I take this?" They both looked up to their server who leaned over the table with her hand on the checkholder. Blair snatched it, scanned it, then placed two crisp hundred-dollar bills inside the binder before telling her she didn't need any change.

Elle reached inside her purse. "How much was it?"

"Don't worry about it. I've got to go." Her eyes avoided Elle's as she flung her jacket over her arm and stomped away.

Before she could even get out of her seat, Elle was staring at the back of her friend's head. "Blair!"

40

Jonathan

"You're what?"

"I'm getting married," he repeated.

"Married? To who?" She uttered a silent prayer for it not to be the woman whom she knew it was.

But he confirmed her fears. "You know who."

"Her?" She didn't recognize her own voice.

"And I know what you're thinking. No, it wasn't going on the whole time. After my son was born and you left, we started spending time together and old feelings resurfaced. It just happened."

"Just like that? I'm gone for a couple of months and you're back in love with your ex and getting married?" Bree crumpled into the dining-room chair. "I never stood a chance, did I?"

"That's not true. You know how strongly I felt about you."

Felt? Her heart sank. He was over her. That's what he was saying. She'd always wished he'd had more of a backbone. How ironic it was that now he did—just in time to tell her it was over.

"Jonathan, please tell me you're not serious. You can't be. You can't do this to me. I don't deserve it." She slammed her palm down on the table. "I don't!"

"And I deserved it when you left? Is that what you wanna talk about? Who deserved what? This is your doing, Bree. Yours! You made your decision when you left." His anger was mounting. Anger not only for her attempt to brand him the bad guy, but for putting him in this situation—again. She'd forced his hand. If only she'd stayed, they'd be together right now. But no, she had to be a brat and run away and now he had no choice—it was too late. He could not hurt Lauryn again. He refused to. Oh, why hadn't Bree just stayed away? He'd never wanted to see that face again. It hurt entirely too much. He'd buried the chapter away and here she was extracting nails from the coffin, forcing him to wonder *what if* and if he was doing the right thing. God, how he hated her and loved her at the same time.

"But I told you why. Can't you understand that? What . . . what if the roles were reversed, huh? What if I got pregnant by my ex and ran off and left every time he called, meanwhile telling you it's all about us. How would you have handled that, huh? You say you understand how I felt, but there's no way you could. Do you have any clue how it feels to watch the man you love create a life with someone else? Any clue at all?"

"Bree, listen—"

"No," she spat. "You listen! I never would have done you like that. Never! And let's not forget how this all started. *You* cheated on me. This is your doing, Jonathan. Yours! I tried to hang in there because I loved you. And the minute I'm out of sight you go right back to her. What the hell does that say to me? And you sit up here and tell me how strongly you *felt* about me. Apparently it wasn't that fuckin' strong."

He searched for a response, but there was none. She was right, he *had* created this monster. In his anger he'd forgotten all he'd put Bree through. He *had* cheated on her and he had withheld the pregnancy from her, but all he'd thought about since the day she left was how she abandoned him and that's what he clung to. In his eyes, *he* was the victim and he'd refused to see the situation from her point of view. His instinct was to reach out and wrap his arms around her, just as he'd yearned to over the past few months, but that would only cause more strife. The love triangle was finally shattered, as it ought to be and needed to remain so. So he fought the urge and channeled his inner asshole.

"Yeah, Bree, this is all my fault. We all know that now. I'm the bad guy who ruined your life." His voice brimmed with hostility. "So, if I'm such a bastard, why are you here? I didn't call you begging for your forgiveness. You came to *my* door. I wanted you in my life and you bowed out. That decision was yours, so you need to put on your big-girl pants and own it."

Bree's eyes grew cold and dark. She stood and faced him. "Who the hell do you think you're talking to? I'm not that gutless bitch you're about to marry—"

"C'mon with all of that." He rolled his eyes. "Are we done here?"

She snatched her jacket from the chair. "Yeah, that's exactly what we are. Done!"

For good measure, he took another swig of his beer and shrugged. She shot him a hateful look before bolting for the front door.

After it slammed behind her, he was finally able to breathe. He hated himself for talking to her like that, but he had no choice. Had he been anything less than an asshole, she would have slithered her way back into his heart and the cycle would have started all over again. But now she hated him, forever scarring even the best of their memories. He grabbed his keys off the counter and rushed out, en route to Lauryn's. He needed an instant distraction from his thoughts.

———————

"You behave yourself tonight," Elle warned as she scanned through Jonathan's DVD collection.

"Don't I always? And no, you can't have that one." He snatched his *An Officer And A Gentleman* DVD from her grip.

"What do you need it for anymore? You've found the love of your life."

"That's my feel-good movie. Take your mitts off it," he said.

"I can't believe you're actually moving out of here. I remember the day you moved in, when I had to convince you that having bean bags in the living room was a bad look."

He glanced around his apartment, nostalgia was setting it. "Yeah, seems like a lifetime ago. Gonna miss this place."

"Well, you won't miss it much after y'all move into that beautiful new condo, courtesy of your soon to be mother-in-law."

"Ugh. Don't remind me about Cruella. Besides that condo has nothing on that estate you'll be living in down south."

"It's nowhere near an estate, silly. Everything down there is huge compared to city living. But how crazy is it that we're both moving? Funny the way things happen."

"Sure is. Speaking of which, you heard from Blair yet?"

She shook her head. The thought of leaving town with things the way they were troubled her, but Blair's insensitive words were etched in her mind. Every time she recalled them, a new wave of anger washed over her. She looked at her watch.

"It's getting late. Shouldn't you be heading out soon? You have a big night ahead of you, bachelor boy."

He placed a lid on the box he'd been packing.

"Shoot, you're right. The guys will be here soon, and I still need to shower."

"Go ahead. I'll finish packing up this stuff before I head out," she said.

"You sure you don't want to come tonight? It won't be all guys there."

"I know, but the women who *will* be there will be sliding down poles. I think I'll sit this one out. Besides, I promised Lauryn I'd drop by and help her with the favors."

"Okay." He headed off to the bathroom. "But don't say I didn't try and get you out of that crap."

She followed him. "Can I ask you something?"

He reached his arm behind the shower curtain and twisted the faucet. "Yeah."

"You sure you're ready for this?"

"For what? The move?" He stepped behind the curtain then tossed his shorts and t-shirt over the rod, narrowly missing Elle's head.

"No, for marriage."

He whipped his head out from behind the curtain. "What makes you ask that?"

"Just asking. I mean, it's a really big move. Just want to make sure you've thought this all through."

"Of course I have."

"And it's not what you think you're supposed to do because of Chris, right?"

The scent of Irish Spring and Pert Plus floated through the steamy air. "I know that I don't have to be married in order to be a father to my son, okay?" His tone was uncharacteristically sharp.

"I'm only asking. Look, I don't mean to overstep my boundaries, but as your friend, I just feel like I need to say something if—"

"If what? What are you getting at?"

"I'm just saying. I know you love Lauryn and since Chris was born, things have been better between you two, but it's okay if you need more time to decide if this is what you really want."

There was a long, uncomfortable silence before she heard the shower stop running.

"Hand me that towel," he said from behind the curtain. She passed a faded, gray one, which had been hanging over the door, into his outreached hand.

"Appreciate your concern, but I'm good with my decision. I love her and we're getting married. That's all there is to it."

"You've always loved her, but are you *in* love with her?"

"What's with all of the questions?" He stepped out of the shower with the towel swathed tightly around his waist.

"I don't want you to do this for the wrong reasons. Four months ago you were in love with another woman, Jon. That doesn't concern you in the least?"

"That's over." He sliced the air with his hand. "I'm marrying Lauryn on Saturday. Subject closed."

"Is it really? Just because Bree ran off on you doesn't change the way you feel about her. I was still in love with Marcus a year after we broke up. You can't turn your feelings off and on like a faucet."

He scrubbed the mirror with his forearm, creating just enough of a fog-free reflection to see his face. "This is not about you and Marcus. It's about me, and I'm over her. She walked out on me with not so much as a goodbye, Elle. I'll never get over that. She's the past. I'm over it *and* her. I just want to move on with my life."

273

"So you think by marrying Lauryn you're moving on with your life? Is that it? If you are, you're just putting a band-aid on this, because a few months from now you won't be happy. Only you'll be married and you won't be able to up and leave." She spoke to his reflection in the mirror. "Look how hard it was for you to break up with her in the first place. You think after everything you two have been through she's just going to let you walk out of her life again?"

He reached for his razor. "*You* say I won't be happy. You don't know what the fuck you're talking about."

Elle's jaw dropped. He had never talked to her that way. What was going on? First Blair, now Jonathan. Just then the doorbell rang. He stalked off, leaving her standing in the bathroom, dazed.

Familiar voices filled the foyer. Her face was flushed with the evidence of her bruised feelings. She grabbed her jacket, intent on making a seamless exit. But before she could make it to the front door, she was stopped by Chuck, who waved a bottle of Patron in her face. "Hey, Elle! You're not leaving are you? Stay and have a shot with us."

She found her voice. "Nah, I can't. I have to run."

Fearfully, her eyes met Jonathan's.

"Good night. Thanks again for your help," he said in a voice she didn't recognize.

———————

All throughout the night, Elle's words resonated in Jonathan's mind. He hadn't told her or anyone about Bree's resurface for fear of bringing it to life. Speaking about it would only awaken all of the feelings he'd spent the past few months burying. The discussion Elle broached was exactly what he sought to avoid.

The events of the evening should have been distraction enough. Despite the throng of half-naked women traipsing about and the insane amount of tequila he consumed, he couldn't shake his thoughts. What would make Elle question his feelings? Up until now she'd been fully supportive of his decision. Why would she wait until two days before the wedding to bring this up? And right on the heels of Bree's visit. Bree. It was just like her to show up unannounced and turn his world upside down. That's exactly what she'd done when they first met. Only then he'd welcomed it. Now it incensed him. Yet since he'd seen her, she was all he could think about. He missed her more than he would admit. Which is probably why he'd lost all interest in the wedding. When Lauryn asked him to help pick their wedding song, he told her it was up to her. He'd given her carte blanche to finalize the menu and had to be reminded to attend his tuxedo fitting. To some that might have served as a sign. But no, hurting Lauryn was out of the question. He refused to revisit all of the drama he'd been through. Since they'd reconciled, life had been peaceful. There was no lying or sneaking around or concealing of things. Now his life was an open book and he was comfortable.

The more he drank, the more he examined the word. *Comfortable.* No one could argue that comfortable was a good thing. But was comfortable something one strived for? Being comfortable wasn't something you would find on anyone's bucket list. He replayed all of the major events of his life and realized one thing—comfortable had never been good enough. It was never good enough to just pass his exams; he had to make the dean's list. It wasn't enough to make the team; he strived to be MVP. And even now, qualifying his team for tournaments wasn't enough; he had to take them to the finals. Why should his marriage be any different? The truth was he loved Lauryn because she was a good woman and a good mother. He felt safe with her, she would always strive to make him happy. She wouldn't betray him and would always be there. His heart didn't race when she entered a room, nor did he long to see her when they were apart. He simply loved her in a safe, calm and comfortable way. But was that good enough? All of those feelings he lacked for Lauryn he still felt for Bree, but he couldn't trust her. How could he build a life with someone who ran away when things became rough?

"J, where are you at? Your head's been in the clouds all night." Chuck stood over him, frustrated with Jonathan's lack of participation in his own bachelor party.

"Ah, my bad. I'm all right. Was just thinking is all. But I'm fine." He stopped the first cocktail waitress he saw and ordered another round. "Now let's get these drinks flowing."

A few hours later he was fumbling with his locks as the hallway spun around him. After several jabs, it finally clicked and he thrust the door open with so much force he nearly fell. Vertigo followed him inside his apartment where he struggled to kick off his boots before stumbling down the hall to the bedroom. He couldn't reach the bed fast enough; he threw himself down and moaned with relief. To undress was asking too much. He lay still, staring up at the metal blades of his ceiling fan, willing the room to stop spinning. Eventually it did, but his thoughts spun on. The liquor had derailed them and the half-naked women on his lap had distracted them, but now as he lay still amidst the quiet of the early morning hours, he was alone with his thoughts. He replayed the events of the night—pre tequila. Guilt washed over him for the way he'd spoken to Elle. He dialed her number, intent on apologizing, but she didn't answer. Before he realized it, he was dialing another familiar number. On the third ring, she *did* answer.

"Jonathan?" Bree's voice was groggy, yet expectant.

"I'm drunk," he slurred.

"Go to hell."

"Whoa, what's that all about?"

"What do you want?" she spat.

"Calm down, baby."

"Oh, now I'm your baby?"

"You've always been my baby."

"Look, I don't have time for this. You spoke to me like I was a piece of garbage last week and now you want to strike up a conversation at five in the morning? Take your drunk ass to sleep."

"I'm not that drunk."

"Not that drunk to *what*?"

"To tell you how I feel."

"Yeah, and how do you feel Jonathan?" she snapped.

"I haven't stopped thinking about you since that day."

"Really?" Her voice revealed a strange blend of anger and hope.

"Yeah, you know you really hurt me, Bree."

"I know—"

"Shh . . . lemme finish. I'm disappointed in you. I thought better of you. Of us. That wasn't cool," he said.

"I know—"

"You know I'm getting married, right?"

She sighed. "Is that what you called me to say? I already got that message loud and clear."

"I said be quiet. I didn't call to argue. I'm getting married to *her*, but I can't stop thinking about *you*. What am I supposed to do about that?" he slurred.

His ceiling fan whirled loudly in the silence.

"You listening, Bree? You hear me?"

"I hear you," she said in a hush.

"So?"

"Jon, you're drunk and I don't like you taunting me like this.

What do you expect me to say? *Don't marry her. Marry me?* Just so tomorrow morning when you're sober you can tell me how you don't even remember this conversation. I wore my heart on my sleeve, I put myself out there and you practically kicked me out of your house. I'm not setting myself up again—"

"Nobody's setting you up, woman! I'm tryna have a conversation with you. Tryna find out what it is you wanna do. Cause this is it, Bree. There's not much more time. You want this or not?"

"*Do I want this?*" She offered a dry laugh. "Why do you think I flew back to New York?"

"Where are you?" he asked. "I wanna see you."

"In the city. Staying with a friend until Saturday."

"Jump in a cab and come here. I wanna see you, I need to see you."

"Now?"

"Yes, now."

"I don't know," she said. "You've been drinking and I don't want to get over there and—"

"Bree, get in a cab and come over here. I'll be waiting for you." He hung up and nodded off. Forty minutes later there was a light knocking on his door.

Eventually the sun broke through the slats of the blinds and beamed warms rays on Jonathan's eyelids. He rubbed them and turned to see Bree's naked body wrapped in his sheets. He jumped out of bed as fast as the banging in his head would allow. In the bathroom, he sat on the edge of the tub with his head cradled in his hands trying to piece together the fragments of the previous night. What had he done? Why was it that each time he pulled himself out of the fire, he quickly found more flames to jump into?

He needed air. He scribbled a quick note, *I'm going out for a run. Will be right back*, and stuck it on the TV screen before bounding out of the front door.

He ran and ran, allowing the fresh spring air to fill his lungs. His head was pounding, but he continued to run until he found himself in a small park, miles from his home. He sat down on the first bench he saw and whipped out his phone to call the woman to whom he owed an apology.

"Hey, it's me. I'm so sorry about last night. I was totally out of line."

Elle told him it was she who should be apologizing for not minding her business. He insisted it was he who'd been wrong and that she was only being a true friend. He went on to tell her about the events of the night, at least as much as he remembered.

"You want to know what I think? I think you should call off the wedding. Tell Lauryn you need time, tell Bree you need time and go do just that. Go away alone for a week and think this all through," she said.

Just then his phone vibrated. The text read: *Good Morning baby. I'm sure you're still sleeping. Just wanted to say I'm so excited and can't wait for Saturday to become Mrs. Jonathan Moore. I love you. Talk to you later xoxo.*

The guilt. It washed over him like a tidal wave. What the hell had he done? That damn tequila. That damn Chuck with all of those freaking shots. And why the hell was Bree still in town? If she hadn't been in New York last night, it would have been a drunken dial at the worst. But no, she was here. In his bed, wrapped in the very sheets Lauryn had washed, folded and laid in only days before. She was there, waiting for him in his room, waiting for him to make good on all of the drunken promises he'd made last night, most of which he couldn't even remember. But what he did recall is the way he felt. The way she felt in his arms, the way he felt inside of her and the indescribable way he felt the moment he woke up besides her. The moment before he remembered he was marrying someone else.

He told Elle he had to hang up, then he perched on a bench with his head slumped low as he weighed his options. If he called off the wedding, even if he just told Lauryn he needed some more time, she was sure to fall to pieces. She would crumple, then Cory, Roslyn and Brandon would wield their torches and lead the witch hunt straight to his front door. As troubling as the thought was, it had nothing on the pain he felt at the thought of Christopher. He was just a baby. He didn't deserve to be caught in the middle of an ugly custody bout nor to be shuttled back and forth between his and Lauryn's homes week to week. He couldn't allow his son to become a pawn in their battle. Christopher deserved the security and stability which came from living with both of his parents, under one roof.

Then there was Bree. She'd flown back to New York with her heart on her sleeve for him. To be with him. Yes, she'd been gone, but what was four months in the grand scheme of things? Did it really matter that she'd left? She was back now and it had been *he* who betrayed her. A fact he'd glossed over, but it was the truth of the matter. There's no way he could have handled it, if Bree was ever pregnant with another man's child, so how was it that he expected her to accept it?

And last night. Last night was indisputable evidence of what it was that still existed between them. The feelings were undeniable and couldn't be set aside or trivialized as mere lust. It was so much more than that.

Another text from Lauryn and a 'Where are you?' text from Bree snapped Jonathan back into reality. He decided to return home and face the music.

Jonathan slowly turned his key in the door. No sooner than he could close it behind him, Bree was on him. She leapt into his arms, plastering kisses on his face. "How was your run baby? Are you hungry? I made you an omelet."

He sat down. "Nah, still a little hung over." The smell of the eggs turned his stomach. "I just need some coffee."

"Coffee it is." She poured a cupful into a green Starbucks mug—Lauryn's mug. More guilt. She leaned over his shoulder and grazed his chest with her fingertips, then whispered in his ear. "Baby, you were so amazing last night. I don't know if it's just because it's been so long or what, but damn . . . " Then she straddled him and began to pull his t-shirt over his head. "I have something for your hangover."

"Bree, no—"

Before he could finish his sentence, she was completely naked. His body pulled rank over his mind, and for the second time that day they were having sex.

41

Elle

They hadn't spoken since their blow-up at the Four Seasons. Despite her hurt feelings, Elle found herself on Blair's doorstep. She was greeted by Vaughn, the new and improved Vaughn, whom she barely had any interaction with in all the years she'd known him. When he greeted her with a firm hug it made her slightly uncomfortable. He told her he was on his way out and that Blair was upstairs.

As soon as Elle stepped inside the foyer, she felt eyes on her. She looked up to see Blair standing on the balcony at the top of the circular staircase.

"Hey," Elle called.

"Nothing." Blair's eyebrows raised. "I was just putting Morgan down. Did we have a lunch date? Did I forget?" She asked as she started down the ivory marble staircase.

"No, we didn't." Elle nervously shifted on her feet. "Just

thought I'd stop by to see you guys."

"Yeah?"

"Yeah." Elle was determined to behave as if everything were normal, as if it were not tearing her apart that she'd gone so long without speaking to her best friend. "Vaughn let me in. It's been a while since I've seen him."

"Yeah, you guys missed each other at the hospital when Morgan was born, right?"

They stood a few feet apart. The air between them remained thick.

Finally Blair broke the silence and said, "I was just about to make some tea. You want?"

The click-clack of Elle's heels reverberated loudly on the wooden floors as they walked to the kitchen. Elle had always thought it lacked warmth. Vaughn and Blair had owned stainless steel appliances way before they became popular and affordable. Those, combined with the stark white walls, black cabinets and white-veined marble countertops, looked like an HGTV showroom. She couldn't imagine many cozy Sunday-morning breakfasts in there. Crumbs and coffee cup rings had no place in this kitchen.

They stood on opposite sides of the island, silently feeling each other out. Blair poured filtered water into a stainless steel teapot, her every move echoed in the loud silence.

"Okay, I lied," Elle finally said. "I didn't come here just to see you. I mean, I did, but the real reason I'm here is because I'm just so upset at the way things went down between us."

"Me too," Blair admitted. "I shouldn't have stormed out like that. It was immature. I'm sorry." She approached Elle, held out her arms then embraced her firmly. "I'm so sorry."

"So what now? Are we good?" Elle asked. "I just want to know I have your support." It was important that Blair be on her side. Her nerves over the move were starting to kick into high gear and she needed her best friend's words of encouragement or at the very least, her silent blessing.

"Of course, you know I'm always behind you," Blair said before a sad expression washed across her face. "But I have to tell you, I really don't want to see you go."

"I know. It's going to be an adjustment for us, for me, for everybody, but it just feels right. I'm going with my gut on this one."

The whistle of the teapot pierced the air. "I know, but Georgia? It's Georgia right?" Blair poured boiling water into two black ceramic mugs. "It's so far away. It's not like you can just get in a car and drive back home for the weekend, you know."

"No, but Georgia will be my home. You can always visit and I'll come back and forth."

"And what about your job?" Blair asked.

"My firm has a small subsidiary in Atlanta. They're letting me transfer." Elle dangled her tea bag in the cup and watched the water turn a pale shade of green. "I'll be making less, but the cost of living is lower so it will all balance itself out."

"And the fact that you'll be living with a doctor doesn't hurt." Blair smirked as she blew at the swirl of steam rising from her cup.

"What's that mean?"

"Just meaning that money will be the least of your concerns."

"Money has nothing to do with this. I don't care about his money."

Blair shrugged as if to say, *if you say so.*

Elle silently scooped a spoonful of brown sugar from a matching ceramic canister, experiencing a nagging sense of déjà vu.

"Okay, money isn't an issue." Blair peered from behind the mug. "So, is he giving you the ring back? Are you guys going to get married?"

"We didn't discuss it."

"You're moving to another state with the man and marriage hasn't come up? I mean, he's already proposed, so what's different now?"

"Nothing. We just didn't talk about it. I don't need a ring to know that he loves me. I wouldn't consider—" Elle's hands flew up. "Wait, what's with all these questions?"

"So, you're still just considering it?" Blair's voice filled with hope.

"No. I'm going."

Blair sighed, opened her mouth to speak then turned her head and looked away.

"What?"

"I have to be honest with you, I think you're making a mistake." There it was—what Blair had been itching to say since day one.

"A mistake?"

"Look, I'm your friend and I just can't let you make this decision without thinking it all the way through—"

"And what makes you think I haven't?"

"What are you getting all worked up for?"

"Because you kill me. How can you stand there and treat me as if I'm some dizzy broad, like I'm some stupid woman with a bad track record? You've known me over ten years Blair. Have a little faith in me." Her voice trembled. "Even if you don't agree, you owe it to me to stand by my side. The same way I've *always* stood by yours!"

A dark shadow cast across Blair's face. "Just what are you implying?"

"Not implying anything. All I'm saying is you're in no position to judge me. No position at all." Elle never thought she'd be brought to say those words, but it was the truth. Because she loved Blair, *only* because she loved Blair, she'd turned a blind eye to a lot of her decisions and it hurt like hell that Blair couldn't do the same.

Blair spoke in a hush. "We said we'd *never* bring this up again. You promised me."

"I haven't brought anything up. That's your guilty conscience."

They locked horns. It was that proverbial fork in the road of friendship. If they spoke their hearts' truths, things may never be the same. But even if they didn't, the die had been cast. The truth bubbled so close to the surface it was liable to spill over at any given moment.

Blair took the first blow. "You know what, Elle? Do whatever the hell you want! If you want to move a thousand miles away for some man you barely know, then fine. I don't care. Just know this—after you realize *again* that he's not the one and you're stuck in some hick town with no life and no friends, don't call me."

"That will never be me, 'cause no matter what ever happened between Luke and I, I'll never be in a position where I need a man. I'll never have to look the other way when a man cheats or mistreats me, just because he pays all the bills. You can count on that." She drove her finger down on the countertop. "That will never be me. Can you say the same?"

"Get the hell out!"

"Fine!" Elle snatched her handbag and stalked out of the kitchen.

A few seconds later, Blair heard her front door slam. She lowered her head onto the counter and sobbed. This was different than the thousand arguments she'd had with Vaughn.

Elle was the only person who'd ever truly been on her side, more so than even her family. And in needing her so much, she'd pushed her away. Just as she considered running after her best friend, she heard her daughter's cries upstairs and knew that no matter what she said or did next, their friendship would never be the same.

Elle sped down the driveway, slowing only once she'd reached a red traffic light. Night after night she had mulled over ways to reconcile with Blair. She'd conceded to be the bigger person, to smooth over their differences and make things right between them. But it was all for nothing. There were so many things she could have said, so many skeletons she could have exhumed, but she hadn't because she knew Blair was already suffering enough. Although she'd never said anything, Elle knew her best friend was ridden with guilt for what she was doing. And that she was living in constant fear of Dylan's threat. For that reason Elle had done just as she'd promised and never spoke Blair's secret aloud even though it racked her own conscience. She had offered unwavering support and now that she needed some, Blair refused it. This move to Georgia was coming at the perfect time. It was time to wash the slate clean and start anew. She couldn't get to Luke fast enough.

42

Jonathan

Jonathan stared at the black suit which laid across his bed. It was nearly ten in the morning. The sun peeked through his blinds; the faint scent of dandelions streamed through his open windows. Without even looking outside, he could tell it was the perfect spring day. A perfect day for a New York City wedding. Next to the suit rested his phone. He knew he needed to pick it up, dial seven digits and break somebody's heart. This was a day he would always remember—the dichotomy was unnerving. Either he would walk down the aisle at four o'clock and commence a life with his son's mother, or he would break her heart, forever marring their relationship, forcing them to co-parent from a distance.

Never before had he viewed his phone with such contempt. At the moment it wasn't merely a communication device, but rather a weapon he was forced to wield. He fought the urge to hurl it against the wall and render it inoperable. Anything to buy him time and delay the inevitable.

Lauryn was none the wiser. At the same moment she was likely at a spa, getting a massage or a pedicure, primping as she drank bellinis with her bridal party. Bree was most likely downtown at her friend's apartment, waiting for Jonathan's call, waiting to hear the story of how he'd called off the wedding. She would feign concern for Lauryn's feelings as she caressed his back and reassured him he'd done the right thing and that all would be okay. Then she would lure him into the bedroom to convince him he'd made the right choice. Neither woman knew her fate still hung in the balance. He had yet to come to a conclusion; in a few hours he was equally likely to be cutting cake with Lauryn as he was to be home eating take-out with Bree.

He would make no calls to Elle or his sister or any of his friends. This had to be his decision and his alone.

He picked up his phone, dialed and the conversation ensued. It was comprised of a slew of remorseful statements like, *I can't do this . . . I'm sorry . . . I just can't . . . I have to be true to my feelings . . . One day you'll be happy I did . . . I never wanted to hurt you . . . Please understand,* and wounded, angry statements like, *What do you mean you can't . . . You can't do this to me again . . . You fucking coward! . . . I'm humiliated!*

Mercifully, the call ended. Before he could second-guess his decision, he escaped his apartment and sought refuge in the arms of the woman he'd finally chosen.

43

Elle

Elle sealed the last of her suitcases and took a final glance around her barren bedroom. All of her furniture and most of her belongings had been shipped down to Georgia the prior week. Only a couple of suitcases remained. Those she would haul into the back of her car for the drive down to Virginia, where Luke was attending a medical conference. They would then drive the rest of the way to Atlanta together.

Just as she was checking her closets for the fifth time to make sure she hadn't forgotten anything, her doorbell rang. Her agent was on the way to conduct the final walk-through with the couple who'd purchased her house.

"I'm coming," she called, as she scrambled downstairs. She swung open the front door to find Blair. She was wrapped in a beige raincoat, cinched tightly around her waist and her eyes were masked with large, round Jackie Onassis-styled sunglasses. They stood in the doorway, awkwardly assessing each other.

"Can I come in?" Blair asked. Elle stepped aside and gestured for her to enter. "Wow. So, you're all ready to go, huh?"

Elle gnawed on her bottom lip, feeling uncomfortable in her own home. She had spent the entire morning psyching herself up for the move, convincing herself she was doing the right thing and willing herself not to cry. She was not up for another battle with Blair; her rattled nerves couldn't handle it. So she sought to busy herself with something, anything to delay a confrontation, which would be their third in a row after ten years of never having argued over anything more than Blair's habitual lateness or Elle's smoking.

Blair avoided direct eye contact with Elle, which was especially hard since the house was all but empty and there was nothing else to focus on. She stood near the staircase, tracing her fingers along the wrought-iron balustrade. "When are you leaving?"

"Sunday morning," Elle said as she meticulously re-taped the box resting on the living room floor.

Blair spun around. "*This* Sunday?"

"Yeah, I start my new job on Thursday."

"When is your flight?"

"Not flying. I'm driving."

"Driving? Alone?"

"Meeting Luke halfway. In Virginia." Elle didn't feel good about her terse replies, but she needed to maintain an emotional distance. They could rehash it all over the phone later, but not today.

A lump formed in Blair's throat. "I can't believe you're really leaving. What's your god-daughter going to do without you?"

The final strip of tape stubbornly refused to affix to the box, forcing Elle to engage; she made eye contact with her friend for the first time. "I'll still be in her life. You know that."

"Yeah, but now she'll only see you on holidays and special occasions. Who's she going to talk to when she needs advice or someone to make her laugh or to vent to when Vaughn gets on her nerves?"

"Well, that's what they have the phone and Skype for. She'll hear from me more than she can imagine." Elle tilted her head up, hoping to capture her tears before they spilled out over her lower lids. "I'm leaving New York, not her. I'll always be there for her and I bet she knows that."

"Yeah, she does, but she's still sad. And she's sorry for being such a selfish bitch. Can you ever forgive her?" Blair removed her sunglasses which no longer served their purpose as two single streams slid down her cheeks.

"Yeah, as long as she can forgive me for saying those horrible things I didn't mean." They hugged and cried in each other's arms.

Blair helped Elle load the last of her boxes into her car. "So this is it?"

"Yeah, I still can't believe I'm moving." Elle shook her head in disbelief. "I feel like this is all some crazy dream."

"Well, call me tomorrow every hour on the hour until you reach Virginia. I want to make sure you're okay. You know, I can drive down with you and just fly back home."

"No, I'll be fine. Besides, I have my audio books all lined up. I'll be all right."

"I'm proud of you. You're so brave. You have so much more courage than I ever could. I'm going to miss the hell out of you, but I know this is the right move. You belong with him."

It was just what Elle needed to hear.

44

Jonathan

"Well, I must say I'm proud of you, Mr. Moore. You followed your heart. I know it wasn't easy." Elle adjusted her strapless dress so the arc of the sweetheart neckline was perfectly centered.

"It sure wasn't, but I know I did the right thing." He brought his cigar to his lips and took a deep draw. "You sure you don't want one? This is good stuff."

She waved away the smoke. "I'll have you know I officially quit. Besides, I don't think this dress exactly goes with a Churchill."

"Don't knock it 'til you try it."

Just then they were interrupted.

"Excuse me, Elle. Do you mind if I steal him away for a minute?" Lauryn beamed, her cheeks still flush with excitement. "I'd like to dance with my *husband*."

Elle smiled. "He's all yours."

Jonathan took his bride by her hand and led her to the dance floor.

45

Elle

Late the following afternoon, Elle was pulling up to the Jefferson Hotel in Richmond, Virginia. She was exhausted from the eight-hour drive, one she'd embarked on after only a few hours sleep, but Jonathan and Lauryn's wedding reception had been worth it. She was delighted to see her friends' lives finally fall into place. Both Jonathan and Blair now had children and were happy in their relationships. While there was no baby in Elle's life, she felt complete and ready to start a new chapter.

She entered the grand hotel lobby and watched a host of well-dressed people mill about. As she looked around, a bellhop eagerly approached her.

"Good day, ma'am. Welcome to the Jefferson. How may I assist you?"

She looked just past him and saw a familiar, handsome face. Luke glimpsed her, waved then started her way.

"Thank you, but I think I have everything I need right here."

46

Blair

The evening they'd brought Morgan Elizabeth Hill home was bittersweet. Blair was thrilled beyond belief to finally begin the next chapter of her life as a mother. Yet, as she gazed upon her daughter, she was overcome with a mixture of regret, sadness and fear, knowing the child would never know her real father and Dylan would never know his daughter. Although she'd come to terms with her decision, Morgan's existence was a daily reminder of what she'd done.

She searched her daughter's face for traces of any resemblance to Dylan and thankfully saw none. She favored Blair—for now.

Vaughn was beside himself with delight. Every time she felt a pang of guilt, she would look at Vaughn, watch the way he doted on their newborn, and the feeling would temporarily dissolve.

Over the next few months, as they witnessed Morgan's development and settled into the joys of parenthood, she and Vaughn grew closer. Their relationship mirrored what it had been early on in their marriage, back when he'd been on his best behavior.

Vaughn was proving to be an incredible father and Morgan adored every second she spent with him. It warmed Blair's heart to watch them together and over time she only rarely thought of her daughter's true paternity. She never heard another word from Dylan after that threatening text message. She often thought about him, where he was, what he was doing and who he was doing it with, but as quickly as the thoughts entered her mind, she would shake them away, taking comfort in the fact that he was not the man for her and God's plan was for her to be exactly where she was. She was content in her marriage and with her life; everything she'd ever hoped for had finally fallen into place. The road had been long, hard and full of heartache, but it was a sweet homecoming.

"My two favorite women," Vaughn said as he stood in the doorway of the nursery, watching as Blair laid Morgan down for the night. He shook his head in disbelief as he approached them. "How did I ever get so lucky?"

"*We* are lucky," Blair said.

"Yes, we are." He squeezed Morgan's tiny hand then kissed Blair on the nape of her neck. "I promise I won't be out long. Once the dinner is over, I'll be right back home."

She told him to send everyone her best and to apologize for her absence, but she just didn't feel right leaving the baby for so long yet. After he left, Blair reveled in her fortune. She never imagined her life would turn out the way it did. They were happy, in love, and had a beautiful little girl. What more could she ask for?

As Vaughn pulled out of the garage, his thoughts echoed his wife's. Finally he had peace back in his home. Just then his cell phone rang.

"*Where are you? You were supposed to be here twenty minutes ago.*"

"Just had some stuff to take care of. I'm on my way, baby." He twisted his ring off his finger and slipped it into his jacket pocket. "And you better be wearing those sexy heels I like."

The voice on the other end purred. "*You know I am. See you soon.*"

Discussion Questions

1. Blair made a controversial decision. What are your thoughts on it? Did you sympathize at all with her position? How do you believe she should have handled it?
2. Did you believe Vaughn was really a changed man? Do you think it's possible for people to change?
3. Do you think Blair ever really loved Dylan? Do you believe she ever had any real intention of leaving Vaughn for him?
4. What are your thoughts on Blair's friendship with Elle? As a friend, how would you have reacted upon learning Blair's secret? What did you think about their argument at the end? Why do you think Blair behaved as such?
5. Who do you believe was a better choice for Jonathan? Do you think he made the right decision at the end? Do you think it's possible to love two people at the same time?
6. Do you believe Jonathan's final decision was based on his son?
7. Why do you think Jonathan stayed with Lauryn as long as he did? Was Roslyn and Cory's disdain for him warranted?
8. What do you think was the driving force behind most of Elle's decisions? Why do you think Elle took Marcus back?
9. What did you think about her reasons for not marrying Luke?
10. Do you believe Luke should have taken her back? Do you think his parents will present an issue for them after she moves to Georgia?

Visit Zoe McKnight's website at:
www.zmcknight.com

Turn the page for a sneak peek at

Zoe McKnight's next book

The sequel to Living in Glass Houses

What Happens In
The Dark

Coming in the Fall of 2012

What Happens in the Dark

I watch her stirring in her sleep. Her hands are balled up into tiny, little fists. Under the sheets I can see her feet flailing. She's a wild sleeper, just as I had been, or so I've been told. She's wearing her favorite nightgown, a pink and chocolate-brown cotton frock. Her initials are inscribed across the front in large cursive letters. Vaughn, my husband, bought it a few months ago. For some reason he's all about monograms with her. All about her room, on just about anything which could be personalized, it reads *MEH*. Morgan Elizabeth Hill. It's on the front of her door, on her towels, her duvet covers, and even on the tiny headboard of the bed she has yet to grow into. When I overhead him on the phone arranging to have her luggage monogrammed, I had to stop him. I'm not sure why she even needs luggage at thirteen months old, never mind monogrammed luggage, but he insisted. And if there's one thing I've learned, it's that there's no point in arguing with Vaughn when his mind is set.

I believe our daughter should have the best, but I don't want her to become one of those spoiled little girls who believes she's entitled to everything she wants simply because her father—well her parents—are rich. Now I know there are people who'll say that I'm spoiled, and yes, I may be, but I've earned every diamond, vehicle, and article of clothing I own. I've put up with a lot these past twelve years, more than I'd like to admit. But that's behind us now. Dr. Lane tells me that forgiving is a decision, one which doesn't just happen overnight, so I had to make a conscious decision to forgive my husband and I have.

Vaughn—the new Vaughn that is—is wonderful. He bursts with charisma and charm. When he enters a room, he commands it and not only because he's six-foot-four and gorgeous, but because he's magnetic. He has a way of drawing people into him and a unique way of making everyone he speaks to feel as if they are the only person in the room. He has a gift for recalling the slightest of details about people—details he easily recites when seeing them again to stroke their egos and have them believe they'd left an impression. I don't know anyone who can work a room the way he does. Still to this day, I watch him in awe. Mostly because I've never been talented in such a way. Over the years I've morphed from the shy, unassuming undergrad I was when he met me, into the worldly, confident woman I am today, but even at my best, I am no Vaughn. A fact he recognizes and I deep down believe is one of the things he loves about me. He could never be with a woman just like him. I've always been content taking a backseat to Vaughn's success. I've never wanted a life in the spotlight and Vaughn never wanted a wife who wanted to be in the spotlight. So in that sense we are a perfect match. What began as passionate puppy love in college has grown into a mature, solid love. One recently cemented by the birth of our daughter.

"Mommy," I hear. Morgan's big brown eyes stare up at me as she rises to her feet and leans agains the banister of her crib. She mumbles something which only I am able to decipher as meaning she's hungry. I nuzzle my nose against her soft, damp forehead and inhale her fresh baby scent. I swoop her up in my arms and we head downstairs. Before we even reach the kitchen, I can hear the whirl of the blender and the distinctive aroma of Rosa's homemade french toast.

"Good Morning Miss Blair," Rosa says. She's holding two clear bowls, each brimming with fresh fruit. "Blueberries or strawberries?"

"Morning Rosa. How about both, I'm starving this morning." I slide Morgan into her high chair and watch as Rosa lays out our breakfast for us, just as she does each morning.

Before I can feed Morgan her first spoonful of oatmeal, Vaughn appears in the doorway. He is dressed in a pair of navy blue slacks. A crisp white collar is peeking out from under his jacket. Although I must have seen him dressed this way a thousand times, I am still impressed with how good he looks in a suit.

"Morning baby." He presses his lips to mine. It's a deep, hard kiss, too hard for so early in the morning, especially since we've already made love twice since the sun rose. So hard in fact that Rosa blushes and turns away as if she walked in on us.

"Good morning you," I say. "You're wearing a suit on the plane?"

"Nah, I have a meeting in the city at noon. Moved my flight back to tonight."

He lifts Morgan out from her seat and playfully tosses her six inches into the air. "How's my baby girl?" Her face lights up and she giggles uncontrollably. I absolutely love to watch them together. There's something about watching a man with his child that warms my heart. "I'll be back around five so can have an early dinner together before I leave," he says with a wink.

"I'd like that. How long will you be in Toronto?" I ask.

He sits beside me. "I'm going to try and wrap things up as soon as I can so I can get back before the weekend. That pumpkin patch thing is Saturday, right?"

I'm impressed he remembers. Details like this he would have glazed over years ago. He never would have cut a business trip short for me and especially not for something as minor as a pumpkin-picking trip. Although I know it's more for Morgan's benefit than it is for mine, I'm still elated. His traveling used to fill me with such angst. But finally that knot in the pit of my stomach, the one which used to wrench every time he was out of my sight, finally uncoiled and eventually faded away. I can now say without a doubt that I am happy. I never thought it would be the case, but here I am, an anomaly—a happily married woman.

"Yup, Saturday. Are you sure you'll be able to make it. It's okay if you can't."

"No," he says as he scarfs down an egg white omelette. "I want to be there. Was even thinking about hiring a photographer for a few hours."

"I really don't think that's necessary. I'll have my Nikon."

"Yeah, but then we can't get shots of all of us together." He pulls out his Blackberry and shoots off a text to his assistant. "So, what do you have you planned for today?"

"Not much, I have yoga in an hour. Then I'm going to shoot over to Nordstrom to return a couple of things I bought online. That's about it."

He gets up and plants a kiss on Morgan's forehead. "I have to run. I'll call you later."

"You've got to stop eating so fast," I scold as pluck a speck of lint from his lapel.

He reaches for my hand. "Walk me to the car."

I walk him to the garage where James, our driver, is leaning against the fender of our black Tahoe. He's tapping away on his phone, most likely engrossed in a game of virtual poker, like he always is when waiting on either of us. Vaughn and I hug, he tells me he loves me and kisses me again before sidling into the back seat of the SUV. I stand in the garage and watch the Tahoe maneuver down our circular driveway until it disappears from my view.

It's amazing how much can change in a short span of time. I can clearly recall the days when just the sight of Vaughn made me sick. Days I wished I could have pushed him in front of a moving car. Days when I believed my life would be so much better if he didn't exist, and not in a I wish-he-had-never-been-born kind of way, more in a I-wished-he-would-have-died-in-a-plane-crash kind of way.

My husband has many attributes, being faithful, however was not always one of them. There have been a slew of random women in and out of our lives for years. According to Dr. Lane, men like Vaughn—who've been judged their whole lives by their achievements—will constantly seek attention in order to feel whole. And unfortunately it often comes in the form of infidelity. She said he got validation from the attention he got from other women. It doesn't make it right, but it does makes sense. Understanding the *why* did help, because at least I knew it wasn't about me and what I was lacking, but rather about him and what he was lacking.

The therapy helped, but it wasn't until a little over a year ago when things finally changed. Vaughn had a revelation of sorts. He finally realized how selfish he'd been and how much his cheating had hurt me. He took me on a surprise trip to the caribbean where he begged for my forgiveness and asked for another chance. As luck would have it, I was pregnant with Morgan, so it seemed like the perfect time to start fresh and on a clean slate. So we did. We renewed our vows and since that day it's been smooth sailing. Everything he's promised, he's delivered on. I no longer doubt his words or question his whereabouts. My closest friend, Elle wasn't so convinced that Vaughn could change, but unlike her, I believe in second chances. After all, all humans are flawed, we *all* make mistakes. I know I've made mine, and while Vaughn doesn't quite know about them, they still haunt me every time I look at my daughter's face.

ABOUT THE AUTHOR

Zoe McKnight was born and raised in New York. After graduating from Hofstra University with a degree in business, she launched a career in marketing and public relations. She currently lives in New York City. Living in Glass Houses is her first novel.